The Truth In Pretending

Juliana Jules

Diamond House Publishing

The Truth In Pretending
Juliana Jules

Images used under license from Shutterstock.com

ISBN-978-0-9938760-2-8

THE TRUTH IN PRETENDING

First edition 14/02/2016

DIAMOND HOUSE PUBLISHING

diamondhousepublishing@hotmail.com

Diamond House Publishing

To my wonderful mother ♥

The Truth
In Pretending

Prologue

Lola Moss felt the hair on her arms rise as she closed her mailbox. She gazed over her shoulder—the world seemed to evaporate. A strong magnetic pull hummed in her core as she turned to face the most enigmatic man she'd ever seen.

Chuck Moran walked into the mailroom of his new apartment building. He was still getting used to having a shared mail area. As he walked in, he noticed a tall blond closing her mailbox. She glanced over her shoulder—the most beautiful brown eyes elicited a humming magnetic pull.

"Hi." She smiled at him, turning her body towards him.

"Hello." He nodded, smiling back and wasn't aware he had taken a step closer.

"Are you new?" She asked, taking a step closer herself.

He nodded and was lost in the way her eyes sparkled. "Yeah, I just moved into apartment eleven."

"Oh, really?" Lola's eyes widened at the news. The man was her next-door neighbor. "I live next door—apartment twelve."

Chuck smiled at his next-door neighbor.

"I'm Lola by, the way." She offered her hand.

"I'm Chuck," he introduced himself as he shook her hand. Since the introductions were over, there was only one thing left. Ask Lola out. She was the kind of woman he'd marry in a second. He knew she was unlike any other woman he'd met.

"Hi, Chuck." Lola smiled at her neighbor. She bit her lip, thinking it was good that David was coming over today to talk about their relationship. Well, soon-to-be-ex relationship. Lola smiled into raven-black eyes.

"Hey, I was wondering if—"

"Lola, there you are, sweetheart." David's familiar voice interrupted Chuck. Lola looked behind Chuck and saw her boyfriend standing there, gazing at her like he loved her.

David's blue eyes sized up Chuck. He gave him that charming half-smile and introduced himself. Lola wasn't sure what happened during the few minutes that followed. She just remembered sitting in front of David, who was telling her he loved her and wanted to take their relationship to the next level—to move in together, starting that very same day.

There came a time in a person's life when they needed to commit. Apparently, the moment had come for Lola, who agreed to move in with David. With a few conditions on both sides.

David would move in with her, but he got to keep his apartment. And they would never, ever talk about their relationship again.

Lola smiled, liking the conditions as she couldn't help but

remember her new next-door neighbor.

In the apartment next door, Chuck sat on his newly bought sofa and shook his head sadly. She had a boyfriend.

Lola was off-limits.

Chapter One

"Yeah... Look, I'm sorry..."

Humph! At least, he could pretend to feel sorry, Lola Moss thought. Was it too much to ask? After everything they had been through, couldn't he at least show some remorse? Really, after living together for almost a year? Sharing a life? No. There was nothing. Not a single trace of guilt on his infuriatingly handsome, godlike face. None. Nothing. God! She was so angry at him. Lola fisted her hands. She still had so many things to yell at him, so many questions... accusations to throw at him, but she bit her tongue, knowing it would only bring another round of useless shouting.

Of course, it was only when they were arguing—and more specifically, when he was defending himself—that David showed any emotion. His liquid blue, mesmerizing eyes went wide and innocent, like those of a child. His mouth snapped shut with indignation while desperation played on his sharp-edged features. Palms raised in the air, half shielding him, half stopping the hard whip lashes of her words. Or at least that's how he made her words seem. Not to mention how he made her feel as she stood gazing at him— like she had brought all this upon herself.

Yeah, right, like it was her fault. *Pff.* She wasn't a "real girl-friend." She didn't act how a "normal girlfriend" should. That one still stung. And he knew it. But even then, he hadn't shown remorse. He felt bad though; Lola knew by the slight way he avoided her hurt gaze. Yet there was no guilt. Never any remorse. Did he even have remorse in him? Was the word even in his vocabulary? Did he even know what it meant? In the two years she had dated him, Lola couldn't think of a time David had shown any remorse.

Either way, his accusations had been a low blow, and he knew it. She didn't act like a "normal" girlfriend. *Urgh!* How dare he throw that in her face!? Wasn't it one of the reasons he had dated her—that it was nothing serious, always a game? And hadn't she dated him for the very same reason—that he was aloof, detached, there but never there?

Yes.

But they shared a life together, an apartment, bills and what-not. Like normal adults. They went grocery shopping with the inten-tion of cooking and always ended up ordering take-out. Lola hated to admit it, but their relationship had changed into something seri-ous. She expected that the least he could do was own up to his ac-tions, instead of standing there, gazing at her like she deserved what happened because of her own negligence.

Urgh! Just remembering his arguments, his excuses angered her even more. Lola looked around her living room, wanting to find something to throw at his perfect face. Her gaze settled on her microwave. That would be good, heavy enough that she couldn't throw it. Gazing with determination, Lola marched off into the kitchen. Or at least she thought she did.

The machine blinked 1:30 and then blinked 1:31. She was still standing in front of David. *Damn.* She was paralyzed. Lola gazed at her coffee table instead; it was at arm's length. There was the newspaper David had been reading in the morning and a heart-shaped metal decoration in the very middle. Newspaper wouldn't hurt; Lola doubted it would even fly across the table and hit David. That left the heart-shaped metal piece. It had belonged to her mother. So no.

Lola gave up. Mycroft, her microwave—a.k.a., her personal cook—was indispensable; she couldn't afford to lose him, even if she'd managed to move him. Everything else in her living room was either expensive or had sentimental value. Lola wasn't going to waste it on David Anderson. So she did the next best thing: stare David down.

Okay, so she didn't exactly decide to stare at him; it was the only thing she could do in her current paralytic state. Having control over one thing, Lola made her stare dull, glazed with accusation and sprinkled with emotionless spark. Eyes wide open, she tried anything and everything to make him somehow feel guilty with her gaze.

Several moments passed in silence and David began fidgeting under Lola's unblinking stare. He glanced from side to side and at the floor, no longer meeting her gaze. A part of her was kind of happy to see him squirm uncomfortably. Good! Go ahead! Squirm! Be uncomfortable, she thought. He deserved it.

Another torturous, silent minute passed. David awkwardly said, "Well… okay… um… I'm off." He walked quickly to the door—practically sprinted to the door—but as he was halfway out, he paused and turned. Lola knew he turned; she could feel his blue gaze on her back, but she refused to turn, even as her curiosity nudged her to. A sad sigh drifted through the air. "I *am* sorry." His voice caressed her ears.

A tear trailed down her cheeks as she heard the soft click of the door closing.

Did his voice have to sound so remorseful? Why? Why did he have to sound genuine, with his swirling guilt? If he wasn't actually sorry, if he didn't care, it would be easier. She could just be angry, but now… a brick lay in her stomach weighing down her with pain.

She had loved him. More than he had her. Obviously. Lola rolled her eyes. But she knew he had loved her, too, in his own way.

Lola plopped down on her couch, feeling her tears roll freely down her face. Her eyes stung and felt oddly dry.

Was she crying because of David or because she had left her eyes open for too long?

Ultimately, Lola decided it was because of David. Of course it was. David had been her boyfriend for almost two years. They had lived together for a year. It was—had been, she corrected herself—a serious relationship. Lola shook her head at the stupid question. It hardly made sense for her to be crying because she had left her eyes open for too long. So with that logic in mind, Lola let her tears run down her face and stain the top of her shirt. She stared into nothingness, just letting her tears run freely.

To her surprise, after a couple of minutes, she realized she wasn't sobbing. Actually, no sounds were coming out of her. Not even a whimper. Weird. People sobbed when they cried. She sobbed when she cried. Why wasn't she now? Weird, she thought once more. Shrugging it off, Lola closed her eyes, feeling relief in her stinging eyes. She sat, crying with closed eyelids.

No! Lola opened her eyes and blinked several times. No, she wasn't going to spend her time crying over him. Smart women didn't cry over men. And she was a smart woman. She had known beforehand that the man was a lying, deceiving… incredibly good-looking cheater! Whispered rumors here and there had reached her ears. David had never had a serious girlfriend. A one-night stand lingered longer than David. David would break her heart. She'd heard the rumors. Women had gone out of their way to inform her about David, but oh… that smile. Blame it on the smile. So charming, so promising. On top of it all, his surfer good looks dressed in sensible clothes. She hadn't been able to help it. And he was the kind of man who beneath his godlike looks was—

No! Get yourself together. Stop praising him, she commanded herself. He was a cheater, and she had known it from the beginning. It had never been a question of whether he would, but rather when. He wasn't worth the cry.

But… She was human, after all. She had the right to cry. If she wasn't crying, then something was wrong with her. A road she didn't want to go down. She had to cry in honor of their relationship, she argued. And she had. Now it was time to stop crying.

Now was the time to be a smart woman, like her father had always taught her. Lola lifted her hand to wipe away her tears. She frowned. Her cheeks were dry. She patted her face, searching for moisture. Underneath and all around her eyes were dry, too. Even her lashes were dry. Her frown deepened. She hadn't realized she had stopped crying.

See? I am a smart woman, after all, she smiled, getting up from the couch and stretching her arms out. Her muscles protested against the sudden demand of flexibility. Aching pain resonated through her stiff arms. They were stiff and aching. How long had she been sitting?

The apartment seemed darker, so Lola concluded that a couple of hours had passed. She stretched, groaning as her muscles protested again, and she reached for her phone in her back jeans pocket to confirm the time.

1:41

What?! Ten minutes! No, there was something wrong with her phone. She double-checked on the clock hanging on the wall. Impossible. Surely she would mourn her relationship for more than ten minutes. Her muscles were stiff; that clearly meant she had been sitting for more than ten minutes. The apartment was dark; clearly it was evening. Light filled the apartment as the dark cloud moved on. Oh. Just a cloud. Right.

Lola sighed, standing in the middle of her living room, gazing around her apartment.

It was the perfect size for her. It wasn't too big or too small. It was a nice, spacious studio apartment. Her living room stood right in the middle, and on her right was her bed, with a nightstand on either side, facing the living room. On her left was the bathroom, near the corner, while her dining/work table was near the entrance door. Beside the entrance door, on her right, was the kitchen. But the best part of her apartment was the back wall, facing the entrance, lined with immense windows. Natural light lit the whole apartment all the time. Even on dull, lightless, grey, cloudy days, the little light there was seemed to find its way into the apartment.

Lola looked around, not knowing what to do. She stared at her bed, hoping it would call her name like it did in the mornings. Unlike those mornings when she needed to get up and go to work, her bed stood there silent, uninviting, in the gloomy greyness of the daylight. It was for the best. She doubted she could sleep; her mind would probably want to think, argue about and remember every little thing possible. Like the time she had fallen down the stairs, or that embarrassing time in kindergarten when who knows what had happened. Maybe she would think about life in general. The purpose of her life, perhaps? In short, not let her sleep at all. It was always when she most desperately needed or wanted to sleep that her brain would remain painfully awake. Knowing her brain, it would probably replay her whole relationship with David. Lola closed her eyes, shuddering at the thought. Sleeping was out of the question. She sighed.

Lola glanced over to her kitchen, hoping she would feel her belly grumble with hunger. Nothing. She wasn't hungry, even though she hadn't eaten anything all day. She should eat lunch; it was almost two o'clock pm, but she was certain that if she ate now, it wouldn't stay down.

Lola sighed again. She had a feeling she would be sighing at lot today.

The price of breaking up with the person you love...

"I think I'll take a shower," she announced, uncertain, and walked towards her bathroom. The world stopped halfway there; a thought fell hard on her, like bricks. She shut her eyes with desperation, groaning out her frustration and fisting her hands.

True. There was no more shampoo, she remembered.

All the morning's events came crashing down.

Chapter Two

Lola had woken up late in the morning, around ten, after a long night of work. She had worked most of the night, finishing one of the interior designs for a new client. Although she would get zero credit for the work, she wanted the design to be special. For some reason, this project meant a lot to her. She was putting everything she had into this project.

After waking up, she grabbed a cup of warm tea that David always prepared for her in the mornings. The liquid was more cool than warm, but warmth still sloshed down her relieved throat. Smiling, she took another sip and wandered over to David. He sat in one of the two armchairs, reading the newspaper. At the sound of her approach, he looked up and smiled at her smiling face. She pressed a soft kiss on his lips and whispered, "I'm sorry about last night. I just had this massive inspiration. I promise I'll make up for it this weekend." Lola wiggled her eyebrows suggestively.

David grinned, pulling her into his lap. "Why wait until this weekend?" he purred, winking. Before Lola could reply, David crushed a sensual and tempting kiss on her lips while his hand teased its way underneath her shirt. A soft moan escaped her lips as he stroked his thumb underneath the mound of her breast.

"Wait." She giggled and gripped his still-caressing hand. With a small tug, she managed to make him stop. "I need to shower," she apologized.

David was about to say something playful—probably suggest they shower together, Lola guessed—but instead, he gazed over her face. His electric-blue eyes searching. An unreadable glaze covered his features. She gazed back, trying to identify the expression in the oceanic depths of his eyes but found only desolation. David looked away and sighed what seemed like defeat. His grip loosened around her waist, and he turned his head, covering his lips with his fingers. Guilt seized her.

"This weekend," she promised, giving him a quick kiss as she stood. David smiled, agreeing to the promise. Guilt eased throughout her body. She disappeared into the bathroom, only to come out a few seconds later.

"Wow, that was a fast shower," David smiled. "Had second thoughts, did you?" He gave her his smoldering, twinkly gaze, leaning forward. He opened his arms in an invitation for her to rejoin him.

Lola couldn't help grinning. "No. Sorry." She tried to fake a pout through her grinning lips. "Ran out of shampoo. Be right back in twenty minutes," she said, pulling on her favorite pair of jeans. Grabbing her sweatshirt from the back of the chair and her keys, she flew out without looking back.

Bam! The door closed behind Lola as she slammed into blackness. The world tilted at her feet, and Lola stumbled back. With her eyes shut tightly, she waited for the impact of the floor on her bottom. It never came. Instead, strong hands gripped her waist and back, bringing a whiff of fresh cologne with a woodsy pine smell. Lola blushed, knowing who it was. She opened one eye after the other, hesitant and fearful. It was indeed her next-door neighbor, Chuck.

Concern darkened Chuck's already dark gaze. He examined her features for a sign of wellness, or perhaps, un-wellness. Her heartbeat picked up as the usual humming ball of energy vibrated in her core. She tried calming her sledgehammering heart. It didn't help that his gaze lingered a second too long on her lips. Lola resisted the urge to lick them.

"I'm sorry." She managed to break free from his gaze. Using his help, she straightened, apologizing once more. "I wasn't looking. I'm sorry. Are you alright? Did I hurt you? It was a good thing you were there..." Lola trailed off. If he hadn't been there, then she wouldn't have fallen, she retorted. If Chuck hadn't been there, she wouldn't have smacked into him and almost fallen, needing his rescue. Lola felt happy, with a tingle of nervousness, at the sight of her neighbor. "Hi," she finished, instead, with a smile, looking up at the man who stared down at her, concerned that she was hurt. Her chest tightened.

"Hello," Chuck greeted her, his raven-black eyes unreadable now. Lola stood, hands twined together and gazing at Chuck, who gazed back at her. Seconds ticked by; Lola was conscious of it; she knew she had to either say something or leave. Leave. She needed to leave before she lost herself in the man's black eyes.

"Were you leaving your apartment, too?" Lola asked instead. He nodded.

They stood gazing at each other for a few more seconds before Chuck gestured for her to go first. Lola gave a polite smile, not knowing if she should say bye now or at the door. At the door, she decided, as she marched the few steps down the hall to the stairs. Because now would just be weird, and she'd have to say goodbye again at the door. If not, she'd come off as rude. She didn't want Chuck to think she was rude—Lola's arm hair rose; time seemed to stop; sound seemed to fade. Her breath caught. Lola gulped.

She walked down the stairs, side by side with Chuck. Every now and then, his arm touched hers for the briefest moment, before he restrained his movements. Lola didn't dare look at Chuck as they went down the final flight of stairs. She was way too aware of him as it was; there was no need to look at his bearded, mysterious face.

At the door, they both stopped simultaneously and turned to one another.

"Bye." Lola bid him farewell with a little hand gesture. He nodded his bye with a fast, almost invisible smile. Seconds ticked by. Lola bit her lips and forced herself to walk out first. She hadn't realized she'd been holding her breath until she marched out onto the Los Angeles street and forcefully had to let go of her breath before she passed out.

Her gaze caught Chuck as he walked down the street to his black truck. He wore a dark green plaid, button-up shirt, dark jeans and well-worn beige construction boots.

He looked very lumbersexual, Lola toyed with the idea as she played with her lip.

A pair of black eyes caught her gazing after him. Lola gasped and turned, blushing, hoping he hadn't noticed. Taking a secretive peek over her shoulder, her blush deepened. He had a slow, lazy, amused smile. *Grr.* Every time she bumped into the man, why did she either act like a fool or become speechless in his presence? Or get caught lusting over him? She couldn't help it; she didn't get to see him every day. Not that she wanted to, but he was a sight for sore eyes standing in the mailroom or the hallway.

Infected by the good mood that normally proceeded after bumping—literally or figuratively—into Chuck, Lola made her way to her new favorite store, Gospella, enjoying the cloudy day. She wondered if a day like this was the kind of day Chuck had been talking about a few months before, in the mailroom. It must be, she concluded, remembering how he had said any day, as long as it was cloudy, was his favorite day.

At the store, Lola took longer than usual, stopping to talk and gossip with some ladies and with Wendy, the cashier and owner of Gospella. Lola remembered that she had been smiling like some idiot. She kept gushing about her plans for the weekend. Oh, god. How she had gushed about her plans… The memory burned Lola's cheeks with embarrassment.

That weekend, one of her best friends, Elena, had planned a massive romantic event. It was to be a whole weekend themed on love and valentines, with an endless list of activities to do as couples. Lola was so happy she had David to go with. She acted like some sick love puppy. It was hard, though, not to feel in love when

JULIANA JULES

hearts hanged from the ceiling. Everything was red and pink, with
bows, kisses and hearts stamped all over. The shelves were stacked
with teddy bears holding heart-shaped chocolate boxes. And every
woman was in love with the idea of love. Everyone had love written
all over them. And Lola was no different.

Finally, after a long chat with Wendy, Lola went to pay, only
to realize she had forgotten her wallet. The lady behind her had
teased lovingly, "Ah, to be in love, on cloud nine." And laughed. Lola
smiled, blushing. She was in love with David, she guessed… It made
sense.

When Lola turned to apologize to Wendy, the cashier stopped
her with one palm in the air. "I'll hold it here for you. I want to know
more about this weekend." Wendy smiled, winking an emerald green
eye.

"Thank you." Lola relaxed, grateful. "I'll be right back," she
promised.

And that's how she had ended up shampoo-less and seeing
her boss's head in her boyfriend's lap, as he groaned.

A definitive groan.

The one she only ever heard in bed.

Now that Lola thought it over, as she walked back to the store
to buy the shampoo, the timing couldn't have been more perfect. A
second later, and she wouldn't have heard the all-too-familiar groan.
A second earlier, and she might have stopped the inevitable from
happening. It also might not even have happened if she'd called her
boss to mention that she wasn't going in that day. Perhaps her boss
wouldn't have dropped by to check whether she was working or taking the day off. Lola rolled her eyes. She was the only employee who

18

her boss felt it necessary to check up on. The perks of "befriending" the boss. It was rare she took a day off. Even on weekends, she'd find a way to work a little.

Of course, her boss, Nicole, had begun to apologize, wiping the dripping white tear off the corner of her smirking mouth. Nicole "tried" to look "ashamed," but Lola could see the deep satisfaction in her dirt-brown eyes. Was this the third boyfriend Nicole had taken from her? The smirk still haunted her. It had always been the same smirk, since college. Lola rolled her eyes. It was always the same story: Nicole would do something with her boyfriend, and Lola would catch her and then she'd leave, like a coward.

This time, her boss cowardly ran out of her apartment. Which only left David. They fought. Naturally. She wasn't going down without a fight. *How could you? You don't care about us. How dare you accuse me of not loving you?*

Gosh, all the things they yelled at each other.

Ding! Dong!

Lola walked into the store. *Urgh.* She stopped and curled her lip in disgust. *Urgh.* Valentine's Day. *Urgh.* Love. *Urgh.* Hearts. *Urgh.* Roses. *Urgh.* Red roses. Double *urgh. Stupid love.*

Lola cursed love, forgetting Wendy had her shampoo at the cash register and she walked towards the shampoo section of the store—which happened to be in the back. Rows of products decorated in pink, red and white hearts mocked her as she made her way down the aisle. She grunted in disgust as she passed anything remotely love- or valentine-related. Condoms=sex=two people=couple. *Urgh.* Pregnancy test. *Urgh.* Lipstick. *Urgh.* Heart. *Blah.* Two days before Valentine's Day; *what a peachy time to break up with my boyfriend,*

Lola thought dryly.

Waiting in line to pay, Lola half listened to the cashier chat with a customer. But after a few seconds, Lola blocked out the two female voices and glanced around, trying to find a distraction from her bitter thoughts. The store had opened a few months before, and ever since Lola had first set foot in the store, she had fallen in love. It was like a pharmacy but built only for women's needs and desires. Wendy had different types of products from around the globe to fit everyone needs. Including Lola's new favorite special shampoo for her blond hair. Not only did it leave her hair shiny and silky-smooth, it left a long-lasting lemony smell with hints of peach. The very subtle hints of peach never failed to remind her of her mother.

Although Lola wasn't really into the whole girly thing, what she did admire was the soft, feminine touches the store had. A flower here and there, a bouquet at the cash register—Lola had thought at first it was from a secret admirer or lover Wendy had. And there was always a pleasant, sweet smell floating through the store. Lola was in love with the color palette. An array of shades of pink with bright white walls.

She also loved the sense of family, community and comfort within the store. Wendy knew almost everything and everyone. She was always trying to help others and creating a sense of family among the women who regularly shopped there. Best of all, Wendy always had stories to tell. No wonder the store was called Gospella. Wendy was like a gossip magazine; she knew everything and anything going on with the women in their neighborhood. But unlike gossip magazines, no names were ever attached to the gossip.

No matter how hard Lola tried to find out who had burned

her boob while straightening her hair, Wendy never revealed anything in her forever-changing answers. The woman in question started out as an elderly lady, then became a young teenager; after that she was Caucasian, Asian, Hispanic, African-American and an array of mixed cultures. But Lola wasn't going to give up; she had a desperate need to know who the woman was. Ah, curiosity.

Under normal circumstances, Lola hated waiting in line—so much time wasted being idle, doing nothing productive. Idleness was her greatest pet peeve. Her life philosophy was to never stay idle. The sole exception to her rule: when she was waiting in line at Gospella. Wendy always made sure to take her time to listen to each customer, never rushing them or making them feel like clients. No, she always made them feel at home, like they were her friends. It was why Lola didn't usually mind waiting, but today, she minded. A lot. The couple extra minutes it took were driving Lola insane.

All she wanted to do was pay and leave as quickly as possible. To stand under the shower, letting the warm water de-stress her body and mind, was all Lola dreamt about. She could already feel her muscles relax, her eyes close as she let the steam play on her skin. Lola sighed, longing for her dream. Soon, she promised herself. She was next in line to pay. Any minute now, she smiled.

One minute passed. Two minutes passed. Three minutes passed.

Lola was getting desperate as each minute ticked by. The temptation to leave was becoming stronger and stronger. No. Wait. *I'm next in line.* It can't possibly take that long. *Distract yourself.* Her gaze traveled to the bold magazine headlines after she had eyed the chocolate bars. "Six Moves He'll Love in Bed." "What He Really

Wants This Valentine's Day." "Plan a Workout Date for This Valentine's Day." "Why She Finally Left Him." "Supermodel Ex Getting Sued." "Caught Him Cheating with the Nanny."

Boring. It was always the same thing.

Lola shifted her feet, impatient, finding nothing else to distract her. Her finger drummed against the oval surface of her shampoo bottle. She gazed out the window to the store in front, then over her shoulder at the lady behind her. She shifted from one foot to the other as her finger drummed faster and faster against the yellow bottle.

Finally, desperation won out. Lola forced herself to listen to the conversation between Wendy and the woman in front of her and tried to figure out how long it would last. If they were in the middle of a conversation, she would just leave, right then and there. Who needed shampoo, anyway? she argued. But if the conversation was almost over, she would give it another minute before leaving. Lola hoped it was the latter; she desperately needed shampoo. Greasy, two-day hair didn't exactly suit her.

"I miss being in love," the customer sighed. A heavy British accent coated her voice.

"I do, too. I've seen so many women in love today, I can't help but wonder when I'll fall in love."

"You've never been in love?"

"Once, but I was young and naïve. I'm not sure it qualifies as love."

"How old were you?"

"I can't remember," Wendy lied with a wink. "But I hope I'll find love again soon. And hopefully, like the kind one of my customers has."

The customer was intrigued, leaning in closer for the little piece of gossip. Wendy did the same. Lola found herself mirroring the women.

"Well, I have one customer who is so in love with her boy-friend. You should hear her talk about him. And oh, they have the most lavish plans for this weekend. A real treat. Anyways, she was so caught up in thinking about him, she forgot her wallet."

"Oh, poor besotted girl."

Wendy shrugged and smiled.

Poor *besotted* girl; Lola pitied her, too, mentally agreeing with the women. In love, and all. Poor thing, when she realized love didn't exist.

Wait a minute.

Her eyes widened in horror. She froze in line. They were talking about her! She had just pitied herself. She had thought of herself as some poor *besotted* girl. She had actually felt sorry for the girl. For herself. A small sound, between mortification and embar-rassment, escaped her mouth.

Wow, this was just an awesome day, she mocked, shrinking into the line, wishing she could disappear. Could this day get any worse? No! Don't think that. Take it back. Something worse could happened. *Sorry, I take it back*, she pleaded looking up.

Too late.

Wendy's green gaze focused on her, as did the customer's. Wendy smiled, elated, as she opened her mouth to say, "Oh, look here—" Lola knew in that split second, Wendy was about to say that she was the poor, besotted girl so in love she had forgotten her wallet. She was also certain they would include her in their conversation about love. And worse, ask her about David. In her current state of mind, it wouldn't be a good idea. Right now, all Lola wanted was to go on a ridiculously long rant about how stupid love was and how it didn't exist. How it had always been some myth, a legend told by sadists. A commercial industry to make money. A way to control the populace. She'd use every single nonsensical and proven reason she'd ever heard to deny that love existed. But, of course, she wouldn't, because it was the equivalent of assembling kindergarten children and announcing that Santa Claus didn't exist. She didn't have the heart to do it. So she was left with one choice, really.

Just as Wendy was finishing "here sh—," Lola threw a ten-dollar bill on the counter and fled the store with an audible swish and clunk of the door shutting behind her.

Soaking in her warm bathtub, Lola thought about Wendy. Did that woman have to remember everything? And repeat it with such accuracy? Hot blood was still pumping through her veins. To say she was mad was an understatement. It wasn't Wendy's fault, but it felt good to blame her, to let her anger out on the woman.

Wendy didn't have to repeat everything, every detail. Sure, Lola liked the store for the gossip, but she liked it when it was about others, not her. *I'm being a hypocrite*, she chided herself. If it had been someone else who it had happened to, she would have gobbled up that piece of gossip, and if it was really juicy, would have repeated it with the same accuracy to her two best friends, Mikaella and Elena. She wasn't being fair. Lola sighed. Wendy's shocked face when she'd run out still haunted her as she lay her hand atop the calm bath water. Wendy was a good person. She hadn't meant Lola any harm or humiliation. Lola briefly closed her eyes in shame and sighed.

"Sorry," she whispered, gazing in the general direction of the store. She hoped good things would happen to Wendy, in compensation for the negative energy she had sent her. Perhaps a sexy man? Or the love of her life? A small weight lifted off her shoulders. Lola smiled, feeling the world become a clearer, more optimistic world as blood pumped through her body and face. Tomorrow, she was going to apologize in person, she decided. She drained the bathtub, picturing the water as all her hate and hurt draining from her. She smiled peacefully as the last drops drained.

Wrapping a towel around her body, she walked into her living room and sat, content, on her couch. She was happy. She felt rage-free. It felt good. She looked around adoringly at her apartment, but her gaze froze on one of her two armchairs. The armchair where that very morning she had been kissing David, the same armchair where she had seen David and Nicole.

Lola felt the betrayal come back bitterly. She glared furiously at the armchair as it reminded her of the afternoon's incident. Well, she had to throw away that chair now.

Great.

She liked that chair; it fit perfectly with her warm, rustic décor, plus it was part of a set. It had an identical twin. Her gaze flickered to the other armchair. Yep, identical, down to the stitching. Both would always remind her of David and her boss. Lola gazed at the chair, praying it would spark another memory. She sighed. Not happening. Just one horrific memory it would always remind her of. Well… that only left one thing to do; she had to redecorate her entire apartment. A smile pulled at the corner of her mouth as she contemplated redecorating her apartment. Such a hard thing for an interior designer to do, Lola giggled. New decoration, new start, new Lola, she thought. Her interior designer mind went straight to work.

Decorating was normally an exciting process, but as she looked around her studio apartment, all her decorations were held together with sentimental value. The armchairs were the set her father and mother had picked out when they had first gotten married. It was in those armchairs that her mother had sung and caressed her belly when Lola was still a fetus. It was the same chair where her father had sat her on his lap when she was scared or sad and had told her lavish made-up stories to make her feel better.

Lola battled with nostalgia and newfound bitter anger at the armchair. No matter how hard she tried to convince herself the chair was innocent, every time she laid her eyes on it, anger bubbled hot inside her as the memory of the afternoon slapped her in the face.

This was completely ridiculous.

Lola stood and strode into her shower and finally shampooed her hair. When she got out of the shower, she got dressed and called her best friend Mikaella with a plan in mind.

Sorrows, be prepared to be drunken away.

Chapter Three

Mikaella Riddler found her best friend already tipsy, slouching at the bar. Cautiously taking Lola's state into consideration, Mikaella walked up to her. Lola never drank, other than at special occasions, and even then, she normally left the wine glass half full. In all the years Mikaella had known Lola, she'd only gotten drunk once—in college, and had learned her lesson quite well.

"Thought you didn't like drinking."

Lola shifted her glazed-over eyes towards Mikaella and gave her a non-committal shrug.

Mikaella quickly understood. "What happened?" she asked, concerned. It must have been something massive to make Lola try to drink her sorrows away.

Lola made a face.

"He... ah... He... well..." Lola cleared her throat, "He... David cheated on me," she finally said, in a single breath.

Mikaella nodded and sat on the stool next to her.

"What? That's all you're going to do? Just nod? Don't you have anything to say?" Lola asked, taken aback.

"Well, can't say I'm surprised," Mikaella admitted as she placed her hands on her lap in a calm manner.

"What's that supposed to mean?" Lola demanded. Mikaella gazed at her significantly. Lola rolled her eyes. "I know, but he changed." Lola defended David.

"He changed?" Mikaella raised a skeptical brow.

"Yes."

"How so?"

"Well… we were living together… He never lived with anyone… That means something… No?" Lola asked, confusion interlaced with desperation.

"I guess," Mikaella replied. She briefly studied Lola. There was a little puffiness and pinkish redness around her brown eyes. "Did you cry?"

"Yes! Of course!" Lola said, offended.

Mikaella frowned. That was odd. It wasn't like Lola to cry over a break-up, much less react this strongly. For a second, Mikaella had thought that something grave—like her father passing away—had happened, but a break-up? With David? Mikaella knew her friend well enough to know she hadn't been in love with David. Lola didn't fall in love. She didn't cry over break-ups. Because who cried at games? Love was a game to Lola. In all the years Mikaella had known Lola, she knew Lola wasn't one for this kind of drama. Was Lola in love with David? They had lived together. Mikaella knew only too well that things changed when people lived together. For better or for worse.

But Mikaella seriously doubted that Lola was in love with David. Did Lola like him? Yes. Had she felt a strong sexual attraction to him? Definitely, yes. But love? No. The answer was automatic. Mikaella knew the answer was no. Something didn't feel right.

When Lola had called her earlier, she had been all melodramatic, but Mikaella had thought it had just been a tactic to get her to the bar. What's really going on? Mikaella wondered.

"What are you thinking?" Lola asked. "Just spit it out, please. I hate it when you go all silent and thoughtful."

Mikaella gazed at her friend, trying to understand. "Well, you guys didn't actually live together. I mean, when he moved in, he only brought some clothes and a toothbrush. He kept his apartment. Not to mention, he would even stay over some nights—"

"That's because it's close to his work. And he didn't cheat on me when he stayed there," Lola interrupted defensively.

"I'm not saying he cheated on you when he stayed at his place. I know he was faithful during your whole relationship." Up until now, she commented to herself. "But what I am saying is it wasn't as serious a relationship as you think it was." Mikaella hated how harsh she sounded.

"But I love him," Lola said, but Mikaella could sense the words were forced. They weren't talking about whether she loved him or not. Something else was going through Lola's head, and Mikaella doubted if Lola even knew what it was. There was something more to this.

"I know you like him." Mikaella chose her words carefully, watching Lola's reaction. Lola nodded, unaffected by her word choice. "And it is a big deal you guys lived together, but—" A bell sounded as the door opened, letting in a group of boasting, testosterone-filled men. They wore green and white rugby uniform shirts—from their rugby practice, Mikaella deduced. Lola's eyes flicked towards the group. A gleam shone through her brown eyes. And half of Lola's attention was lost. Lola's slumped, saddened posture straightened out, becoming more friendly and open. Mikaella held back a smile as she gazed at her friend. Only Lola, she thought lovingly. This was the woman who she knew and loved.

Lola turned to her, asking, "Where were we?"

"I was saying—"

"He passes the puck to number forty-five and oh! Almost scored." The hockey commentator's voice interrupted Mikaella as someone flicked on the TV.

If Mikaella had a quarter of Lola's attention, she had now lost it. Sports and men. She had completely lost Lola.

"Oh, come on! Are you blind?! It clearly went in!" Lola shouted at the referee through the television. She raised her arms in exasperation, shaking her hands. The movement caught the attention of one of the rugby players. A pretty boy. Lola's type. A blond, blue-eyed, preppy-style player who began playing cat and mouse with Lola's gaze.

Oh, yeah, she was in love with David, Mikaella thought with a smile. Seeing Lola like this eased her wariness. Games and good times were what Lola was made of. Lola was harmlessly flirting with the player. Mikaella couldn't blame her for flirting with the rugby player; the whole team was like a dish of muscles with good looks on the side. She even found herself flirting, a little, with one of them.

He kind of reminded her of... that night.

One night with that man, and she couldn't get him out of her head. All week, he had haunted her thoughts. And haunted her skin. She could still faintly feel his touch on her sides.

"Are you paying any attention to anything I'm saying?" Mikaella distracted herself from thoughts of *him*. Lola nodded, not even looking away from the hockey game.

"So I slept with a complete stranger," Mikaella announced casually.

That caught Lola's attention.

"WHAT?!" Lola turned, stunned. Her brown eyes were wide, and a strand of blond hair escaped her ponytail when she turned abruptly. "No! You're lying."

Mikaella smiled. "Yes, I'm lying," she admitted. Well, not completely. He wasn't a complete stranger. He was... she had no idea what he was.

“♥”

Lola narrowed her gaze on Mikaella. She had a feeling Mikaella wasn't completely lying, but she knew better than to push for more information. Mika would tell her when she was ready. Nevertheless, Lola asked, "Why said it, then?"

"I needed to get your attention."

Mikaella had her attention... Okay, maybe not her full attention, but there was a hockey game on, and that cute rugby player kept smiling at her. Still, Mikaella had her attention; she had been talking about... about... What were they talking about? Right. Mika didn't have her attention. Oops.

31

"I'm, worried about you," Mikaella added. Lola sighed. If she was being honest, she was worried about herself, too. She didn't understand her own feelings. She didn't understand what was going on.

"Tell me what happened. How did you find out?" Mika urged. Lola sighed.

"Where to start?" Lola asked, more to herself than to Mikaella. "I walked in on him." Lola paused, trying to find the right words. Mikaella listened with more care than she normally did, shaking her head with compassion. Lola could tell she didn't like the part about her decision to drink away her sorrows. It seemed like the normal thing to do. Wasn't it what great men had done? Great artists? What rappers and singers sang and rapped about? Alcohol, drugs— it all made it go away. Despite her initial thoughts, the drinks weren't helping as she had thought they would. Whoever had come up with the idea that drinking their sorrows away worked, had been lying. It wasn't helping; if anything, her problems seemed to worsen under the inspection of her tipsy brain. Oh, she really should have eaten something that day. She wasn't even done with her second beer.

"Who was the woman?" Mika asked.

"Guess."

Mikaella thought it over and then gasped, "NO! Nicole! Nicole, as in our 'friend' Nicole? As in your boss Nicole?"

"Yep." Lola nodded. Some friend Nicole was. They had met in college, and that had been where their *wonderful* "friendship" had begun. In reality, they weren't friends. They were more enemies than anything else. Nicole was from a wealthy family that had started up a company at her request. Spoiled brat. Lola wouldn't have gone out of her way to work for Nicole, but Nicole had been the only one to give her a job because they had been "friends" in college. No one liked her. Neither Mikaella nor Elena nor she had ever liked Nicole. But even though they weren't the best of friends, a little respect would have been nice. Or, at least, Nicole could have been content with sleeping with just two of her boyfriends.

"Wow, I can't believe it." Mikaella paused. "No. Yes, I can, actually." Mikaella nodded, then asked, "How do you feel?"

Lola gazed at Mikaella's dark brown eyes. She shrugged, uncertain. She didn't know how she felt. She was confused. She was angry, but she wasn't sure about what.

Now that she had had time to digest the day's events, she wasn't sure what she felt. There was something in her she couldn't pinpoint, but it confused her. She wanted to call it relief, but that couldn't be right. She couldn't feel relieved. Relieved about what? That she wasn't actually in love? No, it must be betrayal, heartbreak… Yeah, it must be that— The alcohol was starting to kick in, making her feel loose and happy. Also a little sluggish, but the good part was that her thoughts were starting to make absolutely no sense.

Unsatisfied with the answer her intoxicated brain had come up with, Lola bargained for more time. "I'll tell you if you tell me who the guy is who has you glowing," Lola bargained, desperately wanting to know who he was.

Mikaella blushed a deep burgundy pink. A strong contrast against her pale olive complexion. She was about to deny it, but one good look at Lola's determined face had her backpedaling. Mika's shoulders slumped in defeat. "Well." She took a deep breath and hesitantly told Lola, blushing harder as each word left her mouth, while

Lola looked like a statue, with her mouth open in shock.

"Wow…" Lola sat gazing at her still-blushing, embarrassed friend. "I'm speechless. Never thought you had it in you. I'm so proud," Lola said, sticking out her chest as she placed her palm against her heart and smiled like a proud mother would when watching her child graduate or leave home. Mikaella rolled her eyes but couldn't manage to hide her smile.

"I never thought I would be the kind of girl to do that, but it just happened." Mikaella justified her behavior.

"I'm glad it happened," Lola said, all joking aside. "Ever since you-know-who. You haven't dated anyone. Not even been interested. I was getting worried," Lola confessed. Mikaella looked down, nodding.

Beep! Beep!

Boop! Boop!

Both women instantly reached for their phones. It was a text from Elena. "Valentine Weekend" was all Lola read. She groaned, closing her eyes, wanting to shut out everything. Although she had spent at least a good hour this morning telling everyone about her weekend, she had now completely forgotten about it. The memory brought back a wave of embarrassment.

"Oh, man." Lola pressed her eyes closed more tightly. "The Valentine Weekend," Lola groaned. She had a feeling this weekend would be long and painful. "I completely forgot about it," she whimpered.

Mikaella nodded understandingly. This event would be awesome, if the person was in a relationship. But singles were forced to be matched up, in hopes they would leave with a relationship. Great, if the person was single and ready to mingle.

Neither of their cases.

"Two beers." They both hailed the mustached waiter in unison and laughed, leaning in towards each other.

"Come on," Lola whispered, drunk. "Stop moving. Get in. Come on. Stop moving. Get in already." Hiccup.

The keyhole kept moving, making it impossible for her to get her trembling key in. She jabbed repeatedly at the door, trying to get it in. Hiccup. Come on. She held the key in front of her face to inspect it, her brown eyes narrowed on the shiny, jagged key. She had no idea how many zigzags it should have, but it looked alright to her, and hey! her nostrils were moving. Lola held her breath. Ha! They stopped moving. She let out a series of short breaths. Her nostrils expanded and contracted. Ha! Ha! That's so coo— "Ow!" Lola bumped into the door. She glared at the door as it swayed with the waves while the world turned around her. Whoa. Lola closed her eyes; she opened them and gazed at the brown-painted door.

Right. Key. Keyhole. In. Keyhole, key, in.

Lola inspected the key once more, trying to find the problem. After a careful inspection, she concluded that it was okay. The key looked fine to her. Then why wasn't it going in? Her shaky hand tried again. Poke. Poke. Poke. Again and again, she tried to put the key in the keyhole. Maybe it was the keyhole that had a problem. She hunched and bent to inspect the keyhole.

The door opened.

"Hey! You got the door open," Lola chanted, elongating the words. Joyfully drunk, she passed, hiccupping, by her stunned, dark-green-plaid-wearing neighbor.

Chapter Four

Chuck Moran gazed at the invitation. Pink hearts, arrows, a cupid and many roses decorated the sleek, glossy paper. Bold and cursive typeface invited him to the Valentine Weekend.

A valentine weekend. A weekend filled with romance-inspired activities for couples. He was single and had no prospective valentine in view.

In reality, he had no woman in his life. He hadn't for quite some time. Not since his ex-almost-fiancé. Maybe it was because he'd been alone for so long that he had accepted the invitation.

Despite the fact that he was single, and said as much to Elena—the creator of the Valentine Weekend, who also happened to be looking into constructing a getaway chalet with her boyfriend—she reassured him, saying, "It's no problem. I plan to pair up all my single friends. You must come. It will be amazing. You might find your soulmate."

Soulmate.

The woman actually said "soulmate." Between his loneliness and her enthusiasm— and her boyfriend holding the black pen, about to sign the contract, Chuck had accepted the ridiculous invitation. Now, he regretted it. Big-time.

It was a whole weekend. More than a weekend, he realized, counting—Friday, Saturday, Sunday and Monday. Four days. That was too much time. He could have done other things during those four days, instead of Valentine activities. Why had he accepted? Client. Of course. Chuck sighed.

Interrupting his thoughts, Chuck heard a tapping noise coming from the other side of his door. It sounded like someone was faintly tapping on his door with a sharp object. Who was still up at this hour? Chuck checked his watch. It was 3:30. Probably some drunk, he concluded, curling his lip in disgust. He had no desire to see anyone right now. Much less a drunk.

Ignoring the noise, he focused on the invitation again. It was just four days. It wasn't the end of the world. Sure, he could have worked during the four days, done something productive instead of—he read the invitation closely—instead of going on a boat ride while reading poetry. God, it was worse than he had thought. Chuck sighed. He'd never told a girlfriend he loved her, much less professed his love through poetry.

Maybe he could get out of it. He could call Elena and tell her that some emergency work-related thing had happened and that he needed to take care of it. He would need to word it better, though. A lot better.

He could say— Tap! Silence. Tap! Silence again. Tap! Tap!

Tap!

The noise became harsher, more persistent. Clenching his jaw, Chuck put the invitation on his coffee table and got up, already glaring through the door at the person. As he reached for the doorknob, the noise stopped. He sighed, relaxing his tense chest.

He was in no mood to deal with anyone right now. He was tired. His body hurt from lugging planks of wood all day, and his thoughts were restless, demanding his attention. It wasn't the best cocktail for his mood.

He turned and gazed at the invitation from across his apartment. He wasn't going. It was final.

Hi, Elena. I won't be able to make it to the Valentine Weekend. I am sorry.

There. Perfectly said—simple, with no explanation and to the point. No need to stare at the inoffensive piece of paper anymore. No more wondering if he should or shouldn't go. He had made his decision. It was settled.

Bang! The loud sound hit his ears, followed by silence. Tap! Tap! Tap!

Irritated, Chuck yanked the door open, only to freeze in shock. Lola, his beautiful neighbor, was hunched over, her face at his crotch level. She looked up at him with her big brown eyes, a little cross-eyed.

"Hey!" Lola elongated the word. "You got the door open," she chanted, joyfully drunk.

Stunning him more, she walked past him into his apartment, hiccupping. Chuck's apartment was neither big nor small. It was perfect for him when he'd been kicked out of the house he had built for his ex. The apartment was a spacious brick studio. The bathroom was on the left, along with his kitchen, and on the right was his bed. His bed, which Lola had just bumped into, causing her to hit the floor. She stood up, looking around, clearly confused.

"Why is my bed here? And why is the bathroom on the right?" she asked, getting up. "I thought the bathroom was on the left," she added.

"Well, maybe in your apartment it's on the left, but this is my apartment," he said, heavily emphasizing "my apartment," as if he was trying to explain something difficult to a child.

"This is my apartment," she stated.

"No, this is my apartment," Chuck replied.

"No, this is my apartment," Lola stated again, stubbornly, as she stomped her foot.

Chuck had no patience when it came to drunk people. Especially, drunk women. But he found himself surprisingly calm and amused as he gazed at the flushed, tipsy version of Lola. He bit back a smile; he'd never seen someone actually stomp their foot like that.

"Lola, this is my apartment," he said softly but with firmness.

Lola blinked, confused. "How do you know my name?" Her voice was heavy with distrust. He sighed. She was so drunk; she didn't remember him. Or the fact that they sometimes talked in the mailroom. Or greeted one another every single time they laid eyes on each other, like this morning, when he had caught her gazing after him. Or that he had a crush on her since first meeting her in the mailroom. The last part she didn't know or, at least, he hoped she didn't know it.

"You told me, remember?" he said.

Lola thought about it and then nodded in agreement, with evident suspicion. She studied him closely, her light brown eyes seeing too much. He felt like he was seeing too much of him in the depth of those eyes. "Look, I'm going to go get David, okay?"

Indignation flashed across her face. "He's no longer my boyfriend." She lifted her chin in the air.

His heartbeat picked up as the corner of his mouth tugged upwards. She was single. Oh, Chuck realized. It didn't take a genius to figure out why she was drunk. "So you got drunk because you and your boyfriend broke up?" Chuck asked, to be sure, before making any judgment.

"Of course," Lola said, offended. "That's what people do. They drink away their sorrows. No?"

Chuck nodded. He knew only too well that people liked to drink away their sorrows. He swallowed back the memory.

"I need to use the bathroom," Lola declared out of nowhere, and marched across his apartment to his bathroom. Chuck was left standing alone, near the door and confused, as he gazed after Lola.

The all-too-real stench of alcohol hit Chuck's nose seconds later, after Lola had passed him.

Cheap, empty vodka bottles scattered on the floor in the blue daylight. A woman lying on the couch half-asleep, half-drunk.

Chuck tried to shake the image, but it haunted him as the Valentine Weekend invitation floated through his mind. The images floated back and forth like a tennis ball being hit by the walls of his brain. Both to his relief and horror, his thoughts were mainly filled with Lola. A distraction he jumped on at once.

It was reckless of her to still be in his apartment. She was so vulnerable. Men jumped at the easy opportunity of a drunken woman. The thought set his teeth on edge. He had seen it happen too often. She was really reckless. How easily some bastard could have stopped her in the street? With her brain muddled, her movements uncontrollable. He shuddered at the thought.

Chuck glanced over at the coffee table, where the pink decorated invitation lay. He concentrated hard on it, hoping it would distract him from his thoughts. It worked. Not as much as he had hoped for, but enough for him to calm down with the realization that Lola, at least, was with him. He could take her back to her apartment, where she would be safe. Chuck dropped his shoulders, relieved, as an uncomfortable tug pulled inside him. She'd be out of his apartment. A part of him enjoyed seeing her cheeks flushed and her eyes wide and crossed. A part of him missed seeing a woman moving about in his apartment. How long had it been?

Just over a year, he mentally calculated. That's all? He swore it had been more. He shrugged, shaking his head.

The swishing sound of the toilet's flush broke through Chuck's thoughts. A rhythmic swish followed seconds later. The sound stopped and started, teasing his imagination. He imagined her long fingers playing with the falling water. He saw them twirl through the clear water and then swirl back. He could vividly see the small drop of water, defying gravity and dripping up her arm, to her shoulder. And then Chuck could see himself in the shower behind her, kissing that drop of water off her collarbone.

Sudden silence stunned Chuck out of his fantasy. God. Had it only been one year? One long year. He puffed out his breath, pushing back his desire, and let annoyance settle in as he watched Lola stumble out of the bathroom as if nothing had happened. Well, as if nothing, with a huge touch of tipsiness. She walked past him to his bed, yawning. She over-crossed her legs as she took each step. She wobbled from side to side. She was like a frail tree, swaying and shaking as the wind pushed and tore at it, but surprisingly, no matter how hard the wind blew, the tree never fell down.

Chuck found himself smiling at her dignified stumble. She amused him, he gave her that. She had managed to make him forget he was supposed to be mad at her recklessness.

Lola stopped before his bed, frowning, almost glaring at the poor piece of furniture. She turned, giving him the same stare. A deep "v" formed between her eyebrows.

"Aren't you my neighbor, Chuck?" Lola asked.

"Yes, I am." He nodded, way too pleased she had remembered him, or at least his name. But it was the same thing, right?

"Why are you in my apartment?"

Chuck sighed. Hadn't they gone through this already?

"This is *my* apartment."

"Oh." She breathed like she understood.

Chuck nodded. Finally, she got it.

"So this is your bed?" Lola tried to understand. She placed one hand on his bedsheet and absentmindedly caressed it with small circles.

"Yes." Chuck nodded, trying not to follow the movements of her hand.

Lola nodded, pursing her lips and gazing at his bed. Chuck's eyes went wide as Lola climbed onto his bed. From where he stood by the door, he got a great, split-second view of her bottom in the air.

Lola wasn't voluptuously curvy. She had subtle curves, proportioned to her lean, tall size. She had long legs that could go for miles, which he found a delightful temptation. Chuck thanked the lord that he was a respectable gentleman, because as he watched Lola slip under his sheets, he was more than tempted to join her. Perhaps slide a hand— Chuck took a deep breath. It was always tempting to seduce Lola, but in her current mental state, it would be too easy. Then again— No. He was a gentleman, Chuck repeated to himself. He wasn't going to do anything... unless... What if she wanted him to do something? What if that's what she wanted? He couldn't be rude and ignore her wishes.

No. If she did, then he'd need to hear the words from her mouth, not his lonely lower brain. Still, he glanced hopefully over at Lola, who was snuggling into the sheets. Her expression was serious, her movements precise and strong.

Chuck had the feeling it wouldn't be that easy to seduce Lola. Tension eased throughout him. She, perhaps, wasn't as vulnerable as he thought. He smiled.

"Good night."

What?! Shock tensed his muscles. Was she really going to sleep in his bed? No, she couldn't possibly.

From where Chuck stood, he rose on his toes, trying to catch a glimpse of Lola's face, but it was buried in the pillows. Unsure, he walked up to his bed.

Lola's eyes were closed, and her breath was deep and steady. She might not be vulnerable, but she did look vulnerable lying there in his bed. He watched her breath—out, in and out. He wanted to punch himself for even thinking of wanting to seduce her now. His heart squeezed as he gazed at her. She was beautiful, he thought, gazing at her serious sleeping expression. At least, now he knew she hadn't stayed in his apartment because she wanted him. Of course not. She was just really drunk and truly believed this was her apartment. The thought sank inside him, bringing down his chest.

A year. He shook his head as he poured Lola a glass of water. He hadn't guessed how much he missed a woman in his life. Why had he— Oh, right. He had chosen his solitude, for good reason. And so far, he was liking it. Which was why first thing tomorrow, Lola would be out of his apartment, and he'd be calling Elena.

He placed the cool glass of water on the nightstand beside his bed and put a garbage can beside the bed. Just in case, he murmured softly to her sleeping face. Unable to resist, he pushed a strand of her golden hair back from her forehead.

"Good night," he whispered and pulled back quickly before he kissed her sleeping lips.

Chapter Five

Chuck heard her groaning before he felt the heavy sunlight burn through his closed eyelids. He slowly opened his eyes, squinting into the morning sunshine. Sleepy blurriness blinded him for several seconds until gradually, he came out of the fog and saw the morning sky crisp and clear. He blinked a few times before sitting up on the couch. He groaned both in pain and in horror, realizing his movements were limited by his aching, contracted muscles. Not good. He needed his full range of motion to work today.

Instead of going to the Valentine Weekend, he was going to drive out to the lake and work on his chalet. Like he had yesterday and all week. Like he would for the next weeks to come, until he finished constructing the cottage. He needed to be in top shape.

He could still work, but now, with his aching muscles would be an inconvenience, slowing him down. And although he had just started it, he wanted the chalet to be done already. He sighed internally. His fingers massaged his stiff shoulders loose, and he groaned quietly at the sharp pain it produced. Rolling back his shoulders, he stretched his back. He groaned loudly, stopping mid-stretch. His back cracked in agonizing pain, in protest.

A sharp, frightened gasp pierced his ears, compounding his headache. The pain pumped through his head, making him feel like he had a hangover. Chuck looked up to see Lola sitting up on his bed, with one hand over her mouth and eyes wide in shock, staring at him. She slowly closed her eyes and transitioned her hand over them. "Please, please, please, please, please, please," Chuck could faintly hear Lola whisper. Then a bit louder, she pleaded in a frightened voice, "Please tell me we didn't sleep together," and dropped her hand from her eyes and gazed at him in fearful hope.

"You do realize you're on the bed and I'm on the couch, right?" he replied. Chuck glanced down at the bed. How he wished he had slept in his therapeutic bed. He glanced back at Lola. Her blond, almost golden hair was knotted on her head. Mascara flakes dotted the dark circles under her eyes, and she still seemed a little cross-eyed. He briefly wondered if she was still drunk.

Lola made a face. "So? That means absolutely nothing. You could have slept with me, then gone to sleep on the couch. People do that, you know," she informed him.

People did that? No "people" he knew did that. He gazed at her, trying to understand. What kind of people did she know?

"It's true," she said defensively, after he'd only stared at her like she was a riddle, without saying anything. "People do that." She enforced her point. "Or, at least, David does that." She paused, looking puzzled. "Did that, I mean—at the beginning of our relationship..." She added the awkward explanation, breaking off at the end.

David. Her boyfriend. Her ex-boyfriend, a small voice reminded him. A ball of anxious happiness tickled in his chest. She was single, he internally smiled.

Chuck had spoken with David on more than a few occasions in the mailroom. He had talked more with him than with Lola. Not that he resented the man for it. David had seemed like a good guy. A decent guy. A normal guy. Not someone who would do that. He felt Lola's intent gaze on him while she waited for an answer.

Chuck wanted to roll his eyes but instead settled for a half-amused expression. "You know you have your clothes on, right?" He pointed out the obvious. A pair of classic black sneakers with white shoelaces stuck out of his white covers. "And your shoes," he added.

Lola looked down first at herself, then at her feet and wiggled them to assure that her sneakers were well on. A sigh of relief washed through her body. She shot Chuck an apologetic look. "I'm sorry," she said and squeezed her eyes shut. She rubbed her temples in circles, moaning in pain. Chuck's protective instincts kicked into gear. He edged closed to her from the couch, barely sitting on it anymore.

"Oh," she breathed. "I'm so sorry. I was so drunk last night. I'm so sorry. Did I wake you up last night? Or, should I say, this morning?" She opened her eyes to stare guiltily at him. The sunlight shone on her eyes, making them almost amber. She quickly closed her eyes, moaning again.

Chuck opened his mouth to reassure her, but before he could say anything, she said, "I did, didn't I? Oh," she breathed with guilt. "I am so sorry. I am really sorry. I don't know how it happened. I remember trying to get my key into the keyhole. I vaguely remember you." She waved her hand in his general direction. She opened her eyes and gazed at him apologetically. "No offense." She added, "I don't know what happened. Did I do anything stupid?" She looked down before closing her eyes again.

"No," he replied. Unless he called sleeping in some stranger's bed stupid, which he did. But he didn't have the heart to tell her; she already looked guilty enough. No need to put more on her conscience.

She nodded, not really believing him, and reached over to the glass of water, downing it in seconds.

Wow. No wonder she had gotten so drunk. Chuck watched as Lola gazed into the empty glass in her hands, deep in thought. She moaned and flopped back onto the mattress.

"I am sorry," she said, sitting up again. "I know I should be leaving, but your bed is so comfy." Fifty-thousand-dollar bed; it better be comfy. He glared at the bed, wishing he had slept on it. "My head keeps spinning. Do you mind if I lie here for a few minutes?" she added, lying back down without waiting for an answer.

"Aren't you worried you're in a stranger's apartment?" he had to ask.

"You're not a stranger." A mixture of a smile and disbelief at her bold statement played on his lip. "You're Chuck, my neighbor. We sometimes talk in the mailroom," she replied. "Plus, I'm not scared of you," she added, matter-of-factly.

Chuck let out a low chuckle, shaking his head in amusement. "Do you want some breakfast?" he offered, smiling, suddenly not wanting her to leave his apartment.

"Yes, please." Lola's silvery voice traveled from the bed. She propped herself on her elbows and smiled at him. Her smile was warm, like the sun on his skin.

"Good," he breathed quietly to himself. "Pancakes sound good?" he added, louder.

"Mmmmm. Yes. That sounds delicious."

Chuck stood, ignoring the pain in his muscles, and strode to his kitchen. He grabbed all the ingredients and began preparing the pancakes. The apartment was silent for a few minutes. A soft thump broke the silence, followed by light footsteps. Chuck glanced up at the sound and watched as Lola pulled her hair into a ponytail, her light brown eyes gazing at nothing as she concentrated on the hair band. She was wearing a fitted pale yellow sweater and black jeans. Her clothes hugged her in the right places. Showing a little and setting his imagination into overdrive. Concentrate. Batter. Make pancake batter, he ordered himself.

"You make pancakes from scratch?" she gasped in surprise as she reached him. She leaned over him to get a better view of the pancakes in progress.

"Best kind," he stated with a shrug.

"That is awesome," she said amazed, inspecting the bowl of loose, dry ingredients. "I wish I knew how to make them from scratch. But I don't really cook. I mean, I do but simple, easy, pre-made stuff, you know? Microwavable. But I wish I knew how to cook like this." She glanced up at him.

Whatever he was going to say vanished as he gazed into her sparkling light brown eyes. They were like the shallow end of a pool or ocean; there wasn't any depth. One eye was closer to her nose—

no more than half a millimeter—than the other of her close-set eyes. And he'd been thinking she was cross-eyed from being drunk. Somehow, the barely noticeable offset eye made it impossible for him to look away. He noticed it only when she was gazing upwards; it was unnoticeable as Lola straightened herself out, still gazing at him for an answer.

He simply gave a nod. The strong, ardent scent of alcohol burnt his nostrils as Lola stood beside him, leaning back down to inspect the ingredients. The smell was so strong, it conjured up memories.

The lifeless hand twitching for the half-empty bottle on the ground and knocking it over, spilling the burning smell in the apartment.

"Take a shower," he snapped at the woman in his memory.

Chuck was aware of Lola freezing beside him, snapping him out of the dreaded memory. So many years, pushing back those memories. He did a pretty good job at it, but sometimes, no matter how hard he tried, they still found their way to his brain. Why were the memories so vivid? So clear and crisp? They hadn't been for ages... Of course. His sister's recent visit. Chuck sighed inwardly.

"If you want, you can freshen up in the bathroom." Chuck hesitated, trying to make up for his error. "You could take a shower, if you want." He knew it was too late.

"Are you saying I stink?" Lola demanded with a sour expression, unamused. She glared at him, waiting impatiently for an answer.

Her glare silenced his half-choked words. Damn. He hadn't meant to snap at her like that. Chuck tensed. He was going to lose Lola. It wasn't like he could lose her, because she wasn't his, he clarified to himself. He had meant… What had he meant by that thought? Something different, that was for sure. Chuck's breath became shallow as he tried to apologize and even tried to go back in time.

Lola busted into lighthearted laughter and said, grinning, "Because, I do. You read my mind. I was about to ask you, if I could use your bathroom, to freshen up. The smell of alcohol is making me sick." She laughed. It took a few seconds for Chuck to react to her sudden change, but her smile was playful and harmless.

He smiled, relieved, and nodded. "I have a couple of new toothbrushes in the second drawer, and I'll set out some towels for you."

"Thanks," she replied gratefully, avoiding his gaze. Chuck could hear her thinking away. Suddenly, her face scrunched up, and through a grimace she added, "And I am sorry. I had just had too… It was so much fun. I hope you're not mad."

"Mad? I should be, shouldn't I?"

Lola relaxed, nodding. "Yes, you should, but then again, I really don't mind you not being mad." She gave him a wide smile. Chuck chuckled.

"I'm sorry, too." He sobered up. "I could have said it nicer."

"What? Are you kidding? If you had, then I might have thought it was a pretext to get me naked. And not because I smell nauseating." She made a disgusted face at her smell. "Plus, I would have to bust some serious Kung Fu moves on you before running out." She nodded the sad truth.

"You know Kung Fu?" Chuck raised his eyebrows, surprised.

"I might. I might not." She shrugged. She was playing with him, but something told Chuck she might know a few moves here and there. He found himself studying the tall woman. She was no less than three inches shorter than his six-foot-one. He was puzzled by her—the way words flowed out of her mouth quickly yet completely understandably.

"Prove it."

"And give away my advantage?" Lola raised an eyebrow and then shook her head. "Nope." She smacked the "p." "But just know your size can't take me," she taunted.

"Perhaps. Perhaps not." He mimicked her answer.

Lola's smile widened into a happy, toothy grin, liking that he'd imitated her words. Her smile was like a force pulling him closer. A magnetic pull which hummed him closer to her. Chuck resisted the urge and instead said, "Towels?"

"Yes, please." She smiled and tasted her mouth. "You said the toothbrush was in the second drawer?"

He nodded. "Here. I'll get for you," he added and walked with her to the bathroom. On the way, he made a quick detour to the closet beside the bathroom and took out a set of towels for Lola. When he entered the bathroom, Lola was already looking through the second drawer.

"Wow," she mouthed. "You sure do have a lot of toothbrushes," she added, without looking up. "Many girls come by?" She wiggled her eyebrows at him. Lola tilted her head, inspecting him closely. Like the night before, Chuck felt like Lola was seeing right through him. "Hmm, didn't think you were the playboy type."

"What makes you think I am?"

"The toothbrushes." She pointed at the drawer filled with brand-new packs of toothbrushes. No need to tell her the packs had been on sale. He could have fun, too.

Chuck gazed her up and down and took a long step, closing the space between them. Lola's breath caught at his sudden nearness, but she stayed where she was. Reaching around her, he grabbed the first toothbrush pack and closed the drawer, purposely doing it all slowly, knowing he'd have to lean over Lola. The drawer clicked shut, and he waited a second before whispering in her ear, "If I was a playboy, we'd be taking a shower right about now, after not sleeping on the couch."

Lola shivered, closing her eyes for the briefest moment. It was Chuck's turn to catch his breath. In the mirror, he caught sight of her clutching the counter. Slowly, she released her hand, turning her head into his neck. He barely noticed Lola's warm breath assaulting him down his shirt, as Lola twisted around in one swift movement, grabbing the toothbrush out of his hand. The movement was so sudden, Chuck instinctively took a step back.

"Kung Fu." Lola winked and laughed.

Chuck breathed out a laugh, shaking his head in amusement. He glanced at the shower behind her. "The right faucet is cold water, and—"

"And the left one is warm water. I know. We have the exact same bathroom," Lola pointed out, biting back a smile.

Chuck nodded. Of course. "I'll leave you to it." He stepped out.

Chuck marched back to the kitchen and brewed himself a strong cup of coffee. He needed to wake up. Being around Lola muddled his brain worse than a sleepless night did.

It didn't help that he had always found her interesting, beautiful. If she hadn't had a boyfriend when they had first met, he would have done everything and anything to be hers. He shook his head, trying to clear it. The sound of the shower turning on conjured his fantasy from the night before. Oh, yes. If he was a player, they'd be showering together, with her legs around him and her back pressed against the wall. He felt his groin shift in response. No. Focus. Okay, good. Pancakes. Make pancakes. Good. He focused all his attention on the pancakes. He doubted anyone ever had paid so much attention to making pancakes.

Chuck sighed the biggest sigh of relief when he heard Lola's light step coming out of the bathroom. She sported her yellow hoodie, black jeans and a wet hair bun. He flipped the last pancake onto the stack and turned. "Ready?" he asked.

Lola nodded, eyeing the plate of pancakes he held. A sparkle turned into a million glitters as she licked her lips, anticipating the breakfast. "They look amazing." Lola admired the pancakes as he set them down on the table. He gestured for her to take a seat, and she folded herself into the chair.

"Would you like some coffee?"

"You wouldn't have chamomile tea, by any chance—or green tea?"

He shook his head.

"Coffee is great, then. Don't they always say it's the cure for a hangover?" She added quickly. "I've heard it actually doesn't do anything. I mean, it doesn't help. But I think it does. It might not have antioxidant properties like green tea, but I think the effect is more psychological. You know, comforting."

Chuck listened to her ramble as he poured her a cup of coffee, a smile tracing his features. Lola sat upright, with her legs crossed Indian style, waiting patiently from him to join her. He could tell she was counting down the seconds until she ate.

"Do you prefer butter, peanut butter or jam with your pancakes?" He handed her the cup of coffee.

"Peanut butter?" Her voice was surprised, and she gazed up at him with her big brown eyes. Her lashes were still wet from the shower.

Chuck nodded.

"You eat your pancakes with peanut butter?" she inquired, with curiosity sparkling in her eyes. He nodded again, starting to wonder, if it was weird that he did.

"Me, too!" Lola's eyes widened in delight. "Everyone always thinks it weird but it's so delicious. I think it's better than jam. I never liked the taste of syrup and jam." She shrugged.

"I'd never eat pancakes without good old peanut butter."

"I understand completely. Although I'm not opposed to pancakes with butter. Anything with butter is always delicious."

He nodded, serving a small stack of pancakes on her plate and then fetching the peanut butter.

Silence settled as they ate the first few bites. Lola moaned her appreciation at the first bite. "These are the best pancakes I've ever had." She closed her eyes, savoring the bite. Chuck thanked her, pleased by her gratitude. After a few more silent bites, Lola asked, "So what happened last night?"

"Nothing. Don't worry," he assured her.

"No, I mean, what did I do? I can barely remember anything."

"You really want to know?"

"Oh, god. Was I that bad?" Lola grimaced in horror. "I need every single detail. In return, I'll tell you why I got drunk," she bargained.

It scared Chuck how he could so accurately remember the whole event with Lola and tell it with such ease, as though he had played it over in his mind a gazillion times. In reward, she explained why she had gotten drunk in the first place. Although, quite honestly, seeing her at his kitchen table with her hair wet, in a messy bun, was reward enough. Wait a minute. She said "in return," he reminded himself. Return, reward—it was the same thing, as long as she was here with him, explaining. "Long story short, David cheated on me with my boss."

"Your boss?" Chuck's eyes almost popped out.

"Yep." She smacked her lips on the "p." "My boss. Who also is my friend," Lola said, making quotation marks around "friend" and rolling her eyes.

Chuck didn't believe there was a good reason to get drunk, but hers came close. Her boss. That sucked. He guessed Lola had two options now: quit or continue working with her, knowing she had cheated with Lola's boyfriend.

"You would think that's why I got hammered, and partly it was, but after I talked with Mika—short for Mikaella, my best friend—," she added on the side, "I was ready to leave, but then I got a message from my other best friend, Elena." Lola paused, sipping some warm coffee.

Elena? No, not the same one, he assured himself.

"So Elena texted us, reminding us that today we had promised we would go early, to help her prepare the last-minute details of the Valentine Weekend event she planned."

Chuck frowned. Lola was best friends with Elena. The same Elena who had invited him to the Valentine Weekend?

Going to the event didn't seem like a bad idea anymore.

Thinking he was frowning because he didn't know what "Valentine Weekend" meant, Lola quickly explained. "The Valentine Weekend is this massive event Elena created." Lola used her hands to demonstrate the massiveness of the event. "She's been preparing for months. It's the biggest event she's ever planned. And she's planned birthday parties for Hollywood's finest, along with a couple hundred guests. It's her hopeless romantic side's ultimate dream. Anyway…" She waved off her sudden loss of track. "This weekend is supposed to be filled with romance-inspired activities."

Chuck nodded, knowing too well.

"When you're in a relationship, the idea doesn't sound so bad, but when you've just broken up with your boyfriend who," she pointed one straight finger in the air, "might be there, the whole event starts to sound horrible. Not to mention, on top of everything, now that I'm single, I'll be paired up with someone I don't know and who might be hoping to be paired up with someone who wants a relationship with him." She shook her head.

"And then, I'll either have to be all romantic with the man, or keep my mouth shut and call David and spend the weekend with him. A big no-no." Lola sighed heavily, her body drooping in the seat. "See why I needed alcohol last night? Well, three beers, one shot. I should have really eaten something before," she added to herself. Her gaze was serious as she studied Chuck for a second or two and then added, "Just so you know, I don't drink. I try to avoid it, if possible, but last night I just… I don't know… I just wasn't thinking straight." She shrugged.

A disgust he hadn't realized he'd felt, evaporated. It was his turn to study Lola. Her fair skin with subtle golden tints was smooth—like it was well-kept. Both externally and internally. Not prematurely wrinkled, with more imperfections than possible, like the skin of people who drank excessively.

"I needed to escape my thoughts," Lola continued. "Being paired up with someone who might be hoping to develop a relationship… I don't want another relationship right now. Anyway, it wasn't a pleasant idea, so I thought alcohol would make it pleasant."

Chuck nodded. He still didn't like her logic, but at least he knew she wasn't a drunkard.

"Oh, it's going to be a nightmare," Lola moaned, covering her face with her hands.

He hated seeing the way waves of wrinkles broke out on her forehead as she worried. Casually, he asked, trying to distract her from her tortured thoughts. "Romantic activities, like a boat ride while reading poetry to your beloved?"

Lola froze, dropping her hands and eyeing him with too much intensity.

It worked. Chuck relaxed internally.

"How did you know?" She eyed him suspiciously.

Instead of answering her, Chuck got up and retrieved the invitation from the coffee table. He watched as she gasped, surprised, her eyes zeroing in on the familiar decorated invitation.

"You were invited? Are you going?" she quickly asked.

No. No. No. He was going to call Elena the moment Lola left. He would apologize and tell Elena he couldn't make it. His decision was absolute. It was already made. No change— Chuck nodded.

A slow smile broke across Lola's lips but stopped dead in its tracks as her eyes unfocused on him. They refocused, widening, big and round. "Oh. My. God! Do you have a girlfriend?! If you do, I am so, so, SO, so sorry. I can't believe I spent the night here. Your girlfriend will be so mad—"

"I don't have a girlfriend." Chuck interrupted Lola firmly. He wanted her to understand. There was no one in his life.

"Oh, good" she breathed, relaxing into the chair. "I was so worried there for a second…" Her eyes unfocused again, gazing into space. Chuck could see thinking wheels turning away, manufacturing something.

Run! Came the quick warning. Run, before it's too late. Just run. He didn't listen as he sat, fascinated by how her eyebrows slightly smashed into each other as she concentrated, thinking away. Light brown eyes refocused on him, wide in hope but guarded with fear.

"So I was thinking," she began.

"Uh-huh," Chuck urged with caution and curiosity.

"Since you're going and I'm going, maybe we could go together… as a couple." She gave him a sweet smile, and her words tasted like sugary temptation.

He should have ran, when his instincts had told him to, he thought as he saw Lola's gaze turn persuasively sweet. Gazing at her waiting, hopeful gaze… There was no way he could say no.

Damn.

"Hear me out," Lola said after a few seconds of silence. "We don't actually have to be a real couple. We can just pretend. It'll be fun." She nodded, agreeing with the thought "It will be like a game. Oh. Wait." She paused, thoughtful. "Unless you were hoping to meet someone special there?" She asked, shrugging with anticipated guilt.

Chuck shook his head. On some subconscious level, he had wished it. Even if he missed being with someone, Chuck wasn't the type of man to do a thing like online dating and being set up for a relationship. Love either came on its own or didn't. It was never forced, never sought after. He had learned that lesson.

Lola smiled, optimistic. "I hoped so," she admitted, more to herself than to him, Chuck noted. "Okay, so we pretend to be a couple during the weekend. And get through the weekend alive. What do you say?" she asked hopefully.

Now, there really was no way he could deny her request. She was practically glowing with hope. He couldn't turn down her proposal. He ignored the part of him that was pleased by the idea. If he refused, it would be like crushing a kid's dream. He couldn't do that. She seemed so hopeful.

"We'll keep it PG-rated, but we will have to hold hands, hug and stuff." She licked her lips. "I mean, if we want people to believe it's for real. I hope they do. It will be a nice challenge; don't you think?"

Chuck knew that whatever he said next would answer the question. He should run. He really should, but his feet were planted hard on the floor, pointing towards Lola. *Then say it!* screamed his instincts. *Say you don't think it's a nice challenge. Say it*, begged his instincts. Chuck couldn't.

"I do," he nodded with a smile. It wasn't because he wanted

to spend more time in Lola's presence, he assured himself. It was because his back hurt, so he couldn't work on the chalet. Also, if he went, he would be making a client happy. And happy clients were the best. Going with Lola would just make everything more tolerable. It was an agreeable condition to the trip. It wasn't harmful. It was just pretend.

It wasn't because he wanted to feel her close, like he had in the bathroom. What had he been thinking? He hadn't been thinking. That was the problem.

It didn't matter. He had accepted her invitation, and in less than four hours, they would be heading to the Valentine Weekend hotel.

An hour later, after Lola had left, Chuck remembered how the sunlight had played in her blond hair as she moved her head while she talked. She looked... beautiful. Maybe...

Maybe he should have refused, he thought. But it didn't matter. In a couple of hours, they would be driving down to the hotel.

"No backing out now," he said out loud. It was a lie. He could back out, but he didn't want to. He wanted to see the sunlight play in her hair again. He wanted to see her gaze at him with her sparkly brown eyes. He wanted to be in the presence of a woman. One year of solitude weighed heavily upon him.

Be careful, his instincts warned with the remembrance of the pain he had once felt.

Chapter Six

"I think if you go through east LA, it will be quicker."

Chuck tightened his hands on the steering wheel at Lola's words. She looked up from the map on the phone, waiting for an answer.

"If you want, we can go south. It's a little longer but a better view," he offered instead.

"I don't like the idea of going through the east, but we're already late. But it's up to you. I mean, you're the one driving."

He nodded. She wasn't letting him choose. She was just being polite. He checked the time on the dashboard. It was three pm. They were late. Elena had been expecting Lola three hours earlier. Although Lola had already called and explained before they left the building, he could tell she felt bad.

Her knee bounced as she waited for his answer again. Chuck sighed internally. It would take at least an hour and a half longer if they went south. He knew his way to the hotel. It was farther down from where he was building his cottage. Near the national park. It normally took Chuck three hours to get to his chalet. The hotel was a solid hour farther down than his normal route.

At least there wasn't much traffic on the roads, a rarity on Los Angeles streets.

"Turn left in fifty meters," came the automated voice from Lola's built-in phone GPS.

"Oops!" Lola fumbled with her phone, trying to turn it off. "Sorry. I hit the button by accident," she explained.

"Turn left," the voice commanded.

"Damn!"

Chuck held back a smile and turned left, sobering up again. East LA, it was. There wasn't really a choice, he acknowledged.

Lola glanced up, realizing he had turned. "We're going through the east?" She searched his face. Her eyes might look shallow, but they were the deepest shallow he'd ever seen.

He nodded.

"I've never been," she admitted, with a light tremble in her voice.

"No?" He wished he hadn't.

"My father made it a point for me to never, ever go east. No matter whose party it was. South, yes. North, yes. West, definitely yes. But East? Never." Lola rolled her eyes. "I think my father thought the west side was better suited for his girl. But it's the same thing. The only difference is in West LA, they have money. There, all their partying and drug-taking is justified."

"Having money changes things, doesn't it?"

"It glamourizes things," Lola clarified.

Chuck nodded. How many times had he heard that in school—his classmates dreaming about getting into Hollywood, becoming the next big thing? He never understood why the partying was what they dreamed about most. Paparazzi and partying. That was the mark of making it big. Chuck shook his head.

He despised both. He liked his privacy and hated nothing more than alcohol. Good thing his dream had never been to make it big. He was pleased with running his own construction company. A successful company. His clients were those west LAers looking for that extra something—that renovation or complete new home.

Parked cars, moving cars and houses flashed by Chuck as he concentrated on the roads. He anticipated every move before the GPS announced it, taking shortcuts, because he knew the area well. Lola noticed and soon put her phone away.

There was a gradual change in the housing, the streets and the people, until suddenly, they had no choice but to acknowledge they were smack in the middle of East LA. Lola shrugged, hiding her hands underneath her thighs. Chuck concentrated on the streets even harder, to distract his thoughts from the graffiti-walled streets he'd walked growing up.

The word "Lolita," written in large, red, bold letters, flashed by, with a smacking red kiss next to them.

Chuck automatically gazed at Lola, whose response to the graffiti was the same as his. Her eyes were wide, waiting for it.

"Just say it," she sighed, slumping back into the seat. He didn't say anything. Lola looked at him from underneath her lashes, waiting. He could sense her gaze on him. He knew those deep-shallow depths were waiting, no doubt already creating various different scenarios in response to his thoughts.

"I am not named after Lolita," Lola declared, "if that's what you're thinking."

"Another Dolores, then?" He was curious.

"Nope." She smacked her "p." "I'm not named after a Dolores," she informed him with a huge smile. It took Chuck by surprise, and he loosened his grip on the steering wheel.

"Your real name is Lola?" He guessed it could be a real full name, instead of a nickname.

"Nope." She shook her head.

"Is Lola your nickname?"

"Yes."

"But not for Dolores?"

"Nope." Lola was enjoying this. He could tell by the way her body relaxed in the seat. She looked out the window, her eyes sparkling and her lips trembling with a huge smile. Her knee bounced up and down, anxiously waiting.

"Alright. I give up."

"Lolicia."

"Lolicia?" Chuck smiled, loving the name. It suited her perfectly. It was different, unique like she was. Or he thought she was.

"I'm named after my mother," she informed him. After? The word caught Chuck's attention. He glanced at her—a quick, studying gaze towards Lola. She saw it and in the same breath, continued with, "Hey, do you think it's hard to do graffiti? Have you ever thought of trying it? It looks easy, but I think it must have its science behind it, don't you?" She looked up at him from underneath her lashes. He made the mistake of taking his eyes off the road and gazing into those light brown depths. Lola's eyes flickered briefly to the side; she did a double-take before she yelled, "Be careful!"

Before doing anything else, Chuck slammed on the brakes and looked out the windshield. A man stumbled back until his butt hit the paved road. Chuck's jaw clenched, and he briefly closed his eyes. This was why he didn't want to come through the East. This was why he'd rather drive the extra hour and a half to his cabin. Why he would have preferred to do so today.

"Stay in the car," he commanded Lola, climbing out. He shut the door before Lola could reply.

The drunken man lay on the ground, laughing. He stopped at the sight of Chuck. "Hey, don't I know you?"

"No," Chuck snapped. In one swift movement, he lifted the man and carried him to the sidewalk, holding his breath.

"Yes, I do," the man argued. "You look just like—"

Chuck's nostrils flared, and he unceremoniously dropped the man on the sidewalk.

"Hey! Elder here," the man hiccupped. Chuck raised an eyebrow. The man couldn't be more than forty at most. However, he did look almost sixty.

"Hey, there, pretty lady," the man cooed, looking past him. Chuck froze and turned to find Lola climbing out of the truck.

"Lola, get back in the truck," he ordered.

"But he dropped his wallet," Lola protested, pointing at the black wallet on the road.

"Ooohhh, Lolita." The man smiled and began making kissing noises at her. Chuck's hand fisted and he glared at man, who

67

stopped in his tracks and gave him a sheepish smile.

"Get in the car," Chuck ordered once again. This time, Lola didn't protest. He waited until she was back in the car before fetching the wallet. Chuck opened the wallet. Stolen. Of course. All the money was gone and so were the credit cards. All that was left was a picture of a well-off family. The father in a business suit, the mother in pearls and the little girl a pink princess-style dress. He closed the wallet, disgusted, and threw it to the man, who despite his drunkenness, caught it in midair.

In the car, Chuck didn't utter a word. He gripped the steering wheel tightly, until his knuckles turned white. It wasn't Lola's fault, but he couldn't talk right then. He was too angry at the stench of his memories. Why couldn't they leave him alone? He tightened his grip. Lola's gaze settled on his hands. He tried to force himself to loosen up, but he couldn't.

"You don't like drunk people, do you?"

"You do?"

"No, of course not." She paused. "I am really sorry about last night," Lola added after a few seconds. "Just so you know, I meant it when I said I never drink. Last night was the second time I've ever gotten drunk." Her voice was small, and in his peripheral vision, he saw her head bent low as she gazed at her hands.

He nodded, not trusting his voice.

"Was I anything like that man?" she asked.

Instead of answering right away, he grabbed Lola's hand, the warmth of her skin calming down his heartbeat. He slid his fingers through hers and assured her, "You were nothing like him."

"But still, it mustn't have been fun."

"Under other circumstances, no, but last night was an exception," he allowed.

Lola scrunched up her nose, embarrassed, and laughed. "Thanks for being polite." She read right through him.

Her laughter relaxed his entire body. He kissed her hand, and he found himself smiling as he hit the highway, completely at ease.

Chapter Seven

Lola sat, thoughtful, in Chuck's black four-door truck. The highway passed by in her peripheral vision. Confusion knitted her eyebrows. Thoughts jumbled about, planting endless doubts in her brain. Chuck confused her. One second he was like an emotionless wall and the next, he was cornering her in the bathroom.

Lola bit her lip at the memory. A thrill she'd never felt had shivered up then, like it did now. There was something about Chuck she couldn't grasp logically. It wasn't good. It was making her do crazy things like propose they go on the Valentine Weekend together.

Going with Chuck made perfect sense. It was the greatest alternative to facing happy-go-lucky couples in love for a whole weekend. Less than twenty-four hours had passed since she'd broken up with David. And, well, Chuck—she didn't know what his story was, but he was single, so it made sense for them to go together, instead of being forced to be all romantic with someone they knew they had no future with. Or, at least, Lola thought that was the reason he had agreed to go.

Lola couldn't see Chuck as someone who wanted to participate in such events. In the short—and embarrassing—span she'd spent in his presence, he hadn't seemed the romantic type. The warmth of his hand in hers told her otherwise. At the very least, he wasn't the lovey-dovey, wordy type.

She studied his rough hand intertwined with hers. Oh, god. She'd been a fool. A big one. All because of David. Who was she kidding? It was because of her. Because she didn't know how to handle breaking up with David… how to handle the fact that David had ruined her favorite armchair.

Judging from Chuck's earlier reaction and the way he had snapped at her in the morning, she knew he despised drunk people. Despised with a capital "D." Big and bold. If he hadn't looked so remorseful, she would have marched out of his apartment without ever, ever talking to him again. He really hadn't meant to hurt her. Now that she thought about it, she was surprised he had agreed to go with her, after her drunken episode.

Yet he held her hand as he drove down to the Valentine Hotel. He confused her, and trying to understand the man wasn't going well.

The only conclusion she came up with was that she was going crazy. Nothing made sense anymore, and it was driving her insane. She liked to think she wasn't someone who needed to understand every single detail of her life, but she did need to understand her life in a general sense. Which she had, until yesterday.

It made no sense. Yes, it did, a part of her argued. That part of her enjoyed the idea of being a couple with Chuck. It was why she had insisted on the whole charade. But Lola needed another reason for her newfound insanity. Because that was all this was—insanity.

Stop thinking about it. Let it just be. Okay, Lola thought sternly to herself. It didn't matter, she added.

To distract herself, she looked out the window at the trees flashing by. It helped for a few seconds, but her mind quickly got bored and went back to figuring out the puzzle.

Pff! Some puzzle.

It wasn't like saving the world from hunger. It wasn't even the biggest problem in her life at the moment, but to her heart. Whoa… To her *mind*, it was important to understand.

She wasn't an impulsive person. Total lie. She had her moments, but they were always with food, clothes, furniture. With anything money-related, she had a tendency to be impulsive. But with stuff like this? Definitely no. Well… There was that time senior year… but… well… Maybe sometimes, sh—

STOP THINKING!

Lola closed her eyes, praying it would help. She fidgeted, with her eyes still closed, frustrated it didn't.

"Are you tired?" Concern trembled in Chuck's voice.

Lola opened her eyes and saw Chuck gazing straight ahead at the highway, but she sensed that he was paying attention to her. Lola found herself gazing at his face. He had a handsome face, with his black beard.

Beards were hit-or-miss for Lola, but Chuck's beard was a definite hit. It was thick but not bushy or too long. It was an inch long and perfect. Neat. It just added to his thick, raven-black eyebrows and hair. His hair was casual and simple, shorter on the sides and longer on top. It was slicked back slightly to one side, like he ran his fingers through it. He had an air of darkness, of danger, surrounding him that strangely enough, excited her.

As she gazed at Chuck's profile, black eyes glanced in her direction, before turning back to the road at the speed of light. Raven-black eyes, Lola definitely decided. They were profound eyes. Eyes that revealed he was a dangerous man. A man with a past, she mused.

Wait. He had asked her something. What was it, again? Oh, yeah. Was she tired? Come to think of it... "Just a little," she acknowledged.

She had spent all day running around, packing. Or rather, should she say repacking? All her things had already been packed. She had made sure of it two days before, but that morning, as she checked that she hadn't forgotten anything important, she was suddenly aware that her clothes were inappropriate. So, she repacked everything. Everything. Her socks and jeans—adding her sole dress. Everything, down to her lingerie. She still refused to acknowledge that she had packed her sexiest lingerie and a skimpy nightgown.

She had also gone back to Wendy's store to buy some last-minute items. Condoms. Lola ignored the thought. It had given her a chance to speak with Wendy about the other day.

Wendy's beautiful, freckled face had turned pink with shame the moment she saw her. Immediately, she began apologizing for her careless behavior. The apology was sincere and from the heart. Lola appreciated the gesture, which made her feel good. In return, Lola accepted Wendy's apology and took the moment to apologize for her behavior as well.

"By the way, is there any chance you could tell me who burnt themselves while straightening their hair?" Lola had casually inquired, picking a small white bit of dust off the counter.

Wendy pursed her lips, unsure.

"Hey, remember yesterday, when you almost told that woman about me?" Lola grinned and winked. "You know, the one you were gossiping about?" An amused smiled tugged at Wendy's glossed lips, but she still shook her head. Lola wasn't giving up that easy. "I wonder how people would feel, knowing their gossip had a name and pointed finger."

Wendy narrowed her emerald-green eyes and cooed, "Blackmail? Interesting." She squared her shoulders, raising a perfectly plucked eyebrow. Her amused smile got the better of her, and she laughed.

"I swear I won't tell a single soul. Please." Lola quickly acted on Wendy's good mood.

Wendy hesitated, her lips moving, struggling with the name on her tongue. She gazed searchingly into Lola's eyes and finally sighed, giving up. "Lydia" was the soft reply.

Lola nodded. Lydia. She had no idea who Lydia was. A small drop of disappointment settled in her gut. She had hoped to know who the person was, but unfortunately, she didn't know any Lydias. The name slipped through her mind. Knowing it didn't really add to or subtract from the original story, but it was nice to finally quench her thirst.

"You are the most persistent person I've known," Wendy chuckled.

Lola shrugged, giving her a "Whatcha going to do?" smile, her palms lifting into the air, and she laughed. "But that's why I'm your favorite customer."

Lola winked, and Wendy guffawed in response. "Yes," she admitted through her laughter. Lola joined her, throwing her head back.

It had been an amazing moment and, in all, a nice talk. Lola quickly bonded with Wendy as they continued talking. Wendy was a great woman—on her own, running her own business and without a boyfriend.

"You should come to the Valentine Weekend," Lola insisted, upon hearing that Wendy was single and missed being with someone.

"Your friend wouldn't mind?" Wendy asked, unsure.

"Of course not. Elena is all about the-more-the-merrier. Plus, I think you guys might hit it off. This store looks like what I imagine would be a mini-Valentine Weekend. So what do you say?"

"I wish I could, but Valentine's Day is one of the busiest days for the store. But I'd love to hear all about it when you come back."

"We'll grab coffee when I came back," Lola stated. She wasn't asking her new friend. Consumed with managing the store, Wendy didn't have many friends. Now she did, Lola thought, and told her so.

After their chat, it was official in her mind: Lola liked Wendy. Wendy wa—

Interrupting her train of thought, Chuck proposed, "If you want, you can lie down in the back." He pointed his thumb toward the back seat.

Lola followed his gesture and gazed behind her at the black-back seats. They did look inviting and comfortable. There was definitely enough space for her to lie down. It looked tempting, but Lola was suddenly injected with fresh blood pumping through her, leaving her wide awake and happy. It was sweet of him, she thought, realizing that he had a caring side. Like the way he had protectively commanded her to stay in the car. Granted, if she hadn't known he was being protective, she'd think he was rude. But his features had gone pale, his jaw clenched, way before she'd said anything. Hence, she knew he wasn't angry at her. Then, there was the glass of water by the bed, when she woke up in the morning. And the garbage can. Just in case, no doubt. Embarrassment colored her cheeks. Last time she was ever getting drunk. Better yet, ever picking up a single glass of alcohol.

Chuck had a nice side, which unsettled her.

"No, it's okay. Thank you." She sat up straighter in her seat and turned her whole body to smile at Chuck. He nodded, giving her another lightning-speed glance. His face barely betrayed anything. But she saw his rough features soften at her smile. It was as if he was pleased she had smiled at him.

Or maybe my ego is imagining things.

"So how was your day?" she asked, trying to make some conversation. Up until the little accident, conversation had been flowing and easy, but since then, Chuck hadn't uttered a single word until now. Taking advantage of his loosened tongue, Lola went after the sorely needed conversation.

"Good. Yours?" Chuck replied.

"It was awesome." Lola gave a massive nod.

He hummed a quick agreement along with his nod. Silence settled in the car again.

Okay, so maybe conversation wasn't the wisest idea. Lola was beginning to grasp that Chuck wasn't one for many words. Or it could be that she liked to talk way too much. They still had another two hours and thirty minutes until they arrived at the hotel. Although she wouldn't mind talking the whole trip—she could, in fact, with way too much ease, but awkwardness always followed on one side, and most of the time on both sides.

The awkwardness was too much to bear. She felt awkward just thinking about it. Lola knew herself well enough to know she would end up telling Chuck things he really didn't need to know. She would probably frighten him. Even though he seemed like someone who didn't frighten easily. Lola decided silence was the best route. It would be easier for both of them. He didn't feel like talking. She... She always felt like talking, but that didn't mean she didn't like silence. In fact, she enjoyed it. She bet she could go without saying a single word until they arrived.

Challenge accepted.

An hour later, Lola broke the silence.

"Wow! Look at those colors!" She pointed at the very start of the sunset. "It's going to be a gorgeous sunset; don't you think?" Passion poured through her voice in a squeal. She turned, waiting for Chuck's reply. She expected him to just nod. He didn't disappoint her. She sat back with a smile and watched the soft orange, yellow and pink-red start mixing lightly in the sky. Clouds sifted shades and moved with an invisible wind. They moved to the right as they lowered ever so slightly with every second.

"It's so beautiful," she breathed. "Don't you just love how

the colors mix so well together? I mean, look at those colors, those shades. Nature is so perfect. Look how beautiful it is." Unconsciously, she leaned forward, resting her hands on the dashboard, in awe.

In her mind, Lola saw a room painted a light orange with hues of yellow, a bookshelf with passionate red books and a flirty pink vase. Warm tones, definitely. Balanced with classic white and black, but not too much. No, this room was meant to be colorful, warm and different.

Maybe she could integrate it, somehow, into the project she was working on. Not maybe… She would, Lola decided with determination. She was sure that the client—whoever he or she might be—would love the idea. Or at least she hoped he or she would. Downfall of Nicole imposing her projects on her. Lola did all the work, and Nicole chatted up the clients and took all the credit.

"I know the best spot to watch the sunset. Would you like to go?" Chuck's raspy voice brought her back to reality.

"YES!" she agreed quickly, in a squeal. "I mean, I wouldn't mind," she added too casually, trying to be cool about it, and laughed, making a joke of it. Her chest lifted with glee at the sound of Chuck's low chuckle. It was a nice, deep, throaty chuckle.

The car abruptly turned onto a hidden dirt path surrounded by tall trees. Lola felt a pang of fear, as she only saw trees ahead for what seemed like miles. She was going to miss the sunset, she thought, after an eternity had passed by. Sunsets were so quick—one minute they were there and the next they were gone forever. One sunset was never the same as another. She bit her bottom lip and bounced her knee, waiting in the darkness of the trees.

To her delighted surprise, a lake suddenly came into view,

seconds later, after they had mounted a small hill.

Lola's stomach tingled with butterflies. They were just in time, she thought, as they descended the small hill. The sun was setting, the sky was painted in strong orange, pink and red, with subtle streaks of yellow. It was beautiful. The second the car stopped, Lola jumped out and strode, taking long steps, until she reached the edge of the lake, stopping a few feet away from the water. In the back of her mind, Lola faintly registered that Chuck was following her.

Lola watched, absolutely captivated by the different shades of pink and orange that dominated the sky as scattered red and yellow blended into the clouds. Taking their time, the colors disappeared with the sun. She was fascinated by how the soft hues of orange and pink remained in the sky after the sun had disappeared below the horizon. They slowly mixed with the darkness until the soft colors had completely vanished. Lola was inspired. She had so many ideas running through her head, she wished she could sit down and sketch them out.

Darkness settled around the lake, bringing an instinctive awareness to Lola. Heat registered first, behind her, followed by the realization that it was Chuck. A whole different kind of butterflies tingled in her belly, settling down between her legs. Lola turned her head, opening her mouth to ask what he thought of the sun- set. Her mouth froze, half-open. Not only was he just a mere inch way, but his gaze was intent and unreadable on her. Heat intensified through Lola. She gulped. Escaping the dark intensity of his gaze, she dropped her eyes to his mouth. Three inches was all the difference in their heights—was all that separated her from his plump lips. Lola studied his mouth. His lips were big and full, very kissable.

Would they feel as silky as they looked? Would her lips feel cushioned by his? She hoped they would, licking her lips. Gazing back into his eyes, she watched as his gaze followed her tongue. In the same beat, he imitated her; his tongue moved across his bottom lip. Desire shot through her before settling in between her legs. She closed the space between them, turning her whole body to face him and gazing from underneath her lashes into his raven-black gaze. Mirrored desired reflected in Chuck's features. Like the sunset, taking his sweet time, Chuck brought his plump lips to her waiting ones.

Rough prickles tickled Lola at first, before the smooth pressure of his soft lips consumed all her senses. His kiss was firm and delicious. Warmth radiated from his large hands as he pulled her closer by the waist, deepening the kiss. A small moan bubbled through her. Chuck tightened his hands at the sound, making Lola moan once more.

He broke off the kiss, gently pushing her, putting some space between them. But he kept his hands on her hips. They gazed at each other silently. Lola could still feel the heat radiating from him. She longed to kiss him again. Never had she been kissed like that. Never had she felt a kiss. Kisses weren't something she felt; they were wet, sloppy and at best, like eating someone's face off. Sure, there were the tempting, nerve-awakening kisses here and there. But even those never managed to consume her thoughts to the point of transporting her to a whole her universe. Let's not get crazy here; in short, it was a damn good kiss. One she wanted to repeat. But how?

"What are you thinking?" Chuck asked, breaking the silence. His throaty voice thick with desire.

Yes! My shot!

A slow smile spread across Lola's swollen lips. She hummed and traced a lazy finger across his chest. "Well, since we're pretending to be a real couple, we should practice our pretend kisses. Practice makes perfect, you know. We don't want people to think we're inexperienced, awkward kissers." She casually closed the space between them. Chuck stiffened. Her breath caught in response. But her body melted against his as he pulled her closer to him.

"Yes, you're right," he said in a gentlemanly fashion and then grabbed her face with one hand, placing the other on the small of her back. He pressed her firmly against him, allowing her to feel how hard he was, and lowered his head. He kissed her lips once and another time, and again and again. Lola clutched the front of his shirt, wanting to be even closer than they were already, if possible.

The kiss started light and playful. Sleek pressure darted warm wetness across her lips, parting them. More than willingly, she parted her lips. The kiss deepened and deepened until they both had to break it off, breathing raggedly.

"I" Chuck cleared his throat. "I think that's enough practicing," Chuck said between breaths.

Lola nodded in agreement. That was enough practicing. Any more practicing, and she had a feeling she wouldn't mind suggesting they practice sex.

Actually, she'd love to.

That thought pulled her up short. No, she couldn't have that thought. She had just broken up with David. Her boyfriend whom she had lived with for the last year. She should still be crying over him. Right? Not be completely over him.

Wait. What?

81

She was over David? No, of course not, she reassured herself. Or was she over him? Could she be? No, came the uncertain answer.

Whatever the case, she shouldn't feel so attracted to Chuck, Lola determined. Or have been so pleased that he worried whether she was tired or that he made her delicious pancakes or that he had taken her to a wonderful place like this to watch the sunset. It wasn't right, but in her defense, she'd always been secretly attracted to Chuck. With or without a boyfriend. Yes, but it was different now because—distracting herself from her thoughts, Lola focused on Chuck walking towards what she could only describe as strategically placed random poles.

Wooden structures shot up from the ground, outlining rooms of various shapes. She gazed after him as he moved around the roofless and wall-less house. He inspected the place closely—and she him, from afar.

He was handsome, Lola concluded. So much for distracting herself. She had always found him handsome, ever since she had met him. But since she was with David, she had tried not to think of Chuck as a man, Lola realized. She had tried to think of him as only her neighbor. But being real, no one could ignore a man like Chuck, much less block him out like she tried to do. Not his manliness or the way he made her feel with one insignificant glance.

Nor did it help that she was always secretly pleased to see him in the corridor or to catch a glimpse of him coming in or out of the apartment building. The little chitchats they had in the mailroom of their building never ceased to make her conscious of her pounding heart. That was how she had learned that her heart could do tiny summersaults.

How could her heart not, though? With all his attractiveness. He was taller that she was by a few inches. Which was impressive, since most men she had met had been only an inch or two taller than her five-foot-seven. He was all man, with his broad, muscled shoulders and back and his tapered waist. Easily intimidating anyone, in every sense of the word. His hands were large and rough from hard labor, she guessed. And his mouth was heaven—

"So how do you know about this place?" Lola asked Chuck, distracting herself from lusting thoughts.

"I'm building this chalet," Chuck replied, bent over, concentrating on a wooden post. Concern wrinkling his forehead.

"Oh." Lola inhaled, surprised. "So you're a construction worker?" Lola asked, understanding. His menacing muscles and all-too-manly appearance now made sense to her.

"Yeah, I own my own construction company." He checked a wooden post, shaking it with his hand. Even from where she stood in the dark, Lola could see his thick forearm flex. Lola wasn't sure if her breath caught because of his words or his flexed arm.

"Wow! That's awesome!" Lola exclaimed, her mouth opening into a grin. "What's your company name?" Curious to know more about the flexing man.

"Moran Construction."

"So your last name is Moran?" Lola figured it out, feeling stupid. Chuck Moran. Oh, god, she hadn't even known his last name, and she had been kissing him like that. And still wanted to kiss him like that. Lola stared at a gazing back Chuck. She could tell by his stunned silence that he was thinking the same thing. She hoped he was also thinking the second part, too.

"Yeah," he said, nodding. His eyes darted around his unbuilt chalet one last time before he walked up to Lola and extended his hand to her.

"I'm Chuck Moran, owner of Moran Construction," he introduced himself with professionalism.

Lola grinned and slid her hand into his. "I'm Lola Moss, interior designer." Lola mimicked his mannerisms.

"A pleasure to meet you," he added in a courtly way, with a prompt, firm shake.

Lola's lips quivered, and they both burst into laughter, unable to be serious for long. His laugh warmed her on the cool February evening.

This was absurd!

She knew who he was, and yet, she had absolutely no idea who he was. Chuck wasn't some stranger; she knew him. She had seen him walking into his apartment or checking his mail in the mailroom or walking up or down the stairs. And it wasn't like they'd never talked. Sometimes they did, for the briefest moment, but never long enough to learn more about each other. They had talked about the weather, the building and everything of zero importance. She knew so little about him, Lola realized.

All Lola really knew was, he liked cloudy days best, and now Lola guessed why. It couldn't be much fun working under a hot, scorching sun for hours. She also knew he received an average of three to four letters in the mail at the beginning of each month. Bills, most likely. And lastly, she knew that on Wednesday around ten in the morning, he left the building. Not that she stalked him, or anything. She just happened to be home three Wednesdays in a row and by the window at that time. A mere coincidence. Anyhow, that was when she had noticed his pattern. Lola would never admit that she purposely tried to catch glimpses of him on Wednesdays.

The one person who knew more about Chuck than she did, was David. Most of the information she knew about Chuck came from David. David had told her that he and Chuck had talked on more than a few occasions. He informed her that Chuck was— Come to think of it, actually, he had never mentioned anything of importance about Chuck. Other than that he was doing well. David had never revealed much from their conversations. He had only mentioned that they had talked for several minutes.

Thanks, David.

Chapter Eight

"You know, I just realized I know you, but I don't. Does that make sense? I mean, I see you sometimes, around our building. And we sometimes make small talk, but I didn't even know your last name or what you do for a living. I know you without knowing you. Isn't that weird? Is that even possible?" Lola asked him.

It was, he realized, as his thoughts mirrored hers. He knew Lola but didn't know anything about her. He didn't know what she liked and disliked. But he had always paid attention to her. More than he liked. The fact that he knew that every two weeks on Thursdays, Lola received packages from online orders was a little unnerving.

The most important information he needed to know had been that she had boyfriend. In other words, he steered clear out of her way. The moment he had met her, Chuck had known that Lola was different. He liked her more than anyone he had met, in a matter of seconds. Although Chuck didn't dare to admit that at the time—

or now. Now, he assured himself, it was the solitude speaking. But he couldn't deny that staring into her eyes that day, he felt something in him he'd never felt. A sort of calmness in his chest.

Even now, he was feeling something he couldn't describe. She had this effect on him. Even when he had tried to steer clear of her, every time he caught a glimpse of her or talked with her about the weather, his heart squeezed happily. He always found himself smiling after a mere glimpse of her beautiful, round brown eyes or golden hair. It was nearly impossible to avoid her, so Chuck constantly reminded himself that she had a boyfriend. She was off-limits. Not anymore, a small voice reminded him. Chuck smiled.

"Yes." He answered all her questions.

"I think we should get to know each other," Lola announced, resolute.

"We should," he agreed. He wanted to know what she liked and disliked. Why? He didn't know, but he just needed to know about the mystery Lola inspired in him.

The evening was much darker, and Chuck could barely see Lola's features, but he could see her outline. He could feel her thinking away. Just like she had earlier, as she watched the sunset. She had looked so beautiful, he had been drawn to her, literally. Before he knew what he had done, he was standing so close behind her, he could feel a soft heat radiating from her side. Then she had looked at him and licked her lips! It had been too much for him. He couldn't have kept himself from kissing her even if he had wanted to. Then, hearing her moan had almost destroyed him. He would have taken her right there. Almost did, too, when they kissed again. But he had to stop before it went further. He didn't want to push things and most certainly, he didn't want her to think he was the type of man who was just going to have fun with her for the weekend and then leave.

"Do you want a tour?" Chuck pointed at his chalet, after a minute of silence had passed. Normally, he would have welcomed the silence, but he wanted to hear her voice again. God. He sounded like some infatuated fool. And only after one—well, two—kisses.

"Sure," Lola said, uncertain, but he could faintly see her smile. "But it's kind of dark. I don't think I could see much."

Of course. Damn, he needed to think things through more thoroughly.

"You're right," he simply replied, thankful that it was dark and she couldn't see his embarrassed features.

"But when we come back down from the weekend, can we stop by? And you can give me a tour then?" Lola offered the alternative as they headed towards the truck.

"Of course." Chuck nodded.

"Wait," Lola said, stopping outright for a second before continuing her steps. "You said 'my chalet,' as in you're building it for you? Or are you building it and therefore feel it's yours? Like when I design something for someone else, I always feel like it's mine."

"It's my chalet, as in I'm building it for me," he said. He heard her stop again. He stopped and turned towards her. It was almost pitch black now. All he could see was her black silhouette. Worried, he asked, "You okay?"

"You're building, your own chalet?" she asked, astonished.

He wanted to only nod, but he knew she wouldn't see it. He settled for "Yes," with an unseen nod.

"Wow. That's really impressive." She let the words come out slowly, in astonishment, and began walking again. In a few steps, she reached him, and side by side they finished walking the last few steps. "So you designed your own place, and stuff? Or did you hire an architect? Does your team help you? How does it work?" She bombarded him with questions as she climbed into the car.

"Yes and no. I had the idea and a mock-up sketch, but my freelance architect designed it for me. He helped me improve it. I'm building it on my own." He answered each question in order, one by one.

It would have been a lot faster if he'd hired his team to build it, but he stubbornly wanted to do it on his own. He needed to prove to himself that he could make something of his life.

"Y-y-ou're building it alone?" Lola stuttered, stunned.

"Yeah, it would be quicker if I hired my team, but I build it on the side, as a hobby." He explained the half-truth. He didn't want to go into why he had decided to build it alone. He, himself, hadn't gone down that road. He liked to think he was building it because it gave him something to do, other than think about— Don't go there. Not know.

His knuckles whitened as he gripped the steering wheel more tightly. He felt Lola's gaze settle on his hands, and like earlier he forced himself to loosen his grip.

"So are you going to hire an interior designer? Because I know this girl who's amazing, if you're looking," he heard Lola say. He couldn't restrain the smile spreading across his lips.

"I actually already did," he admitted with guilt. "If I had known you were an interior designer, I would have hired you without

89

a second thought," he said, apologetic. He would fire the one he had hired, but the designs were supposed to come through in a month or so. Apparently, it was almost done, according to the lady.

"You keep surprising me," she admitted. "You don't seem like a guy to hire a decorator. Who did you hire?" Lola asked, surprised and a little upset.

Lola was right; he wasn't one to hire interior designers, but he wasn't opposed to harmonized beauty, either. And one of his newest and most important client's girlfriend had sold him on this interior design company.

"It's called Va—" He was interrupted by Lola's phone beeping.

Lola instinctively reached for the phone in her pocket. The light of the phone briefly illuminated her face in the darkness of the truck. Silence settled as Lola's eyes scanned her phone. "Oh, man," she groaned.

"Everything alright?" he asked, concerned.

"Yeah." Lola pouted. "It's just that La Liga lost their soccer match," Lola sniffed, still pouting as she glanced at her phone. Repulsed, she turned off her phone, taking away all the light from the car.

She liked soccer. Not only did she like soccer, but she liked Spain's La Liga. They weren't bad but he preferred the United Kingdom's Brighton Roses.

"You like soccer?" Chuck asked her.

"Of course," Lola stated, offended by the lack of obviousness on his part. "You?"

"Yes. La Liga aren't bad, but I prefer the Brighton Roses,"

he replied.

"Well, then, you'll be happy to know they beat us today," she informed him sourly, crossing her arms against her chest. So Lola was a true soccer fan, he noted with a smile.

"Of course I am. But I can't say I'm surprised. We are much better. No offense," he teased, not able to help himself. If she was a true fan, she would get mad at him. He heard her gasp in outrage.

"That's what you think, but we have the best goalie," Lola began, in the heat of passion.

Chuck grinned, already coming up with his next comeback: They obviously had the best goalie—but for the other team.

For the rest of the ride, they argued about who was the best team. It was friendly banter between them. Near the end, they couldn't stop laughing.

Ultimately, over a quick supper at the restaurant beside the gas station, when they stopped to refill the truck's tank, they decided each team was good in its own way.

Chuck pulled onto the road that led up to the hotel. Christmas lights were swirled around the tree-lined path leading up to the hotel. Floral garlands hung from one side of the road to the other above them, creating a tunnel for the passing car.

"Wow," an astonished Lola breathed beside him. He couldn't blame her. The "hotel" wasn't a hotel, but rather, a huge mansion. In the darkness of the night, they could only see the windows lit up, uniform squares in vertical pairs running along in massive horizontal rows. It was huge. Chuck found himself in awe as well.

"Wow, this is ridiculously incredible." Lola's eyes were almost bugging out as they got their suitcases from the back of the truck.

"I know," he admired.

Lola gazed at the mansion while her hand patted his truck, trying to find the luggage. A smile tugged at his cheeks. He lifted her purse and set it near her patting hand. He shook his head, amused, watching as Lola patted her purse before tightening her fingers around it and lugging it out with a sense of accomplishment that she had helped.

Standing close to each other, they took a moment to admire the mansion. Lanterns stuck out from the windows, illuminating the night. It was painted a soft yellow, and all the window frames, along with the doors and their decorative porticoes were painted white. It looked Victorian and charming.

"It feels magical," Lola announced, taking it all in as she turned to look at Chuck. He gazed into her eyes, longing to kiss her again. As if sensing his desire, she tilted her head to give him better access.

No need for more invitation.

Chuck lowered his head—

"LOLA!" He heard a female voice shriek from the mansion.

Chuck looked up to see Elena and another woman at the door. Chuck glanced back down at Lola, but she was gone, walking towards her friends.

"Hey, I'm reporting for duty." She greeted them with a grinning army salute.

He followed behind with the luggage.

"Ha! I hate to tell you this, but you're late for duty," Elena laughed. "Mika and I already finished everything."

"Aaaww, you guys," Lola whined. "You know how much I wanted to help." She sarcastically faked her disappointment. She burst into laughter with a fake-devastated Elena, who hugged her laughing friend, joining in the laughter. "Sorry, we're late. We took a little detour," she added sincerely.

"It's okay," Elena assured Lola. "By the way, he's an a-hole," Elena said. Lola looked at her, confused, and glanced worriedly at Chuck. "Mika told me all about David." Understanding dawned on Lola's face, and she relaxed, shrugging her slender shoulders. She went to greet the other girl, who Chuck assumed was her other best friend. Mikaella, if he wasn't mistaken.

"Hi, Chuck!" Elena turned to him with a joyful smile. "I'm so glad you came."

"Hi, Elena. Thank you for inviting me," he said. "How is Larry?"

Elena's soft, almost fairy-like features fell at the mention of her boyfriend. "He's good. Working," she said quickly. Too quickly. Chuck wasn't the only one to notice. Lola's head snapped up, and she gazed intently at her friend before exchanging a loaded stare with her other best friend Mikaella.

"Chuck, have you met Mikaella?" Elena swiftly changed the subject.

"No, I don't believe I've had the opportunity," he said and extended his hand to Mikaella. "Chuck Moran," he said, shaking her hand.

"Mikaella Riddler," Mikaella said, scrutinizing him. Chuck was uncomfortable under her intent gaze. The woman had a la-ser-sharp, scanning gaze. The kind that saw more than anyone else could in a mere second. Thankfully, Lola came and stood beside him and asked Elena, "Can you give us a tour of the place? It looks so beautiful."

Elena smiled. "I know. I can't believe my luck. All of this for free," she added, disbelief thick in her chirpy voice.

"Free?" Chucked echoed, surprised, raising his eyebrows.

"Yep." Lola smacked her "p." "Elena was desperately looking for a place to host the event that wouldn't go over budget and also that was nice and not too small. After weeks and weeks of searching, one day, someone anonymously gave her permission to use this place for free. Amazing, right?" Lola informed him.

Chuck nodded.

"It's all thanks to Mack," Elena added, referring to his free-lance architect and one of her best friends. "He was the one who found out about the place. We looked around, and I knew it was too expensive, but then the letter showed up, solving all my prob- lems." She smiled. "Anyways, come this way. I'll give you a tour be- fore showing you your bedroom. I chose it especially for you, Lola." Elena smiled at her friend. "Come," Elena urged them, and they made their way through the maze of the mansion.

It wasn't lost on Chuck that both of Lola's friends snuck studying gazes at him as they toured the mansion. One more scruti-nizing than the other.

This will be interesting.

Chapter Nine

Lola was impressed.

The inside of the mansion was even bigger than the outside. It was impossible, but that's how she felt, gazing up at the two floors with their high ceilings. The main entrance stood in the middle of the grand house, with two massive staircases leading upwards, forming a half-circle on each side. As they walked in, a servant appeared out of nowhere, taking their bags to their room while they toured the place.

"Wow, you have servants?" Lola asked, even more impressed.

"I know," Elena said happily. "Another pleasant surprise. And a huge help to my volunteers."

Lola smiled, nodding. If she only knew. Mikaella caught her eye and gazed at her meaningfully. Lola gave her a slight nod. They had a suspicion who the generous anonymous donor might be.

The small group of four toured the basic essentials of the

mansion, like the kitchen, dining area, the living room… a drawing room, the biggest home library ever, and of course, the 150-meter-long indoor pool. A must in every home. Lola was stupefied by the grandeur of the mansion.

"And here," Elena pushed open a heavy oak door, "is your room."

Lola's mouth popped open.

Gorgeous. Simply Gorgeous. Could she marry this room?

Lola was in love. The room—and the house—was like stepping back in time and landing in an interior designer's paradise. Although she personally preferred contemporary, rustic-style décor, she was absolutely enchanted by the house's Victorian charm. So much so that she found herself wishing for a "home" like this.

Victorian antiques decorated the soft, feminine, cream-paletted room while golden hues added prestige. It was the size of her apartment, with a sofa set in the corner, near the changing screen and en-suite bathroom. It was elegant and feminine. If it wasn't for the antique Victorian furniture, Lola would have sworn she was staying at le Château Versailles. And better yet, she dared say it was like Marie Antoinette's room.

And the bed—Lola ran, jumping into the air and flopping down on the bed, her back first, laughing. It was gigantic! Lola laughed. It was at least four meters wide by six meters long, Lola estimated. One thing she was sure about, was that the bed was hard to resist.

"Wow!" she sang through her laughter. "This is awesome." Her nose crunched up in excitement as she playfully squirmed on the bed. The bedding was silky-smooth under her hands. It must feel nice sleeping naked on these sheets, she mused. She imaged herself snaking around the bed, feeling the softness on her body.

You can't, a small voice reminded her. Oh, yeah. She was sleeping with Chuck. Right.

Her eyes widened. Oh, my god! She was going to share a bed with Chuck!

Somewhere inside her, she had known they would be sharing a room, but for some reason, she hadn't thought they would share a bed. She hadn't thought things through. There were major implications to sharing a bed with someone. And major self-control.

Lola caressed the golden bedsheet and sighed internally; it would have been nice to sleep alone and naked. Lola sighed—a small drawback to her whole pretending charade. The worst part was that she knew she could sleep naked and Chuck wouldn't do anything. But that was just it; she wanted him to do something. Or even worse, she wanted to make a shameless move on him.

Definitely. Major, MAJOR self-control.

"Sorry, Chuck." Elena's apology came as her salvation. "But tonight, you'll be sleeping alone," she announced. "I'm stealing Lola for a sleepover."

Relieved gloominess washed through Lola as disappointment settled in her belly. It was good that she wasn't spending a night with Chuck. Hopefully by the next day, when she'd share the bed with Chuck, she would have mastered self- control.

Swinging her legs off the bed, Lola strode to the luggage, which sat by her two best friends, who stood waiting for her. As she grabbed her duffle bag, Lola glanced towards Chuck. His brooding figure stood in the middle of the large room as he looked around, taking everything in. He looked so handsomely out of place. Chuck belonged in the wilderness, surrounded by trees and a lake—like where he was building his chalet—not by flamboyant, superficial, delicate floral décor. Real wild flowers, yes. Floral print, no.

Lola had wondered why he had chosen such a far-away and isolated place to construct his chalet, but seeing him surrounded by antiques, she understood that he was a man of nature. At the lake, he had fit in so well. He had been just as much a part of the scenery as the trees. She imagined him looking quite sexy—like a lumberjack— as he built his chalet.

Flickering black eyes jumped from one place to another, searching. His thick eyebrows smashed into each other, trembling with anxiety. He looked like a lost child, innocence and worry playing on his hard and mysterious features.

Endearment propelled her towards Chuck, with a surprise kiss in mind. His back was turned to her as he gazed at the bed. Lola smiled, anticipating his surprised shock at her kiss.

The surprised one was her. As she reached up on her toes to plant a kiss on Chuck's unsuspecting cheek, he turned his head at the sound of her approach. His lips meeting hers, shock froze their locked lips together.

Might as well kiss him, Lola mentally shrugged. Her lips softened, molding into his, urging him to follow. Chuck replied with tender pressure. She smiled into the kiss, placing her hand on his chest. She pushed herself back, using her free hand, and smiled into his eyes. Her heart pounded in her chest in a steady, strong rhythm. It stopped and went into overdrive as Chuck twirled a stand of her blond hair and gently pushed it behind her ear. A smile lifted his bearded lips.

"Good night," Lola breathed, longing to share the bed with him, to sleep in his arms.

"Night." He nodded, smiling. It was quite a full smile, but it was the most enigmatic smile Lola had the pleasure to lay her eyes upon. So elusive, and unavoidably infectious.

Using all the emotional strength she had, Lola stepped out of Chuck's warm aura. If she stayed a minute longer, she might attack him with more kisses. Forcing herself with all her might, she turned her body toward her best friends.

Oh, no.

Mikaella and Elena were in the middle of sharing a loaded stare. A stare Lola knew all too well.

Uh-oh.

Sure enough, they hadn't even taken three steps out of the bedroom when Elena nonchalantly asked, with too much meaning, "So you and Chuck, huh?"

Lola cursed her red cheeks. "Yeah. No! I mean… I… He and I… Well… I mean," she mumbled nervously.

"Wow! Lola Moss is tongue-tied. My, my," Mikaella teased with a southern accent, making Lola blush a deep shade of red.

Oh, God. It was going to be a long night.

"But seriously, what's up between you and Chuck?" Elena prompted.

"We're just playing a little game of pretend." "Why?"

"Because it's fun."

"Why?" came Elena's soft but serious voice.

"Because, spending the Valentine Weekend alone doesn't

sound appealing to me. Plus, I don't want to date anyone right now."

"Why?" This time it was Mikaella's inquiring voice. The same one she had used the night before.

Exasperated, Lola glared at Mikaella; they were not about do this again. "Gee, I don't know. It might be because I broke up with David."

"Speaking of David..." Elena opened the door to her bedroom. "Is it horrible of me—"

"Yes." Mikaella's voice interrupted Elena.

Elena ignored Mikaella and continued, "To ask David to fill in for one of my singletons?" Elena's face scrunched up, waiting for Lola's reply.

"You had another cancelation?" Lola asked.

Elena nodded sadly. "It worked out perfectly. I had two singletellas cancel and three singletons. One was supposed to be with Chuck, but that worked itself out. One canceled the other out, and now I have one left, with no match."

"I'm sure David won't mind," Lola assured Elena, knowing David really wouldn't.

"But will you?"

Lola shrugged her shoulders. "I don't know," she admitted. "But I think it's unfair that someone will miss out on all the fun because of me."

"Don't you think it'll be awkward, with you and Chuck?"

"No, Chuck and I are just pretending to be a couple. There's no reason there should be any awkwardness."

Elena's amber eyes flashed to Mikaella, who passed her a silent message.

"If you say so." Elena bit her lip and occupied herself with sending a text to David while Lola wandered over to the gigantic bed filled with flimsy bags and packets of heart-shaped candy.

"I thought you said you'd done everything," Lola grumbled, knowing what their sleepover would entail.

Mikaella hugged her from behind, laughing "What? And let you miss all the fun?"

Beep! Beep!

Lola's phone announced a new text message. From David.

Should I go?

It's up to you.

Are you there alone?

No. I'm with Chuck.

Our neighbor?

Yes.

Ex-neighbor to you, Lola thought. Several moments passed in silence. Was he mad? Did he still love her? Was he jealous? Did she care if he was? Lola chewed her lip, waiting for his answer. A whole infinite minute passed, and Lola was two seconds from going crazy, waiting for his reply.

Are you going to come?

I'm not sure.

Lola read and reread the four words, trying her best not to read too much into them. He was unsure. Right. Normal response. If she was being honest, she was unsure, too. Unsure of herself, unsure of Chuck, unsure of her life and most of all, unsure of how she felt about David. Lola puffed out her breath. Two pairs of eyes snapped to her face, one lifting her eyebrow while the other narrowed her intent gaze.

"So he says he is unsure," Lola announced, shrugging off her sudden unease. Her announcement was met by silence. Lola hated it. Her eyebrow twitched as she waited for someone to say something. To change the subject. The more silence there was, the more she was tempted to think. She didn't want to think. She didn't want to feel. At least, not about anything other than amusement and joy.

A quick gaze to Mikaella eased her body, because Mikaella gave her an understanding nod after a quick assessment of her twitching eyebrow. That was why she loved Mikaella.

"So I'm in love," Mikaella announced.

Lola's eyes glittered at the news. "Please, tell me it's…" Lola looked at her significantly, remembering the man Mikaella had told her about.

"No" was Mikaella's curt reply. Lola dropped her shoulders, disappointed, and flopped onto the bed.

"Who?" Elena hooted, wanting to know. "Who? Who? What did I miss? Who is the man?"

"No one." Mikaella looked pointedly at both women in a warning to drop it. "It's just a man who I spent a night with."

"You mean…" Elena's mouth popped open, almost as wide as her round eyes. "No! I can't believe it! You? Now this calls for serious celebration."

"Yes, let's bring out the champagne," Lola agreed, getting up at once.

Mikaella was not amused. Lola bit her lip, trying to hold back her laughter at her blushing friend.

"If you do, I won't tell you with whom I'm in love," Mikaella threatened.

Lola hummed, thinking it over. "Champagne or knowing? Toughie, but you're lucky I've decided to give up alcohol completely."

The image of Chuck's disgust at her in the morning and at the drunken man still burned in her memory. Alcohol didn't have its appeal anymore.

"It's fine by me. I want to know who captured Mikaella's heart," Elena grinned, climbing on the bed beside Lola. Their arms intertwined as they waited for Mikaella's answer.

Mikaella took a deep breath. Holding it in, she said, "I am in love with Edward Fairfax Rochester."

Lola rolled her eyes as Elena said, unimpressed, "Again?"

Mikaella giggled, nodding. "Always."

"You and Jane Eyre." Lola shook her head, smiling. "Remember how every month, Mika had a new fictional crush?"

Elena nodded, grinning at the memory. "I remember it used to annoy what's-his-face."

"True. I had forgotten about him" Mikaella said, shaking her head as she remembered her high school boyfriend.

"Speaking of boyfriends, I want to know more about you and Chuck." Elena wiggled her eyebrows.

"Well…" Lola gave a cheeky smile and winked. "Where to start?"

The question was asked playfully, but Lola truly wondered where to start. When she met him, or when she spent a night in his apartment? Lola decided it was best to start from the day before— less "history."

She, Elena and Mikaella spent all night talking and talking. Lola was transported back to their high school years, when every Friday they had a sleepover where no one ever slept. It had been forever since they had last spent a night together. It was exactly like when they were in high school. Except they no longer talked about whether the hockey's team goalie was going to ask her out to the school's movie night or whether Mikaella would finally get a kiss from her steady bookish boyfriend or whether Elena's crush would finally talk to her in math class.

No, this time, it was a juicier conversation. Kisses, lingerie and secret fantasies were thrown into the conversation, mixed with fears, doubts and the future.

Although Lola gave a detailed description of her first kiss with Chuck, she kept many details of her time with Chuck to herself—like the way he made her feel with one glance. The feeling reached depths inside of her that she didn't dare think about, much less feel. She also didn't tell her friends the fear that lurked around his name. The way it made her heart beat faster, stronger and truly alive. Or how the world seemed clearer, better, in his presence. Or the doubts waiting to haunt her at the first chance.

Chuck was dangerous; she had always known it. A man she should stay away from and keep at arm's length. A man to only have fun with. An easy task with such a man.

How could she explain such a man to her friends? If she did, then she'd have to admit there was something private between Chuck and her. A bond. A silent and unavoidable bond. They might take it the wrong way and tease the petunias out of her.

However, their teasing was inevitable, Lola learned, as she

dropped two heart-shaped candies in the flimsy white bag.

"Hey, out of curiosity, what do you guys think of Chuck?" Lola tried to sound casual and not like it was the most vital information in the world. She failed. Both saw right through her. Smiles teased their lips as they shrugged like it wasn't important, saying he was nice.

Nice?

Grr. Generic answers. Everyone was nice. Even people who weren't. On top of it all, it wasn't like it was a surprise. She had been the one who he had cooked pancakes for. She knew he was nice. Sooner or later, Lola knew, she would know how they truly felt about Chuck.

"Oh, speaking of Chuck, his sister is coming," Elena informed her.

"He has a sister?"

Elena nodded. "She is super sweet. You'll like her when you meet her. By the way, remind me to tell Chuck."

Lola nodded. An anxious, anticipating fear clutched her gut.

It's fine, don't worry. It's just his sister. And apparently she's super sweet. Yeah, but Elena found everyone super sweet. Hush. Let's just hope she was right. Lola plopped a chocolate candy in her mouth. Lola had a system of her own—two heart candies in bag, one candy in her mouth. Lola smiled sheepishly at Elena's unamused, narrowed gaze, after she had caught her eating the little chocolate hearts for the fifth time.

"If I were you, I'd be eating chocolate, too." Elena brushed off her annoyance. "After all, you're meeting Chuck's sister tomorrow."

"Tomorrow?" Lola gulped down the candy. It no longer tasted like sugary cream down her throat but like a brick of bitter cocoa. "Why tomorrow?"

"Because everyone arrives tomorrow, at noon."

"Tomorrow, at noon!" Oh, god. That was too soon. What should she wear? Should she be casual about it? Formal? Oh, dear lord, help.

"How many couples are coming?" Lola asked.

"About fifty. Why?"

"Just calculating the chance of meeting her tomorrow, in the sea of people."

"Oh, don't worry. I'll make sure you guys meet." Elena gave her that sweet, menacing smile. Lola gulped back her fear with a nod and gave a faint-hearted smile to Elena. Her light brown gaze flickered to Mikaella, who couldn't hold back her grin. And after that, every five minutes, they teased her about Chuck.

The last thing Lola remembered, she was cuddling with Mika, mumbling a series of incoherent words, stopping her friends from teasing her as the world darkened in a blur around her.

Chapter Ten

Soft, clunking noises and the lightest shuffled footsteps boomed through Lola's ear, waking her up. The world was a blurry confusion. Exhaustion fell heavy on her eyes. She wasn't ready to wake up. After a long night of laughter, teasing and sharing, it was an understatement to say they were all exhausted. Except Elena, who by default was naturally born a *cheerful* early riser. "Cheerful" with a massive capital "C." The woman could sleep an hour and still wake up at six in the morning with a smile on her lips and bouncing about, bursting with cheerful life. Like she was right now. Her movements were lively with joy, precision and energy.

"Good morning," Elena chirped, smiling when she saw Lola's half-opened eyes.

"What time is it?" Lola grumbled sleepily, squinting her blurry sight eyes.

"Six in the morning" came the annoyed reply from Mikaella

as she gazed at her phone, eyes heavy with sleep.

"What?!" Lola's eyes widened. "Really? Elena, I love you, but six in the morning?" Lola whined, mirroring Mikaella's annoyance. "Really?" she sobbed, shutting her eyes, and covered them with her forearm.

"Sorry" was Elena's unapologetic-sounding apology. If Lola hadn't known any better, she might have glared at the small woman. But to accommodate them, Elena made as little noise as she could as she continued to get ready. Lola tried to go back to sleep.

Almost inaudible clunking noises pounded through her tired brain. Reluctantly, she opened her eyes at the same time Mikaella did. After several attempts at falling back asleep, Lola gazed at Mikaella's bloodshot eyes, knowing they were a reflection of hers. Groaning simultaneously, they rolled off the bed, glaring at their friend as they walked out of the room. Elena shrugged her shoulders with guilt, but her lips were still turned up.

Almost sleepwalking, Mikaella and Lola made their way through the mansion to their assigned rooms. Mikaella had to go a little farther than Lola, since she resided on the left side of the mansion, where all the singletons were staying. One of the perks of being a singleton was that they got a whole room to themselves.

Lola stumbled into her room, her vision heavy, almost blinded by blurred sleepiness. She bumped into the bed, waking Chuck up. "Lola?" he grumbled, disoriented, through half-opened eyes.

"Sorry," she whispered. "Elena woke us up. I'm so tired," she yawned, crawling into bed. She snuggled up against Chuck's side. She was faintly aware of his arm wrapping around her. Lola quickly fell asleep in the warmth of his giant body.

11:17 am

Tight, snuggled, warm pressure was the first thing Chuck registered as he opened his eyes. The second was Lola's soft, lemony scent. The third was the realization that her head lay on his chest as her steady breath blew on him. Chuck smiled, briefly remembering Lola entering the room in the early morning and wrapping his arm around her after she nestled against him. He could still feel her smile as she had fallen asleep in his arms. Contentment washed through him, and he sighed.

11:18 am

Lola's eyes slowly popped open as she registered the sound of a steady beating heart beneath her ear. Snuggled between Chuck's body and arm, Lola sneaked a quick peek at his sleeping face. Dark, wide eyes met hers. Embarrassed that she had been caught, a coral blush colored her cheeks. She smiled groggily at him.

"Morning," he greeted her.

"Good morning," she grinned, yawning, and without thinking, she reached up to kiss him. He kissed her back sweetly and tightened his grip on her, making her smile.

"Had some night?" he asked. Lola simply nodded and sat up, yawning. She turned to stare at him teasingly. She said playfully, "Spent quite some time talking about you."

She laughed when Chuck's eyebrows shot up, his eyes wide, alert. He practically blared with sirens of alarm.

"I'm just kidding," Lola assured him. "Well, not really. I mean, we did talk about you, but it was all good. I promise." And she plopped down to give him another kiss.

She had to stop kissing him. From now on, no more kissing… Okay, maybe some kissing, she allowed, for keeping up appearances, but not like this. Not like he's my boyfriend. Because I don't want one. A real one. This is all pretend, just a fun way to get through the weekend. Nothing serious, she felt the need to remind herself, for some reason. Don't forget. It's only for the Valentine Weekend.

On that note, she sat up again. Lola glanced at the clock on the nightstand. Eleven twenty-one. The guests would start arriving around twelve, but she was spared from greeting them with Elena. The duty had fallen on Larry, which meant Lola could sneak in some work before the first activity started in the afternoon. Yay!

"People will start arriving at noon. And the first activity is at two. I have some work to finish up," she informed Chuck. "So would you mind meeting me outside at one forty-five?" she proposed.

"Sure." He sat up beside her, rubbing smooth circles on the small of her back.

Lola smiled at Chuck, her gaze roaming over him. Thick raven-black bed hair lay flat against his head; his black eyes were still a little foggy, but his beard was surprisingly neat. Only one particular patch stood out, facing the opposite direction from the rest. Lola smiled. Soft coarseness met her finger as she smoothed it back, unable to resist. His beard was soft. She stroked it again, wanting to feel its softness. Absentmindedly, she found herself caressing his beard. Enjoying the silky, coarse feeling against her fingers, she leaned in, distracted by her rhythmic strokes, and softly sank a kiss on Chuck's lips. Pulling back, she now stroked with both her hands. She smiled, enjoying the numbness of its softness.

Strong fingers gripped her hands, freezing her own on his beard. She gazed into his dark eyes questioningly, coming out of her hypnotic trance.

"Work?" Chuck reminded her, his eyes searching hers.

A jolt of realization straightened her out. "Right. Work." She nodded and leaned in, kissing him softly. "See you soon." Lola jumped off the bed, internally kicking herself for kissing him again. Twice and almost a third time, if he hadn't brought her back to reality.

She would need to establish some ground rules. If her heart wanted to survive. Whoa. Wait, of course her heart would survive. Where had that thought come from? She shook her head. She needed to establish ground rules for the sake of... of... Well... of... of her dignity? Like there was any even left? Yes. Yes, there was. Out of respect for... For Chuck. And David.

Chuck didn't deserve to be a rebound guy. Rebounds never lasted. As for David, despite the recent incident, he had been a good boyfriend. A candidate for a life partner. Out of respect for what had been, she felt she should slow down with Chuck. And apparently, her heart would appreciate it. Her libido, on the other hand, wouldn't.

Heart or libido?

Tough decision.

At one forty-five, Lola spotted Chuck, Mikaella, Elena and Larry all talking outside in a loose circle. Rather, Chuck and Larry were talking while Elena and Mikaella stood by them, clearly bored.

Elena saw her first, lighting up. "Lola! Come save us!" Elena

111

said, faking melodrama. Lola rolled her eyes. A reaction like that meant the men were probably talking business.

Before Lola reached them, Larry's phone rang, and he left abruptly, speaking harshly into the phone. "What do you mean you aren't going to do it? Ly— I swea— Will you let me talk!? Damn it!" he snapped, his hands turning white, then whiter as he gripped the phone, while his other hand fisted in frustration at the caller. Trembling with anger, he disappeared into the mansion.

Lola watched as Elena's fearful gaze flickered around the unsuspecting group that gazed after Larry. Her mouth opened to apologize for Larry's behavior. Lola couldn't let Elena do that again. It wasn't her job. Before she said anything, Lola cut her off with a question for Elena and Chuck. "How do you know each other?" As the words came out, Lola realized she should have asked it at the beginning.

"Chuck is building us a chalet close to the city." Elena relaxed into the question, eyeing her gratefully.

"Not too far from where I'm building my chalet, actually," Chuck added.

"Oh." Lola relaxed, too. Right. Lola remembered. Elena had mentioned in passing something about Larry wanting to build a chalet. A few months ago? Quite honestly, she hadn't paid much attention. Ever since then, Larry had increasingly become a workaholic— and therefore, distant. Lola didn't care what he did or didn't do. As long as he wasn't hurting Elena.

Lola decided to stand beside Mikaella, even though Chuck stepped to the side, giving her space beside him. She didn't trust herself to be close to Chuck yet. She didn't want to make a fool of herself like she had this morning.

"I feel like I've seen you before." Mikaella narrowed her eyes on Chuck, "remembering." Lola's breath caught. Oh, no. She knew that look.

"We're neighbors," Lola reminded her quickly, giving her a meaningful stare.

Mikaella nodded with a sly smile, already aware of the fact. Lola clenched her teeth and widened her eyes, shaking her head ever so slightly in warning. Mikaella ignored her. "That's it!" Mikaella snapped her fingers, remembering. "I saw you from Lola's window, coming out of the apartment building." Mikaella acted satisfied by her remembrance, pointing her finger in the air at the memory. Lola knew better. Mikaella had caught her one Wednesday morning, gazing after Chuck. And then another, on New Year's Eve. Hot embarrassment flushed through Lola.

Chuck nodded slowly, unsure what to do with the information. He gazed questioningly at Lola's tomato-red face. Lola shrugged her shoulders, as if in ignorance of what Mikaella was talking about. She gave him that "she's crazy" smile with a pointed thumb towards Mikaella. Chuck wasn't convinced; Lola could tell by his scrutinizing gaze.

"Chuck!" Mack's familiar voice shouted in delight as he came out the front door of the mansion, behind Chuck. "My man, how are you?" Mack greeted Chuck with pat on the back and a firm handshake.

Lola took a moment to furiously glare at Mikaella for her audacity. Mikaella brushed off her glare with a swift shrug while she read deep into her eyes. A smile pulled up her cheeks, after seeing something she liked, and she winked good-naturedly. Lola rolled her eyes and glared once more, with the warning that whatever she had seen or noted, she better keep it to herself. Her warning was cut short as Mack went to hug Mikaella, and followed by her.

"David is a jerk," Mack whispered in Lola's ear as his tall, lanky frame hugged her.

"How—" she began. Mack laughed, his gaze betraying him as it settled on Elena, whose delicate features turned pink with guilt.

"Of course." Lola shook her head, amused, watching Elena's gaze chide a wolfishly grinning Mack.

Lola didn't mind. Mack was bound to know sooner or later. He was the completion of the best friends' circle they'd had since their first year of college. They pretty much knew everything there was to know about each other. But if they were being honest, Elena was the closest to Mack and probably knew more about him than they did. It never failed to amaze Lola the ease and complicity they had with one another.

"Lola," Mack wrapped an arm around Elena's waist, "you have chosen wisely." Mack mimicked how wise men sounded, pointing at Chuck. His voice was slow and purposeful. Mack even relaxed his eyes and tried to look through his "years" of "wisdom."

Lola blushed, laughing.

∽♥∽

Mikaella observed as Lola's blush deepened as she gazed shy- ly for Chuck's reaction to Mack's teasing. At the sight of Chuck's proud, puffed-up chest, Lola relaxed into a smile, puffing up her chest, too. Mikaella held back a smile. It was official. Lola had finally—

"Oh, my god! You made it!" Elena said cheerfully, looking over Mikaella's shoulder.

"Of course. Wouldn't miss it for the world," came a husky, smooth voice from behind Mikaella.

Shivers ran up her spine.

No. Please. No, no, no. Please. She'd recognize that smooth, husky voice anywhere. Please let it be her imagination. Please. She wasn't sure she could handle seeing him right now. Slowly, Mikaella turned her head. She sucked in a breath.

Chadwick Maddin stood behind her, in all his glory. Mikaella watched as his expression went from surprise to wickedness. Chadwick deliberately took his time gazing at her from head to toe and back. He gave her that smile, his eyes shining mischievously. She gulped. No doubt, he was thinking about… Great.

"Mikaella, what a pleasure to see you here," Chadwick grinned, almost purring the words, taking a step closer.

Mikaella mustered a faint smile, shifting backwards as she nodded. From the corner of her eye, she saw Lola gazing at her curiously. Mikaella ignored her for the moment. Although she had already told Lola about her one-and-only wild night, Mikaella hadn't quite mentioned the man in question. She hadn't mentioned him at all, other than that he existed—but no name, no description. There hadn't been a need, really. Lola didn't know him, and… and if she had mentioned Chadwick, then it would be like admitting she had lost control. Something she never did. And still refused to admit.

Standing so near him, Mikaella felt her self-control waver as her body shivered with betrayal again at the thought. Mikaella slid closer to Lola for protection, deciding that the best course of action was to avoid all conversation with Chadwick. Relief pulsed through her as Lola instinctively linked arms with her. She was safe.

"Chadwick, how are you?" Mack greeted the man, shaking his hand. Chadwick turned and greeted Chuck. "Chuck, good to see you again." Both men hugged each other like old friends, while Chuck replied, "Likewise."

Mikaella and Lola gazed at one another, each with one eyebrow shot up in the sky and the other pulling downwards with confusion. So both men knew each other. How? Chuck knew Chadwick, Mack knew Chadwick, and Elena knew Chadwick. Everyone knew everyone. Huh? Interesting. A small world or was fate playing a trick on them? Mikaella briefly speculated, gazing at the group as Chadwick greeted Elena and asked her about Larry.

How Mikaella wished he would take forever to greet Elena, because as he finished, Chadwick turned his full attention to Mikaella. Not good. He gazed at her expectantly, with his dark blue eyes shimmering with mischief in the sunlight. Chadwick's tempting lips opened to reveal his mischievous thoughts. She had a feeling they weren't something she wanted to hear. Or more accurately, her friends to hear. Impulsively, Mikaella cut him off as he brought his tongue to his teeth, making a hissing sound.

"Mr. Maddin, I don't believe you've met my best friend Lola. Lola, this is Chadwick Maddin." Mikaella gestured between both of them. They shook hands cordially. Lola eyed Chadwick suspiciously as Chadwick sized up Lola's protective arm linked through Mikaella's. Lola noticed and tightened her grip, stepping slightly forward, shielding her from Chadwick. What did Lola see? Mikaella wondered. Sure, Chadwick wasn't a man to trust, but to bring out such a reaction in Lola?

Mikaella found herself gazing intently at Chadwick, trying to figure him out. She met his dark blue eyes framed by black lashes. She searched deep in his eyes, only come up with tempting mischief. Chadwick winked, grinning, guessing her thoughts.

Mikaella gulped.

Chapter Eleven

Lola walked close beside Chuck as they headed around the soft-yellow mansion to the back yard to meet up with the rest of the guests.

It was weird, Lola thought, still dazed by the recent encounter. Chuck knew Mack, Elena and this Chadwick guy, who she wasn't sure she liked very much. The way he had stared at Mikaella—she hadn't liked it one bit. It was somewhere between a predator hunting its prey and a sort of fascination. The two added up to no good. Anyhow, most importantly, Mack and Elena had known Chuck. How come she hadn't known?

"Isn't weird you know all my friends? And I didn't even know. I feel like they know you better than I do. How did you meet them?" Lola voiced her thoughts to Chuck.

Chuck shrugged his shoulders, explaining. "Larry hired my company to build his chalet, and through Larry, I met Elena. Elena introduced me to Mack. Mack actually helped me design my chalet and now does some freelance work for my company when needed."

Lola nodded, taking in all the information.

Mack was a freelance architect who worked for various construction companies. Lola doubted he gave more importance to one job or another. Still, it would have been nice if he had showed enough interest in Chuck's company to mention him. She'd ask him about it later, she promised herself.

"You know," Chuck continued side-tracked, "I had actually talked with him before, on the phone. Chadwick referred him after Mack had done some work for him."

"Oh," Lola breathed, curious. "That's so cool," she laughed, thinking about the peculiarity of their meeting. Networking at its best. But why hadn't it extended to her?

Wait. Lola was catching on late. The name "Chadwick" sounded familiar in his voice. Lola remembered their easy embrace. Maybe they knew each other well enough; Chuck might have more information on this predator. Lola inquired, "So how do you know Chadwick?" She narrowed her eyes at Chuck.

"Chadwick is an old friend. He actually called me Friday morning, asking about the Valentine Weekend."

Lola nodded. Chadwick couldn't be that bad if he was an old friend of Chuck. But still, it was to be confirmed.

So they all knew each other and she hadn't known. She thought she would have heard Chuck's name come up in conversation with Mack. Or when Elena had mentioned that Larry was having a chalet built. But Lola had never heard Chuck's name or his company name come up when Elena mentioned the chalet. Maybe

119

she had, but she hadn't paid attention. And as for Larry mentioning his name, Lola doubted it. Until recently, she had barely spoken with the ma— Oh. Wait. Yep. There it was. The memory of Larry answering "Moran Construction" after someone had asked him a question at a New Year's get-together they had at her place. Lola had been in the kitchen, talking with Mikaella, and had barely heard it.

It didn't really matter how they had all met; Lola was happy her friends knew Chuck—except Mikaella—and clearly liked him.

Even though Mikaella studied him with caution and precision, Lola knew by her embarrassing teasing that Mikaella approved of Chuck. Her three best friends approved of Chuck, Lola smiled, showing teeth.

Approved? The word snapped her out of her toothy grin. Why did it matter if they approved? It didn't. It shouldn't. It doesn't. Her relationship— "*relationship*"—with Chuck was only for this weekend. They would most likely continue with their own lives afterwards. Without one another. An uncomfortable tug weighed in her chest as she gazed at the moving green grass underneath her feet.

"What are you thinking?" she heard Chuck ask her, his deep voice sounding concerned. She looked up from the green grass, realizing that it had stopped moving. They stood at the edge of the huge back yard, where about a hundred guests were loosely scattered on the back terrace.

On the lawn, dispersed strategically around the fresh green grass, were pairs of easels standing back-to-back, with large white sheets hanging over them. A black pen lay on the little beige stool on each side. Lola turned her attention to Chuck and found dark, studying eyes on her. She wondered what could possibly be going through his head, with his gaze so intent.

"Ah, hm. Nothing, really." She shrugged, assuring him it wasn't important.

He didn't look convinced. Chuck raised his thick black eyebrow, waiting for the real reply.

"It's nothing, really," Lola said defensively. He didn't budge. "It's true," she persisted. It didn't work. Sighing in frustration, she gave up. "Fine. I was just thinking about this weekend, that's all." She looked down at the green grass.

"What about it?"

Lola wanted to glare at Chuck for making her say it. Wasn't her answer enough for him? Apparently not. His gazed deep into her eyes waiting for the answer.

"About us."

Chuck nodded, waiting for more. Lola glared at the ground and managed to say, "And how it's only for one weekend." She kicked a patch of grass.

"How do you know it's only for a weekend?"

Her heartbeat picked up rhythm.

"Because it has to be like that," she explained with finality.

Chuck nodded. "If you say so." He shrugged his massive, uncaring shoulders.

No, she didn't want to say so. But it had to be like that. There was no other possibility, because— Fear gripped her. Whatever, it didn't matter why. Either way, by rule, she never dated anyone within two weeks of breaking up with someone. If she did, it was automatically categorized as meaningless. Chuck wasn't someone meaningless. But for her, he would be. He had to be. He just had to. She gazed down at the grass.

The green grass suddenly became a gloomy room where a man sat on the bed, gazing out the window. Not here, not there.

Lola shook the image out of her head. She swallowed back the lump in her throat. Fearing that if she gazed at the grass any longer, more memories would find their way back to her, Lola tried to find solace in Chuck's features, but a movement behind him on the back terrace caught her attention.

David's familiar silhouette weaved through the crowd. He had come, after all. She looked away as tight relief wash through her.

Warm fingers cupped her face, forcing her to gaze into black eyes. They were soft and tender. Chuck gently stroked her blushing cheek. He gently kissed her half-open lips. As he pulled back, he said, "Let's enjoy this weekend. We'll worry about the rest after."

Lola bit the edge of her bottom lip, liking how "we" sounded on Chuck's plump lips. She had come here for fun, and she wasn't leaving without it. Pushing back everything that didn't belong in the moment, Lola let herself slip into the role of Chuck's girlfriend. Only to find that she had already shifted modes.

She smiled up at him, caressing his beard with one hand and agreed. "You're right. Let's have fun."

A content smile traced Chuck's lips and he nodded. He then guided her to the back porch, with his hand on the small of her back. Lola's skin tightened at his touch as he guided her onto the back terrace. His hand rested ever so lightly on the small of her back, but a kilo's worth of temptation weighed between her legs.

Standing among the other lovers, Lola and Chuck listened to the hostess welcome everyone and explain the first activity. While

Elena spoke, Lola subconsciously leaned in on Chuck, settling comfortably beside him while he wrapped his arm around her waist.

Oh, no. Lola held back her groan as Elena finished explaining the first activity, in which each couple had to draw their significant other. She should have guessed they would do something art-related.

A little warning on Elena's part would have been nice. Lola could have practiced her life sketching skills—which were nonexistent. Lola was an abstract painter. She managed colors better than lines. Sure, she could draw, but her drawing skills were limited and trained for interior design. There was something about drawing people that caused her hand to act like a five-year-old's.

The worst was, Elena was no better at drawing, so Lola wodered why she would choose this as an activity. Elena was a sculptor with a passion for crafts. Her ability came in handy when she planned small, intimate events and the clients wanted something homey. Nothing better than handmade decorations. Mikaella, on the other hand, was a cartoonist with the capacity to draw anything painstakingly realistic. She was the drawer of the group. And Mack was also a good drawer. The activity must be for them, Lola thought with a smile, liking that she had found the logic in it quickly.

꙰ ♥ ꙰

"This should be interesting," Lola muttered. Chuck nodded through his fear at Elena's announcement.

He couldn't draw. At all.

Murmuring, excited and terrified voices mingled in the air as they all waited for the volunteers to hand out the number of the

123

easel that belonged to them.

"You know what would be interesting?" Lola thought out loud, her eyes widening with excitement. "If we went all *Titanic* and did it naked." She smiled up at Chuck, playfully wiggling her eyebrows at the suggestion. He liked the idea. And he liked even more the way Lola enticed him with her playful gaze.

"I would appreciate it if you didn't." Elena broke the moment, handing them a card with the number two written bold and large, scattered pink hearts framing the card. "I don't think the guests want to see you naked."

"But you do," Lola teased her friend, winking.

"Always." Elena puckered up her lips at Lola and laughed. "But I don't think everyone wants to see Chuck naked." She turned to him. "No offense."

"None taken." He turned back to Lola.

Lola gazed at him, her head tilted and her gaze speculative as she gave him a slow once-over, starting from the bottom and lingering a little too long at his hips and biting her lip. She finished her scan and licked her lips. Lola would love to see him naked; Chuck read her thoughts. He winked at her with the promise that she would. Lola pursed her lips, smiling with anticipation.

God. How enticing she was. Lola wasn't like anyone he'd ever met. In her presence, he never felt bored, never felt alone, like he tended to feel despite the presence of other people. Lola was someone everyone gravitated towards, that person everyone wanted to be around. He did, too. Which meant only one thing. He was a man on a mission. He had to convince Lola that there could be more to them than this weekend. He knew there could.

Chuck could feel it, deep inside him, where truthful knowledge resided. He knew it. It was only a matter of making Lola realize it, too. They had to give this a chance beyond the Valentine Weekend, Chuck thought as they made their way to easel number two.

Chuck sat in front of Lola as she silently began sketching him. They each had thirty minutes to sketch the other. Elena had said it was to represent how they saw each other. Lola had volunteered to go first. She gazed at Chuck's face, then at her easel and drew something, looking back up at him.

Lola studied what she had done so far and shrank back on her stool with guilt. Her long legs pointing at angles to the side as she gazed at her drawing.

"I think I should apologize. I'm not a good drawer, so be warned. I'll try to do my best." She tried smiling through her guilt and ended up grimacing. She shrugged. "My best will look like a five-year-old drew you," she added, laughing. Chuck smiled. He knew his wouldn't be any better.

"You know, I met Mikaella and Elena in art class in high school. We all loved art so much that we bonded over it and became inseparable that very same day. I don't have any siblings, so I think of them as my sisters." Lola conversed as she continued sketching. "We're all only children in our families, you know." She paused, concentrating on a spot she was drawing.

Chuck loved it when Lola talked. She had a tendency to talk too much. She was able to answer yes or no questions with essay-long answers. He enjoyed her bubbly banter and worried when she spent long periods without uttering a single sound. He could see her thinking and thinking away. It was a danger when she was thinking away.

He was constantly drawn to her while she thought. Literally and figuratively. It didn't help he was both worried and curious to know what kinds of thoughts passed through her mind. He wanted to know her.

If he wanted to know her, there was no more perfect time than the present, as they said. "That means you're an only child." Chuck closed his eyes at his own obviousness. Of course she was, Captain Obvious. She had just said it. Pay a little more attention. Or better yet, think before speaking. Yeah, right. Around Lola? Good luck.

"Mmm?" she hummed, raising her eyebrows as she concentrated on drawing. Good. She hadn't heard him. He could pretend he hadn't said anything. She looked up at him questioningly, after a few seconds of silence. Or not. He cleared his throat. "How's the drawing going?" he asked instead.

Lola made a face and laughed. "I'm really sorry, but I think I deformed your face," she said, then added, "I don't see you like this, by the way."

"It's okay. I can't draw at all. Whatever you drew will be better than mine," he assured her. Sunlight sparkled on Lola's amber, chocolatey-brown gaze. A breeze shook a strand of golden hair loose from her ponytail, and it swished down her face. Delicately, Lola tucked it behind her ear with her slender fingers. Chuck's mesmerized gaze followed her movement with close attention.

"Are you close to your sister?" Lola asked as she continued on the drawing.

Surprise momentarily stung him as he tilted his head, wondering how she knew he had a sister. "Sister?"

"Yeah, Gabriella, right?" Lola asked, looking up at him. Her features fell as the understanding of her words dawned on her. Her light brown eyes widened in horror at her realization. She began shaking her head, trying to explain but silent, inchoate words mumbled out.

Chuck bit his lips to keep from laughing. She looked so adorable when she was anxious. Chuck wanted to draw it out, see her flushed face a little longer, but luck was on her side.

Not far away from them, Elena made rounds, making sure her guests were alright. At the mention of Gabriella's name, Elena's head snapped up. She apologized to the model-looking guest and made her way to Lola and Chuck.

"Oh, I forgot to tell you. Gabriella is here," Elena announced once she reached them.

An anxious jolt stung Chuck's heart. Gabriella had to work. She didn't have the luxury of taking time off... Unless. He sighed. Unless she had gotten fired.

Again.

Maybe he was jumping to conclusions. He would give her the benefit of the doubt.

"She's on the other side of the yard," Elena informed him. "She wanted me to tell you she needs to speak with you."

Chuck nodded, giving Elena a tight, forced smile. He'd talk to Gabriella later. Right now, he was concerned. A thin line had replaced Lola's smile. She shook her head and looked up at her best friend. "How come you're not with Larry?" she inquired.

Elena's cheerful smile drooped.

"He had to take a call." She shrugged. "Anyway, I'll let you lovebirds continue," she added and walked off quickly. Lovebirds.

Not quite yet.

Lola gazed after her friend, fear heavy on her face. "I'm worried about her." She frowned. "Lately, she's been avoiding the topic of Larry. Last time I talked about him, merely stating that it wasn't right that he takes calls during their meals, she got mad at me, telling me I was wrong and that he was perfect. She actually said, 'He's perfect.' It was so unlike her. I don't know. I find it abnormal," Lola commented.

Chuck had noted the same. But Chuck wasn't in a position to come up with any conclusions. He barely knew Elena.

The scratchy sound of the pen flying across the paper snapped Chuck's attention back. Lola's hand moved roughly against the paper until she sighed, dropping her exhausted hand. Chuck waited anxiously. She sighed restlessly, looking down at her lap. Thinking it was the drawing that had upset her, Chuck thought to comfort her. The drawing couldn't be that bad, surely, he thought. But her saddened eyes said otherwise.

"Hey, don't worry about the drawing—"

"What?" Lola looked around, confused. "Oh. No. It's not that…" She sighed. "It's just that I feel like everyone knows you, and I don't. I mean, I was the one living beside you. Should I know you better? It's starting to be unfair." She stomped her foot lightly. "I mean, Elena was the one who told me about Gabriella. And I'm sure Mack knows more about you than I do. Even Larry, I'd venture to say. It's just… I… um… I don't know. I guess I wish I knew more about you," she admitted in a small voice.

"You know I have an amazing taste when it comes down to soccer teams," he teased, lightening up the mood. And that right there was more than all her friends knew about him. He was very careful with what information he shared, especially with clients and co-workers. It was more a habit of self-preservation than professionalism.

"Okay, let's not exaggerate." Lola stopped the idea with her palm. "You have acceptable taste in soccer teams," she laughed. Chuck chuckled, loving the unapologetic laugh she had. It was deep and natural, coming from the back of her throat.

"How about this? You tell me more about you, and I'll tell you about me," Chuck proposed.

"Deal," she said, picking up the black pen and continuing to draw. "So what do you wanna know?"

"Let's start with the basics."

"You mean like my name is Lola Moss, and I blah, blah, blah? Like in school? After every single summer?"

Chuck chuckled at the half-horrified, half-amused face she made at the memory. He nodded.

"Alright, then brace yourself. Some seriously boring and obvious information is coming your way." She paused, sitting up straighter and pasting a forced, fake smile on her face. "Hi, my name is Lola Moss. I'm an interior designer, and I am from Los Angeles."

"Hi, my name is Chuck Moran. I'm the owner of Moran Construction, and I'm also from Los Angeles."

Lola burst into laughter, throwing her head back. She shook her head as laughter sized her. "I think we should try another tactic," she giggled. "Oh!" She widened her eyes, and her mouth formed an "o" as she had an idea. "How about we do it in chronological order?" She smiled, liking the idea.

Chuck nodded. Could he skip the first eighteen years? Wanting to prolong his fate, he asked Lola, "You said you were named after your mother, right?"

Lola nodded, avoiding his gaze by suddenly seeming very interested in the drawing.

"Yep." She smacked the "p." "I come from a long line of Lolicias. I am Lolicia the third."

Chuck narrowed his eyes. He couldn't tell if she was lying or playing. But one thing was for sure: she wasn't telling him the truth. Finally, she met his gaze. Her quick gaze read his in seconds.

"It's true! My grandmother's name was Lolicia, and so was my mother's."

Chuck waited, knowing there was more. "Was?"

Now it was Lola's turn to narrow her gaze at him. It might have been a glare, for all he knew. She concentrated on the drawing. He was patient; he had no problem waiting her out.

"I was named after my mother. She died giving birth to me." Lola shrugged her hunched shoulders. "My father raised me on his own."

There, on the outer edge of fifty couples, while they were deforming one another's faces, they found out more about each other.

"I'm sorry," Chuck said, wanting to hug her.

"Don't be," she pleaded with a soft smile. "I loved living with my father. He raised me on his own. And before you ask, no, he never remarried. I don't think he ever even considered the idea," Lola realized. Love softened her expression, tenderness sparkling in her brown eyes.

"He must love you a lot." Chuck didn't blame her father.

Who wouldn't love her?

"I think so." She smiled. "I mean he did try his best to teach me how to be a proper woman. The best he managed was getting the semi-tomboy out of me after trying to get me into a beauty pageant."

"You were in a beauty pageant?" Chuck smiled at the idea. Lola, who'd he always seen in jeans, sneakers and t-shirt or sweatshirt, wasn't someone who he'd think was the typical beauty pageant girl.

"*Tried*," Lola clarified, "to get me into a beauty pageant. I was disqualified when I arrived covered in mud after playing soccer with the neighborhood boys," Lola explained. "Poor Dad. I think that's when he realized he wasn't going to have a little princess girl. But deep down, it was a relief for him that I was more tomboyish than girlish. He didn't have to try so hard to find things to please me. I liked sports, he liked sports. We were able to bond closer. Something I'm very grateful for." Lola smiled and paused, fixing something on the drawing.

"You know," she said after two seconds of silence. Chuck smiled, loving the sound of her voice. "When I was little, my father had a furniture shop, and after school, I would help him arrange the store, so it was more appealing to the eye. A.k.a., brought in more paying customers." She smiled at the memory. "I owe my love of decorating to him. It was always a challenge when he received new stock. I loved battling with the old color palette and the current trend in colors to create harmonic displays—inviting and comfortable."

Chuck envisioned a tiny mud-covered Lola, running around couches with lamps in each hand, deciding which one went best with the black leather couch.

"He moved to Florida three years ago. I visit him every chance I get—which has been two, to date—and he visited me once, six months ago. I try to visit him as much as I can. I sometimes miss him so much." Lola's brown eyes gazed down as she remembered. Shrugging, she stared at Chuck with her round, almond-shaped eyes and asked, "What about you? Are you close to your parents?"

Chuck hesitated, fear punching his stomach. He tried his best not to recoil from the blow. "I owe my love of construction to my father." He maneuvered a semi-honest answer without revealing too much information. Lola smiled at the insignificant piece of information. Guilt poured salt on his wounds. She was honest—granted, not right away—but he should be, too. If she had told him about her mother when she didn't want to, then he had to tell her about his father. His past. Fear gripped him again.

"Did you inherit your father's company?" she asked.

He shook his head. Chuck had inherited nothing but his genes.

"So you constructed your own company?" she asked. "Pun intended." She winked at him.

He nodded, grinning a chuckle.

"Why did you decide to start your own company?" Lola searched his face. His knee bounced up and down. His grin disappeared. Here goes. Please don't run away. "Where I'm from—"

"Los Angeles?"

"East Los Angeles."

And there it was. Lola's gaze unfocused on him as she leaned away from him. "Oh," she breathed. "No wonder you knew your way so well there." She half smiled at the realization.

132

Chuck let go of the breath he hadn't known he'd been holding.

"Continue," she urged, with curiosity lighting her eyes.

Chuck cleared his throat. "People liked to take the easy way out. They either lived off the government or bounced from job to job." Or did illegal jobs, Chuck thought. "I used to think you weren't allowed to keep a job for more than three months." Chuck shook his head, remembering his childish thoughts. "Silly. I know."

"Not silly," Lola assured him compassionately. "You didn't know better. I think it's cute." Lola smiled warmly. "So did you think the only way to have a stable job was to be an owner of a company?" Lola asked.

Chuck smiled at her quick mind. "Almost. I had a steady job for two years in high school. I learned you were allowed to work more than three months. But it also taught me how easy it was to settle for a mediocre life with a steady job. I didn't want to settle in my neighborhood. I wanted another life." He forced his knee to stop bouncing. "I vowed to work hard until I reached the top. Starting my own company was the ultimate goal."

"So you're at the top?" Lola raised an eyebrow. Chuck nodded. "Wow." Lola nodded, amazed. "You fulfilled all your goals."

"Not all," Chuck realized.

"Like what?" Lola leaned forward, curious, eyes widening in anticipation.

"A family." His gazed roamed her features.

Lola blushed, dropping her gaze to the ground. "Oh," she breathed, smiling, and bit her lip. She bore her eyes into his, searching. "Haven't found the right woman?" she teased.

Gazing into her golden hair, backlit by the sun, and her round brown eyes sparkling with playfulness, Chuck stood and leaned down over Lola. With a smacking sound, he stole a kiss from her lips. "Perhaps I have," he teased back.

Lola burst into laughter, shaking her head with a toothy grin. "You have, until you see what I've done to you." She pointed at her drawing. "Your turn," she announced, reaching for the sky with her long arms. She moved from side to side, stretching, and let her hands drop around Chuck as he took a step back to sit down. With a slight pull, she brought herself to his lips, kissing the surprise out him.

"I can steal kisses, too," she warned, giggling.

As Chuck deformed Lola's face on the white paper, she inquired about him some more.

"Are you close to your sister?" Lola asked again.

Chuck nodded, relaxing into the change of subject. "Growing up, we practically only had each other." The information slipped out. Lola frowned. Before she could ask him what he meant—as he knew she was going to—Chuck continued in the same beat. "Gabriella's really great. She's smart. Had the highest grades in school. I used to try to help with her homework, and she'd end up helping me with mine." Chuck boasted about his sister's qualities, in an effort to ignore his anxious wonderment. Why was his sister here and not working? Why did he have to love his sister so much? Worry about her so much?

Chuck was laughing so hard, he was sure he almost peed his pants. Their drawings were so horrible, he actually felt bad for the pieces of paper, which were marred for life with the hideous assault.

Elena's voice drifted among the couples, announcing that the next activity was to create a frame for one another—to frame their masterpieces, as she put it. She clearly hadn't seen their drawings. They had completely deformed one another. Chuck looked like a deformed, crooked head with a beard. Lola looked as though a toddler no older than three had drawn her. There were no words to explain the wiggly, uneven lines he dared to call her face. It was just too funny. In between fits of laughter, Lola kept apologizing. Her nose scrunched up as she guffawed. Chuck's hand rested on his sore core as he laughed. He couldn't even talk; he was laughing so much.

Holding Lola's hand in one of his hands, and the two atrocious drawings in the other, Chuck guided them back into the mansion. As he was mentioning that he needed to speak with his sister, Gabriella spotted them in the sea of people. Making her way through the crowd, she greeted him. "Chuck!"

"Gabby, it's good to see you," Chuck grinned, hugging his little sister tightly. "Gabby, this is Lola. Lola, this is Gabriella." Chuck released her, presenting Lola.

Lola's cheeks turned slightly pink as she extended her hand to greet Gabriella. Her whole stance and allure become formal, with a hint of nervousness. To his and Lola's surprise, Gabriella ignored her extended hand and hugged her warmly.

"I can't believe my brother finally found someone," Gabriella announced, elated. Chuck rolled his eyes. Gabriella made it sound like he had been single for years and years. It had only been one. Granted, one long, long, eternal year after having dated his ex for seven years.

Lola returned Gabriella's hug, struggling to respond. Chuck

guessed that Lola didn't know how to say that they weren't together, that this was only for the weekend. It was pretend. Although there was no fooling him. Those kisses were anything but fake. He'd loved this morning and last night, when she'd kissed him so openly. Her lips were so soft, he could kiss her for days and days. A voice cautioned him that their initial deal was for the best.

Lola looked at him for help. He smiled and leaned in and kissed her surprised lips. He turned his attention back to his sister.

"How come you're not at work?" Chuck asked.

"You know, it's been a month and a half since I last saw you. Since—" Gabriella ignored his question.

He cut her off sharply. "Gabs, don't," he warned. He knew where she was going, and he didn't want to go there. Not with Lola beside him. Determined black eyes stared down at her stubborn black eyes. Seconds ticked by. Chuck felt Lola stare between his sister and him.

"You can't ignore it forever." His sister gave up, exasperated.

He nodded. He knew he couldn't, but he wasn't ready to face it yet. He still needed time. Who was he kidding? He'd never be ready. Not even if he actually tried. He needed to man up and face it. Simple… Just not now.

Soon. Soon, he promised.

Chapter Twelve

Lola walked silently beside Chuck through the woods. After making frames for their horrific drawings, Elena had announced that there was nothing more romantic than sleeping under the stars. Yep, they were going camping. Lola smiled. She was glad Elena had taken her suggestion. She had always wanted to go camping.

That was romantic.

They had to build a fire and roast hot dogs for dinner, with s'mores for dessert. Plus, they had to set up a tent, something Lola had always wanted to do. She was more than a little excited, her small skips of anticipation adding bounce to her steps.

Elena had given them a list of questions to ask one another as a game to get to know each other. The list was meant only for the singletons set up as couples, but Elena had felt it necessary to give it to them, too. Lola didn't mind; she wanted to know more about the mysterious man walking beside her. If it was anything like Lola had envisioned—conquering the mystery of Chuck—the night was planning out to be fun.

Or so she hoped.

In theory, the idea sounded amusing. Chuck, the woods and her. Definitely fun. But ever since Chuck had his stare-down with his sister in the mansion, he had been even more silent than normal. If that was even possible. It was. And it radiated a certain frustration. Lola didn't understand it. He couldn't be mad at his sister. Chuck had been talking earlier about his sister, saying how smart she was and well, just listing off her achievements and qualities, all brotherly and proud. She'd be a fool not to realize how much Chuck loved his sister. When they had left, he hadn't seemed angry at Gabriella at all. It had to be something else. But since then, he hadn't uttered a single word, not even as they made the frames for their horrendous drawings.

Before they had left the mansion to go into the woods behind it, Lola had a little chat with Gabriella, when Chuck went back to their room to get something. They talked a bit about the guy Gabriella was paired up with. Gabriella told her that the guy was nice and that they had tried to make it work, but there was no chemistry. It was awkward between them, and they had decided to just pretend. But even pretending was awkward.

Pretending?

The word caught Lola's attention. She and Chuck were pretending, but it wasn't awkward between them. It felt normal, actually. And very nice. Granted, Lola didn't have the heart to tell Chuck's sister that she and he were also pretending. Although she wished she had. When they went to say goodbye, the woman had actually threatened her.

"Oh, and if you hurt my brother, I will have to hurt you," she menaced and then laughed lightly, winking at Lola and wishing her a good night with another warm hug. Instead of feeling scared that Gabriella had threatened her, deep down Lola was pleased that Gabriella had threatened her, because it meant that she loved her brother. And if she loved her brother that much, it meant Chuck was a good guy. Lola knew he was a good guy, but confirming it with a close relative didn't hurt. She glanced at Chuck and found him so deep in thought, he almost looked mad. Maybe he was. She wondered. Looking closely at him, she saw pain burning deep in his dark eyes.

Wanting to distract him from whatever he was thinking, Lola laced her fingers in his and said, "I hope we get there soon. I'm hungry."

They had been walking for a couple of minutes, following the red bows taped to the trees, to the campsite where they would spend the night. Lola had hoped Chuck would say something, but he just nodded, like always. And went back to his thoughts. At least he kept his hand in hers, but she was a little frustrated that he had just nodded.

I am going to make you talk if it's the last thing I do!

Right. She needed food in her system. Urgently. She had gotten irritable way too fast there.

Thankfully, a few minutes later, they reached the campsite. It was a circle, not too big or too small. It was nice and cozy. There was a small pre-made fire pit with cut-up logs beside it. Lola walked around, scanning the woods for places she could change without Chuck seeing. And most importantly, where she could pee if she needed to.

"I'll start making the fire," Chuck said at once, dropping to his knees, placing the logs in a tippy formation on the fire pit. His movements were swift and precise. With calm hurry, his hands flew quickly across and over the fire pit. Gazing at him, Lola realized that he hadn't even taken off the backpack Elena had given him. Lola put hers down and went over to Chuck. She placed a kiss on his cheek. "I'll set up the tent, then," she said, tugging off his backpack, where the tent was. Lola felt Chuck's gaze as she walked away. She flicked her hips from side to side with slow, seductive precision. With all the time in the world, she bent over and shot Chuck a seductive gaze.

Mortification balled in her stomach as she realized Chuck wasn't gazing at her anymore. Right. Lola tried to silently laugh off her sense of stupidity.

Five minutes later, Lola groaned out her frustration. Setting up a tent was anything but easy. And to make things worse, she was seriously starving now. She thought she might cry, because she was so hungry. Everything lay at her feet, mocking her. Lola held a foldable pole that had smacked her in the face more than once.

This wasn't fun.

Lola felt Chuck come up behind her and take the pole from her hand. She happily let go of the infernal stick and leaned back on Chuck. "I'm so hungry," she whimpered softly, closing her eyes. Her stomach rumbled loudly in agreement. She hadn't eaten all day, but she didn't regret it.

She'd officially finished the design layout, color palette and mock-ups for her most recent client project, in the morning. She had worked on it so hard; she prayed the client would like it, if not adore it. It was her ultimate masterpiece.

Tender, moist pressure pressed atop Lola's head as Chuck murmured, "The fire's ready."

She smiled, turning and pressing another kiss on his cheek. "Thank you," she whispered gratefully and went to retrieve the food from her backpack. As she did, Chuck fumbled around with the tent pieces. Familiar snip-snapping noises filed the air. Good luck. Lola rolled her eyes. At any moment, she would hear the smack of a pole hitting him. By the time Lola turned around with the food in her hands, the tent stood strong and study, with Chuck standing beside it, unhurt. Her mouth popped open. "H-how you do that?" she choked out.

Chuck shrugged his large shoulders, a little bit pleased by her reaction, Lola noted. He studied her stupefied face and offered to teach her after they ate. Nodding excitedly at the proposal, Lola plunged into roasting her dinner.

Lola was amazed at how quickly Chuck set up the tent again, after they had eaten. "It just takes practice," he told her as he undid it a second time. More amazingly, he was a patient teacher. He taught her the basics of assembling a tent and turned it into an art, giving her tips as she practiced.

After they had finished setting up the tent for a third time— that time she did it all by herself, while Chuck supervised—they sat down on opposite sides of the small orange fire.

The sky was a matte, dark navy blue fading slowly into black- ness. The evening was cool, and mosquitos were starting to come out. Smoke travelled up to reach the sky, evaporating as it reached the height of the surrounding trees. Silently, Lola gazed into the yellow-orange flames, sighing contently.

Smack!

Her hand fell flat on her arm. Slowly, she lifted her hand, eyeing the little squashed dot with a broken wing. Blood scorched underneath the tiny, swelling bump on her forearm.

Smack! came a harsher, quicker sound from the other side of the flames. Lola's head snapped up as Chuck flicked off the tiny bug.

Smack! In unison, they smacked their legs. Blood tingled in her thigh, under her slap. Gradually, it was replaced by a pounding-hot mosquito bite.

Clap! She clapped one dead before it bit her nose.

Lola crawled to her backpack, remembering that she had seen bug repellant. Rummaging through her bag, a smile broke out as her fingers grasped the metal cylinder.

Pressing hard on the little white spout, Lola found herself in an excessive cloud of clinically lemon-scented bug spray. Nothing like her sweet, lemony-smelling shampoo. The misty cloud soon evaporated. Next up, Chuck. Lola lifted a malicious eyebrow. She glanced over her shoulder at the large man sitting on the ground. With calculated slowness, she turned her body to face him as she held the bug spray can like a gun, pointed upward. Black eyes shot up to her face. She narrowed her eyes at Chuck, taking a slow, deliberate step. A bushy, raven-black eyebrow rose.

"Are you ready?" Lola took another step closer. Chuck looked around, confused. Lola pointed the bug spray at him. "Boy, don't play with me," she warned, fighting the tug on her cheeks. "I asked you a simple question," she snarled, her voice dropping in menace.

Chuck gulped. Lola bit her cheeks to keep from smiling. He looked so scared.

"Are you telling me you'd rather be bitten by mosquitoes than be ready?" Lola taunted. To prove her point, another mosquito bit his arm. "I'll ask you once more. Are you ready?" Lola raised an eyebrow. Realization dawned on Chuck.

Chuck nodded, acting nervous. He got up, fidgeting, playing along. Lola took two quick steps and paused before Chuck, adding suspense. She gazed into his black, almost pupil-less eyes, fighting hard against her smile. They stood a mere foot away from each other. Lola watched as his chest heaved heavily with each breath, waiting for her next move. Lola let the silence stretch out longer, making him nervous for real.

Out of nowhere, she yelled, "Yaaww!" spraying Chuck all over. Chuck tumbled backwards at her cry, but his laugh filled her ears. She twirled around Chuck, jumping from side to side, every now and then giving a Kung Fu "kick," laughing. She finally stopped when the can sizzled out pure air.

"Silly." Chuck grabbed her waist as she laughed, and he pulled her closer. Lola grinned, letting the can fall from her hand with an audible plink, and wrapped her arms around his neck. She reached up on her toes, puckering her lips for a kiss. Chuck chuckled his throaty laugh and shook his head. Closing the space between them, Chuck kissed her hard, with passion and longing. Just how she liked it.

Pulling back, Lola ran her fingers over his beard, enjoying the coarse softness.

"Want to play the game?" she asked, flicking her eyes from side to side into his. Chuck nodded, smiling. Lola got the question sheet from her bag and settled down on her side of the fire. Distance. She needed some distance from the man.

"Okay, do you want to start, or should I?" she asked Chuck.

Chuck smiled. "You already started," he said, referring to her question.

Lola grinned, throwing her head back, laughing. "Okay, so it's your turn, then."

Chuck nodded, laughing as she passed him his sheet of questions with the scattered red-dot border. Hers was decorated with pink arrows.

He read the question. "What's your favorite color?"

"I don't really have one. I love all the colors. You?"

"Green."

"Why?"

"Because I like nature," he replied simply.

"Okay, um, what's your favorite food?" Lola asked.

"Pizza. You?"

"Grilled cheese sandwich. And that's only because it's one of the only things I can cook," Lola said and added, "but I must say your pancakes were delicious." Chuck's eyes lit up, and a smile teased the outer edges of his plump lips.

Do not jump over the fire to kiss him. Don't. Lola resisted the urge.

He looked down and frowned. "These are a lot of questions," he said. "How about we each ask a question and then both answer the first thing that comes to mind?" he suggested.

"Yes! That's an awesome idea! It'll go faster. I'll start," Lola said. "What city would you like to visit?"

"Amsterdam," he said.

"Rome," she said.

"Would you rather be an animal, a food or an object?" Chuck asked.

"Animal," they said in unison. They looked at each other.

"Bear." Chuck answered their unspoken question.

"Dog," Lola answered, grinning impishly. "I just love those little noses." She touched her own nose, wiggling her fingers. "And floppy ears." She used her hands as ears on top of her head, flicking them downward and back up, demonstrating floppy ears. Chuck laughed quietly.

They continued their questions. Read an eBook or a paperback book? eBook when traveling, paperback at home. Go to a play or musical? Play. Go to the theater or a movie? Movie. Hike or bike? Hike. Go to a comedy club or dance club? Comedy club, Chuck said, and Lola said dance club, but they both decided they would go to neither. Watch sports or play sports? They both hesitated at that one. Chuck was like Lola, who loved to watch sports but also enjoyed playing them. What was the one thing they would change, if they could do it all over? They both skipped the question. If you were to create a piece of art, what would the theme be? Stability. Who would you want with you, if you were stranded on a desert island?

"You," Lola almost blurted out, but she held back and replied instead, "I don't know."

"Me, either," Chuck said.

If she was stranded on a desert island, she would want to be with Chuck. It was logical. She knew that with Chuck, she would be safe. In the span of the few hours she had spent in his company, Chuck had more than demonstrated his capacities to survive in the wild. It was logical that she wanted him. Stranded on an island, she clarified to herself. Plus, if they needed to reproduce, she really wouldn't mind. Lola eyed those thick, pulsating veins on those rough hands. Was she breathing? Nope. Breathe in and breathe out.

Thank god, silence settled around them. Lola welcomed it. Heavenly. Lola was sure her voice would tremble with desire, giving her away. They had been talking for at least two hours. Or maybe longer. It was hard to tell; the sky had been dark for quite some time. The only light came from the fire, helped by a million stars in the black sky. The cool breeze swirled around her, but near the fire, Lola barely felt it. Lola drifted into the universe of her thoughts, conscious that Chuck was doing the same.

A few minutes later, Lola's gaze flickered from the flames to Chuck's face. Chuck sat staring into the flames with the same expression he'd had earlier—seemingly hard and cold, lost, with hints of despair. Something tugged at Lola's insides, at the sight of his strong features struggling with pain. Head held high, jaw clenched, it was a dignified pain. Subtle but undeniable. A lump lodged in her throat. Was it because of what his sister had been about to say when he cut her off? It must be. She had a feeling it was. Surely it couldn't be that bad.

Only one way to find out.

Lola crawled around the fire, dragging her blanket behind her. She carefully laid it on the ground beside Chuck before lying down. His lifted a questioning eyebrow, gazing down at her. Prop-ping herself on her elbows, she lightly tapped the ground, inviting him. Chuck lay down, leaving his arm slightly open as an invitation to snuggle against him. *No need to do more.* Lola snuggled beside him, setting her head on his hard chest.

Lola gazed up at the stars for a few minutes, listening to his heartbeat, getting the courage to ask him. She didn't want to be shut down, but she had to ask. If not, she'd blame Gabriella for a crime she might not even have committed. Lola would understand if he chose not to answer. Or worse, stayed completely silent, leav- ing her hanging. Lola held back the shudder at the thought.

Taking in a deep, steadying breath, Lola softly asked, "Can I ask you one last question?"

"Of course."

"What was your sister talking about earlier?" She prayed he understood what she meant.

Her prayer was answered.

Chapter Thirteen

Chuck gritted his teeth and closed his eyes, wanting to shut everything out. Everything except the warmth of Lola's body against his right side or the weight of her head on his chest. He didn't want to answer the question. He didn't want her to know, because then, things would change. He still wanted to enjoy the moment longer with Lola. Pretend or not. He still wanted to believe she was his and that she accepted him for himself. But there was a part of him that didn't want to believe; he wanted to know. If his mission was to keep her company for longer, then she had to know. Both the good and the horrible.

Chuck waited for the fear of confiding in Lola to seize him. It didn't come. Instead, the need to confide in her battled with his desire for her to never, ever, under any circumstances, find out. Yet he found himself seizing every ounce of courage. He took a deep breath. Here goes. "She... ah." He cleared his throat. "Gabby was talking about our mother," he said in one shot.

"Oh, my god!" Lola propped herself up on one elbow, her wide eyes looking down at him. "Your mom? Is she okay? Is she hurt? You have a mom? Is she alright?" Lola exclaimed with worry. Her sparkly brown eyes glittered with concern. Flicking from one eye to the other, they searched for his reaction. A strand of golden blond hair fell in front of her face; he gently pushed it back behind her ear and slowly caressed her cheek and then her bottom lip. He felt her breath catch slightly as his hand traveled down her neck, pushing back her hair.

"If you want to know, you'll have to let me get through it first," he said gently. Lola nodded, understanding. She laid her head back down on his chest and waited for him to continue. With his arm wrapped around her, he softly played with her blond hair as he talked distantly, with words like he had been an unattached observer, rather than having lived it. It was his way of protecting himself from the cutting pain in his heart.

"My mother is as good as she'll ever be. Putting it nicely, my mother is a drunk. Ever since I can remember, she's always been drunk." Or getting drunk, he thought. When she wasn't getting drunk, she was tricking people out of their money to buy more alcohol.

"My father wasn't much help. He loves my mother so much he does whatever she wants. Gives her whatever she needs. He worked day and night for her." Chuck paused. Always building a safe haven for others while he failed to do so for his own family. Chuck wanted to shake the irony out of his head.

"He would always take my mother's side, always defend

her." He paused. "When Gabriella and I were both old enough to work, we started saving all our money, thinking maybe if we moved, they... She would change." Chuck remembered how Gabby and he would whisper into the night, dreaming that their mother would stop drinking and change. Become a real mother. Chuck closed his eyes at his own stupidity in thinking it would happen. "But she refused. She was outraged by our even suggesting such a thing." To teach them their lesson, she had taken all their money and wasted it on cheap vodka. "She loves her neighborhood, the dirty building. All her drunken friends are there—never judging, always encouraging." He gritted his teeth. *Come on, that wasn't a sip. Bet you can chug down the whole bottle. Ha ha! Don't listen to them, they're young. They don't know what they're talking about. Drinking does nothing to the baby. Mom, stop. Think about the baby. You heard him, it does nothing.* Chuck knew *he* was wrong.

"My father seconded her decisions." Chuck paused again, unsure how to tell Lola the rest. The part that made people run away. The part that answered her question, and possibly might drive her away.

"The thing is my mother is an aggressive drunk. She and my father always fought." He paused, forcing out the next word. "Physically." Lola froze. Chuck gulped. Please. Don't run away.

"About a month and a half ago, they got in a huge fight, resulting in both going to the hospital." Chuck still remembered the cold, empty feeling settling in his stomach as Gabriella, ashamed, had told him as she sat across his desk. His father was in a coma, and his mother had a broken leg and three broken fingers and was severely bruised. No surprise when they found out she had serious liver failure. He cleared his throat, waiting for Lola's reaction. She was calm, her breathing a little shallow, waiting for him to continue.

Boom. Boom. Boom. His heart pounded. Crawling anxiety gradually seized his heart, his jaw set straight and hard.

"She wants to see me. My mother. But I have sort of been ignoring the request." He hadn't seen her since the day he left. He couldn't face her without remembering everything she had put Gabriella and him through. And still was putting him through. The shame he carried. The quick judgment people made of him because of her or the all-too-quick pity followed by the need to patch him up. A waste of time. Seven years. Chuck ignored the thought. No one could help him, because he wasn't broken. He just needed to learn how to live with the scars. Scars were easily handled in solitude. Chuck took a deep, shaky breath.

Lola's finger gently stroked small circles on his shirt. A calm smile spread across Chuck's lips. She wasn't running. She wasn't running. He relaxed. Lightening the mood, he added a little trivia. "That's how I actually started building the chalet. I cut off all communication with everyone and immersed myself in building it. I figured I was going to do it sooner or later, and I had the plans already done."

He felt Lola smile.

She was silent for what seemed like a lifetime to Chuck. He remembered her tiny, almost inaudible, shocked gasp. What if he had scared her away? What if she was waiting for the right moment to leave? What if she was thinking of a way to tell him that she never wanted to see him again? Like his ex-had. No, Lola wasn't anything like the petit, proper brunette he had dated. He held his breath, waiting for her reaction.

"I'm sorry."

Chuck closed his eyes. Here comes pity. Warmth softly caressed his chest in reassurance. Lola's hand stopped moving, her hand heating his heart.

"… It makes sense," she breathed. "I mean, it's horrible, what you've been through." She paused, searching for words. "But I understand now why when you talked—well, briefly mentioned—your father and not your mother this afternoon, I saw a certain anger and resistance in you. And then, the way you talk about your sister with admiration… I… It… Err… It just makes sense… No, I mean… I don't know. I don't think I'm expressing myself well, but you know what I mean?" she asked him anxiously, her hand clutching his shirt.

He didn't have the slightest clue, but he released his breath, feeling a weight lift off his shoulders. She wasn't running away. She was, instead, playing with the creases of his shirt, snuggled closer to him. Her touch was tender and accepting. He wanted to burst into joyous laughter and squish Lola in a bear hug. Why had he been so worried? Lola wasn't like the rest.

"Are you going to visit them?" she asked, shifting and putting her chin on his chest as she gazed at him.

"I thought you said one last question," he joked. Lola grimaced, gently poking him with her knee. He laughed lightly, tightening his grip on her waist. "No." His response was automatic. "… I don't know," he replied truthfully, his deep throaty voice shivering with uncertainty.

"If you do decide to go and need someone to go with you,

I would be more than happy to go with you," Lola offered, with sincerity burning in her seemingly shallow brown eyes.

His heart fluttered the truth throughout his body. Gazing into her eyes, he realized he loved her. He had loved her from the moment he had met her, almost a year before.

He loved her.

ৡ ♥ ৶

Lola gazed at Chuck's face. He was such a strong man, she thought. A man of few words, carrying tomes' worth of words in experience. Chuck had come a long way; she would never have guessed that he had come from that kind of background. He was refined, with his mysterious air. But somehow, in her twisted sense of logic, it made sense. His strength was much more than the hard muscles covering his large body. His strength was rooted in him; it was a part of him, like his raven-black eyes or his high cheekbones. It was who he was. It was a strength built when he had no other choice but to be strong. An invisible, unbreakable strength, Lola contemplated.

He was a man who didn't go around... revealing— Her heart squeezed against her chest— He wasn't a man who revealed his vulnerability. His weakness lay in her knowledge. He trusted her. The thought shook her out of the universe of her thoughts. Fear pumped through her heart. This trust wasn't the normal trust she was used to. This trust implied much more. Gazing at him, she saw his black eyes stare into nothingness, deep in thought, too.

"You know, when you're deep in thought, your eyebrows smash into each other," she grinned, placing one finger in between

153

his eyebrows, separating them.

Chuck's eyebrows sprang up high on his forehead at her touch. Lola laughed, propping herself up into a sitting position. Sitting up along with her, Chuck took her hand in his, weaving his fingers in hers and said, "You know, when you're thinking, I swear I can hear wheels turning," he teased.

Lola faked surprised outrage. Her! Please! She broke into laughter, throwing her head back. "Mikaella and Elena say the same thing," she said, smiling, unable to keep up the charade for longer than three seconds.

Chuck chuckled his deep, throaty laugh. Lola's smile deepened. She loved how his laughter sounded. He slowly caressed her cheek like he couldn't resist, then down her jaw line. He grabbed her chin with his thumb and forefinger, bringing her head to his. He stopped a few inches from her lips and gazed at every inch of her face with admiration, with desire. Lola felt a small humming between her legs. Chuck let go of her chin and continued to stroke her cheek, pulling slightly back from her face. He brought his thumb to her lips and gently outlined her lips. She could feel her heartbeat in her lips and wondered if he could, too. Lola's lips parted, and Chuck softly traced her bottom lip over and over, his thumb edging onto the moist sheen of her satin inner lip. Lola shuddered slightly, tightening her thighs.

His touch was so soft and light, leaving her aching for more. She wanted to inch forward, to close the space between them, to feel whether his lips were pumping hot with blood, like hers. But she didn't want to kiss first. She wanted him to kiss her. She needed to know that he wanted her as much as she wanted him.

Lola gazed into his raven-black eyes in the light of the fire in front of them. He gazed back into hers. The moment held such intimacy; it undressed their souls. Chuck gently cupped Lola's face, finally closing the space between their beating lips.

Chuck kissed her gently at first, slowly sliding his tongue, then darting it across her lips, parting them. Lola moaned as she felt a flush of excitement when Chuck began teasing her tongue. She played along with the chocolatey-tasting tongue. She shifted and swung one leg over him, straddling him. Another moan escaped her lips as she felt the warmth of his hardness between her legs.

Lola wrapped her arms around his neck as he grabbed her waist, pulling her closer to him. His hands began wandering up and down her back, making her squirm in delight. Chuck groaned—almost a growl. Blood pumped between her thighs at the sound. The more she squirmed, the more ragged his breath became, the more he groaned.

The more he groaned, the more her breasts ached desperately for his touch. She wanted him to touch. She wanted to feel him.

Wanting more of him, Lola began making small circles with her hips, rubbing against him. Unable to stop herself, she moaned softly. Pressure gripped her sides, and she felt his breath become raggedy. Lola smiled against his lips.

Her breasts felt swollen, and she became more desperate for his touch.

Thankfully, Chuck broke off their steamy kiss and began kissing down her neck. Lola threw back her head, giving him more access. His slid his tongue up and down her neck, making her shudder with desire. His hands slowly began travelling up her body, over

155

her grey fitted sweater, stopping underneath her breasts. Slowly, he slid his hands down to her jeans, making her moan, half in frustration, half in desire. He slid his hands underneath her sweater and shirt. He lightly trailed up her belly, stroking it up and down, without any purpose other than to torture her. Lola wanted to whimper each time he slid his hands back down, without the slightest touch to her swollen mountains, always just millimeters away. Without warning, he slid his hand underneath her bra. Lola gasped, clutching flannel fabric in her hands.

Chuck kissed down her neck, and with a quick movement, unhooked her bra and took off her sweater and shirt. Shrugging off her bra, Lola felt a soft shiver as the cool night breeze touched her bare body.

"Beautiful," she heard Chuck say as he gazed at her perked-up nipples. He closed his mouth over her watermelon-pink peaks. Another kind of shiver ran through Lola's body. She moaned loudly, her head thrown backwards, as he sucked, licked and teased her. As he brought his lips to hers, she took off his jacket and shirt. She briefly admired the smooth, hard plane of his chest and shoulders. Chuck kissed her again, pressing her breast against his chest. Lola moaned again, feeling the warmth of his skin pressed against hers.

Lola let her hand wander, touching him, teasing him, always going far down but never close enough to his bulging hardness. She rubbed herself against his hardness, loving how he tightened his grip on her.

Chuck shifted, laying her down on the blanket alongside the fire. He settled above her, kissing her lips over and over again, playing passionately with her mouth. He slid his tongue down her neck, in between her breasts, down her stomach. He trailed his tongue along the edge of her jeans. Lola shivered, biting her lip as she moaned. Her skin tightened at the warmth of his breath. Sliding off her jeans, he lifted her hips high in the air, settling her legs on his shoulders. Lola moaned loudly as she felt his hot breath against her wet, beatin— "Ah!"

Chuck slid his tongue between her swollen folds. He sucked, licked and teased her down below. He slid his tongue in her over and over again. Lola moaned and squirmed herself closer to his mouth, wanting more. She heard Chuck groan. She felt herself get closer and closer, higher and higher. She wanted him. She wanted him in- side her.

"Chuck," she whimpered. "Please," she moaned, feeling the hotness of his breath.

Chuck settled above her again as she slid her hand down his bare chest to unbutton his jeans. She felt his muscles ripple at her touch and his breath catch. She stopped. "Condom," she breathed. Chuck nodded. She was about to say she had some in her backpack, but Chuck was already up and rummaging through his. He took off his jeans, shoes and socks and slid on the condom.

Lola bit her lip in excitement.

In the glow of the firelight, vibrating from Lola and Chuck's passionate embrace, the bug spray can rolled until it hit the edge of the fire pit. Momentum built, and it got hotter and hotter until under the passionate pressure, the bug spray can exploded seconds after Lola and Chuck did.

Screaming for her life, Lola clutched Chuck harder and

threw her head back, laughing hard as she realized the small can had ex- ploded. Laughing along with her, Chuck kissed Lola, and round two began with a bigger explosion.

Chapter Fourteen

Lola woke up the next morning feeling wonderfully alive. Her body ached deliciously in the right places. She smiled, opening her eyes, nestled against Chuck. She felt his chest rise up and down as he breathed. Raising her head, she gazed at Chuck's sleeping face. He was so handsome. And an amazing lover. She shivered, remembering his large hands on her body, holding her strongly to him.

Lola felt wonderful, happy and alive… And confused.

She frowned.

Lola hadn't expected to actually sleep with Chuck. Sure, she had fantasized about it, but it was one thing to want it and another for it to happen. When she was with Chuck, she always had either a dull burning desire to be with him or an actual full-blown passion to touch, to kiss him. But Chuck was a good guy. She hadn't wanted to use him as a rebound. Because being realistic, that was what he was. A rebound. The only plausible explanation for her behavior. And they had no future together. They couldn't.

It had all happened so suddenly; one minute they were talking, and the next he had been caressing her, making her tremble with desire, making her cry out for more. Being with him had been nothing like she was used to. He kissed her like no one ever had before. He made her feel like... like... She was wanted. Not only physically. It was like he wanted her. For being her.

Who liked her for her, other than people who had to? Other than her best friends and father? No one did. Then why did Chuck make her feel that way?

Grr. It was confusing.

Not in her wildest dreams did she think that after sleeping with Chuck, she would be so confused. Why was she confused? She didn't understand. She would have thought that after sleeping with Chuck, she would feel alive and happy and wonderful. Granted, she was feeling all those things, but her mind just got stuck on the confusion part.

Okay, let's analyze this.

In order, Lola had broken up with her boyfriend. Then she had gotten drunk and ended up staying at Chuck's house. Chuck had agreed to pretend to be her boyfriend. Then—

There it was!

She'd broken up with her boyfriend—what, like two days ago? —then she had proposed to Chuck that he be her pretend boyfriend... But last night didn't feel pretend to her. Nothing with Chuck felt like pretend to her. But it was. Don't forget that, she reminded herself.

It felt, at times, too real— Even through the closed door,

pain-filled sobs resonated through the silent house. Lola shook the sound out of her mind, ignoring it and continuing her initial train of thought. She had to hand it to him; Chuck was an amazing actor. But it was time to put some reins on those talents.

From now on, Lola vowed, she wouldn't kiss him. There wasn't a need, really. There were plenty of couples who were together in public, and they weren't kissing each other. Did that make them less of a couple? No, of course not. No more lovey-dovey touches. Just no more! She almost yelled the thought, trying to drown out the echo of her sobs.

Distance. Distance was needed, she frantically thought. How hard could it be?

∿ ♥ ∿

Smiling, Chuck woke up with his eyes still closed. He tightened his grip on Lola, hugging her closer to him. His hand slammed into his chest, after finding zero resistance in the air. Chuck opened his eyes, expecting to see Lola sleeping beside him, then rolled over to his other side, but instead, he saw an empty tent. He sat up quickly, looking around as if she might suddenly appear. But she didn't. An invisible force punched his heart.

He had fallen asleep hoping to wake up and see her in his arms, to see her smile at him, sleepy and satisfied from their night together.

Maybe she had just gone to pee and didn't know he would wake up. Now there was a perfect explanation. One he liked better than Lola waking and realizing it had been a mistake, or something along those lines. Or worse, leaving because of his past. His heritage.

161

Chuck shuddered at the bitter taste the thought brought. He gulped. Yeah, he definitely preferred his first theory. Or maybe she was hungry and had gone to eat. See? There were a million explanations for why she was not there with him, so no need to panic. But his instincts incited him to panic. His heart began beating faster and faster, and it squeezed with every beat. He felt a cold sweat slide down his back as he tried to think of other reasons why she might not be in the tent with him, in his arms. Mayb—

This was ridiculous, he chided himself. Quickly getting dressed in the small, confined space of the tent, Chuck stepped out to find out what was happening. He knew something was up. He could feel it. And confirmed it when he saw Lola sitting on the ground, staring into the dead fire pit, her eyebrows knitted together as she concentrated on whatever was going through her mind. It wasn't a good sign.

"Morning," Chuck greeted her, eyeing her reaction.

Lola looked up, startled, with her wonderful brown eyes. She quickly averted her gaze to the side, then down to the ground and replied cheerfully, "Good morning."

She was avoiding his gaze, he realized, and she was preoccupied with nothing. Something was definitely wrong. He walked over to her, with the intention of kissing her silly until she told him what was going through her amazing mind.

Sensing he was too close, Lola looked up and gazed into his eyes. Searching? He leaned down to plant a kiss on her soft lips. He was relieved when she inched forward a little to meet his lips, but just as he puckered his lips, millimeters away from kissing the heaven of her lips, Lola turned her face. Chuck ended up kissing her sweet cheek. Although, at the moment, he didn't think it was sweet. He wanted her sweet lips.

So it had been pity. Last night had only been pity. He should have known. How stupid he was to believe for a second she didn't care about his past. All women cared, all women pitied. Some tried to mend him, while others... while others, like Lola, comforted him for a night with the desire to bolt at the first opportunity.

Disdain, hatred towards nothing and everything, needled its way through his heart. Shame ripped at his heart, battling the new-found love he felt for Lola. Damn it.

His heart sank, drowning his feelings in the pit of his stomach.

☙ ♥ ❧

Lola felt horrible. Chuck mumbled something about the tent and began undoing the tent. His actions were sharp and harsh. His face was like a stone. Hard and cold. Emotionless. Lola desperately looked at his thick, raven-black eyebrows. His wonderful eyebrows that always told her if he was thinking or if he was mad. But they stayed where they were supposed to stay, between his dark eyes and his forehead. *Thanks*, she thought sarcastically, angry. Why was she getting mad? She was the one who had turned her head when she had been about to kiss his big plump lips. She was the one who wanted distance between them.

But the need to kiss him had almost overwhelmed her. If it hadn't been for her trusty inner voice shouting from a distance in the back of her mind, alongside the still-echoing sobs, Lola would have kissed him senseless. If she had, then he wouldn't have understood her need for distance.

Lola wanted him to understand without her saying anything. And from the looks of it, he did. Why wasn't she happy, then? She had wanted it, no? She had, but she wasn't feeling the normal relief she should; instead a painful porcupine ball weighed in her core.

It didn't help that she could feel the distance grow bigger as the seconds ticked by. The distance was cold and rigid. Lola shivered involuntarily at the thought.

Lola sighed.

If she had wanted distance, she had gotten it, in what felt like the distance between the top of Canada to the bottom tip of Argentina.

The silence stretched between them as Chuck finished packing the tent. Silence. One second, two seconds, three seconds passed by. Silence. More seconds passed by, four seconds. Silence. More seco—

Oh, my god! She was going insane! She was actually counting the seconds. She had to say something, anything. She couldn't stand the silence anymore.

"Hm, I think someone dropped off breakfast this morning," she said, pointing at the blue cooler by the path they had come along the night before. Lola knew someone had; she had already taken a quick sneak peek when she spotted it as she searched for a place to pee. It was filled with cut-up fruit and a couple of mouthwatering patisseries. They looked good. There was some juice, too, and she wasn't sure, but a thermos bottle gleamed in the middle of all the delicious food, with what she imaged would be coffee or tea.

Lola had to hand it to Elena; everything was extremely well-planned. Although she had thought camping would be romantic, Lola had her share of worries, mainly about food, and she hadn't thought about bugs, but she always would now. Lola scratched her arm. A smiled threatened when she remembered the explosion—and the many, many after. But Elena had provided them with everything they needed. Lola knew she would never forget last night. *It's because of Chuck,* a voice inside her chanted, *not because of Elena's preparations.*

Sssshhh!

It was everything Lola didn't want to acknowledge. She was trying really hard not to remember his large hands on her body, his mouth on her lips, on her aching breasts, on her burning wet— She moaned almost inaudibly, remembering the delicious sensation. She could still feel the hot, tickling sensations torturing her between her legs. Tightening her thighs, she bit her lip. She felt blood flow to her cheeks. Please don't notice, she prayed.

Chucked briefly gazed at her and simply nodded at her words.

Not knowing what else to say, Lola contented herself with setting breakfast out for them. She should have guessed he would just nod. Chuck really wasn't a talker, she acknowledged. The most he'd ever spoken had been last night, when he had told her about his parents.

She admired Chuck. He had made something of himself; he didn't let his past slow him down. Despite the hardship he had lived—the kind she'd only heard about in stories but that no one she had ever met had lived through. Realization dawned on Lola; despite it all, her father had sheltered her from the worst.

Thank you.

Even though in her teenage years, she had complained about

the hardship, she'd had it easy. To endure such suffering like Chuck— Lola wasn't sure she would have been capable of handling it. Which only added to her admiration of the man. Lola bet he'd make a great father, do everything his parents never did.

Whoa. Not that she cared if he would make a great father, because she didn't want kids—more like give birth. He did, she remembered. The only missing part of his life was a family, he had told her. Distance was starting to sound good again.

Lola carefully set out the two bowls of fruit, using the cooler as a table. She placed them on either side of the cooler, along with a box of orange juice, and laid out the patisseries in between. Thin golden crusts, sprinkled with powdery sugar and hints of red, fruity jam bubbling out on the sides. Lola was certain she was drooling as she stared at the patisseries. She glanced up to check if Chuck was done with the tent. She smiled as he walked towards her. *Patisseries, here I come.* He was taking his sweet time.

Lola become impatient and was left with nothing else to do but stare at him. He looked good, she noted. Chuck wore a red-and-black plaid flannel button-up, long-sleeved shirt with his dark wash jeans and beige construction boots. He ran his hand through his hair as he walked towards her, coiffing it messily sexy. When he sat down opposite her, Lola said, "Looks good, huh? Bon appétit."

Chuck nodded.

Being a good girl, Lola picked up her fruit salad first, while she eyed the cheese Danish. She tried making conversation. "So what do you think we'll be doing today?"

Chuck shrugged and said, uninterested, "I don't know" as he placed a strawberry in his mouth.

Lola felt a pang of stupid jealousy of the damn ruby-red strawberry. She wanted his lips on her, not the strawberry. *I wanted this, remember?* Distance. No, she didn't remember. At the moment, she was mad at the strawberry. Ruby-red, golden-speckled, vibrant-green-leafed strawberry. She glared at it with envy. Whatever. He could eat and enjoy his damn strawberry. She didn't care.

And enjoying them, he was. His lips turned upwards as he chewed. A drop of red, juicy syrup bubbled on the edge of his tinted red lips. Calm and peaceful, his features relaxed into the taste.

Her eyes narrowed at his chewing mouth. She'd ask him if he really liked strawberries. The word "strawberry" tasted like acid in her mouth.

"So, you like strawberries," she accused. Surprised by her tone, Chuck froze mid-bite. Oops. So much for asking him casually, like she didn't care. And she didn't, for the record. She just wanted to… to start a conversation. With the non-talking, strawberry-eating, tempting-the-hell-out-of-her man. Not her fault it came out all bitter; the man had provoked her. Really… Oh, god, he was seeing right through her.

Nodding, unsure whether he should answer, Chuck searched her features with intensity.

God, she was so obvious. Instead of putting more of her foot in her mouth, Lola nodded, too, stuffing her face with the fruit salad. With every single delicious, sweet piece of fruit. Except the strawberries. She studiously ignored them. She didn't care how ripe or juicy they looked.

Chuck noticed, making her blush as she caught him eyeing the strawberries, confused, and then glanced at her quickly to search for more clues. Lola avoided his dark gaze. It held too much intensity, too much knowledge.

Her foul mood lightened considerably when it was time to eat the patisseries. Lola's eyes sparkled at the possibilities. There was so much to choose from; there were croissants, a cheese croissant, raspberry Danish, a cheese Danish and small chocolate chip croissants. It was rare moments like these where she thanked her mom for giving her the type of body where she could eat whatever she wanted and not gain a single pound. That's what her father always told her—she had the same body as her mother. At times, she wished she could gain a few pounds. But no matter how hard she tried, it never happened. She just wanted enough to fill out her curves. Men always stared longer at women with curves, even if they had a little belly along with those curves, in her experience.

"Ladies first," Chuck gallantly offered.

Oh, yes!

Licking her lips, she picked up the cheese Danish and bit into it. Yep. She moaned. And wasn't the slightest bit ashamed. Even if Chuck raised a quizzical black brow at her. It was so beyond deli- cious. It was sugary, soft and creamy and just plain delicious.

"Wow," she moaned again, closing her eyes for the briefest moment. "You have to try this. It is *so* good," she said, bringing the bitten cheese Danish to his lips for a bite, before Chuck could reply. Unable to reject it when it was practically pushed in his mouth, he took a small bite, which she appreciated. David always took huge chunks whenever she offered him anything.

The second her mind conjured up David alongside Chuck, she couldn't help but compare both men.

David was charming, sexy and always made tea for her in the morning. Chuck was handsome, very manly and made the best pancakes she'd ever eaten. But he was also very silent, whereas David was talkative—they could have long, equal-sided conversations. However, when she talked with Chuck, it always felt intimate and nice. She felt like she could share things with him and he would always understand her, never judge her. With David, when they talked, it felt like they were good friends, gossiping away. Lola never told David her biggest fears or her deepest secrets. It wasn't because she didn't trust David; on the contrary, David was one of the most trustworthy people she knew. It was just that she never felt like confiding in him. It never crossed her mind.

With Chuck, she did. She wanted to tell him things she had once only told Mikaella and Elena. And even though at times his silence drove Lola insane—like now, when Chuck wouldn't talk—Lola acknowledged it that it was part of his mysterious charm. But more importantly, it was who he was. She liked that he didn't talk as much. It suited him. And she liked him the way he was.

She liked him?

Of course she did. What a silly thing to question. Of course she liked him. If she didn't, she would never have slept with the man. Some of her earlier confusion eased. Of course she liked him, she thought, realizing how true the statement was. She liked Chuck. She smiled. Actually, she liked him more than David. Pancakes over tea.

That thought pulled her up straight.

She liked Chuck more than David?

That probably said more about her relationship with David than her relationship with Chuck. She calmed herself. But the thought opened up a whole new kind of question. If that said more about her relationship with David than with Chuck, then had she really loved David as she thought she had? Had she been in denial? It made sense to be in love with David. They lived together, for crying out loud. But that didn't explain why she had moved on so quickly from David. Wait. Had she really moved on?

Now she was confused.

Thanks. Lola's mouth soured. Could her mind ever stop from over-thinking and questioning and trying to understand everything? She wished she could let things happen without worrying, without thinking, without analyzing.

Ha! Like she analyzed.

Chapter Fifteen

The walk back to the mansion was silent. Of course. Lola rolled her eyes. Did she think he would suddenly start talking, out of the blue? Couldn't blame a girl for hoping. Lola did try more than once to start a conversation with him, but he simply nodded or gave her a cold, monosyllabic answer.

She sighed.

Had she known he would have reacted like this, she would have kissed him. But she knew she had made the right decision to put distance between them. Their relationship was only for the weekend; they didn't need to complicate things. Stop thinking. Obediently, she concentrated on the feeling of the sun on her skin. It was nice and warm on her exposed skin. Lola wore a spaghetti-strap floral dress with a sweetheart neckline and circle skirt that stopped two inches above her knees. She briefly closed her eyes, enjoying the moment, regaining her initial good mood.

Now this—this was what she liked to call a good time.

The mansion looked beautiful in the bright sunlight, the white window frames seemed to glitter in the sun, Lola thought. Without thinking, she grabbed Chuck's hand as he walked right beside her. "Isn't it beautiful?" she asked, wanting to share the moment with him. She looked up, expecting to see him nod, but instead found him staring down at her. Cold and confused was the best she could describe his expression. He looked away, not answering, not giving anything away.

"Right," Lola muttered under her breath.

In one swift step, Chuck swung around and faced her. Lola smacked into his chest and tumbled back into his waiting palm.

"What game are you playing?" he snapped. "Is this about what I told you yesterday? Why the sudden change?"

There were few moments in her life when Lola had been truly afraid, but this came near. Dignity shot her up.

"What do you mean?" She puffed her chest out, accepting the challenge.

"You know what I mean," he retorted.

No, she really didn't know. For all she knew—oh. Lola looked down. They had been playing a game, and she'd changed all the rules without his consent. Oops. Raising her gaze to apologize to Chuck, Lola caught sight of a familiar form. Gazing over his shoulder, she saw the last person on earth she wanted to see talking with Elena. And clearly, judging by Elena's body language, she wasn't happy with the newly arrived guest.

Lola's blood drained, leaving her looking sickly pale, as her knees buckled underneath her.

"Is everything alright?" Chuck asked, grabbing her by the waist, steadying her. Lola hadn't been aware that she was falling. Chuck hovered over her, blocking her view of Elena and the new guest. Lola nodded. But she couldn't talk as shock morphed into anger. She was too furious to talk. Blood scorched through her, pumping adrenaline throughout her body.

Lola walked around Chuck and stalked towards the pair. She felt Chuck behind her, a foot away. She could feel his confused, startled gaze on her back. In a few strides, he was beside her.

"Lola," Elena began saying in warning, but then the guest cut her off.

"Lola," the woman cooed, opening her arms for a welcoming embrace. Lola scoffed—sure, like she was going to hug her. *Pff.* Like they ever hugged.

"Nicole," she countered, calmly and coldly, ignoring Nicole's open arms. Lola felt Chuck stiffen at her side. Half of Nicole's lip turned up in a smug smile, and she turned her attention to Chuck.

"Chuck, good to see you again." Nicole gazed seductively. Lola almost lost it right then and there. Nicole knew Chuck? Why? How? Had the entire universe met Chuck before her? Lola's heart squeezed.

"Miss Vance," Chuck replied.

"Please, I have told you before, call me Nicole," Nicole said and actually batted her eyelashes at him. Did the woman have a death wish, or what? Lola took a deep breath to calm herself. Unconsciously, she stepped in front of Chuck, blocking Nicole from him.

"I thought you weren't coming," Lola stated.

"I wasn't, but then I changed my mind." Nicole looked at

Elena, pointedly annoyed. "I am allowed to change my mind, you know," she said, her voice sounding fake and light, as always. Condescending. "Anyway," she sounded out each syllable, annoyed, "I came here to talk to you," she said to Lola.

"I don't want to talk to you." It slipped out. Mistake. Big mistake.

Nicole grinned with all the smugness in the world. Then Nicole made her face fall a little in absolute tragedy, like Lola had hurt her. Pff. Lola wished. "Is that a way to talk to your boss?" she asked, offended.

Lola held back a frustrated groan. She wanted to retort that it was the way she would talk to her friend, Nicole. But who was she kidding? They weren't friends, even if they tried to pretend.

The only reason Nicole was in Lola's life was because for one, she was Lola's boss, as she smugly pointed out, and two, because no matter what Lola did, Nicole would find out and try to make her life a living hell. Because of that, Lola had only gone to work for Nicole after Nicole had sabotaged all her other opportunities. The thought "Keep your friends close and your enemies closer" had come to her mind, and she had finally accepted Nicole's job offer.

After a long silence, Nicole looked arrogantly triumphant. "I need to talk to you," Nicole said, breaking the silence. "As your boss." She lifted her pointed chin.

Lola groaned. Great. Whatever it is, please, let it be quick. "What is it?" she asked, a bit sharply. She couldn't help it. At the moment, all she wanted to do was tackle the woman to the ground if she continued giving flirtatious glances at Chuck.

"I need to talk to you alone," Nicole said, annoyed, gazing

pointedly at Elena. Elena glared back at Nicole but did as she bid. Knowing Elena, she would probably be watching from the window. Nicole turned her gaze to Chuck, and it turned sweet. "Would you mind giving us some privacy?" She sweetly batted her eyes again.

Breathe. Breathe. Breathe. Brea—

Lola felt Chuck's lips press a kiss on her head and softly whisper in her ear, "If you need anything, I'll be inside." She nodded, looking into his concerned eyes.

Her heart swelled with gratitude as she watched Chuck walk into the mansion. He had calmed her with one little kiss and whisper. Lola didn't know whether to run after him and kiss him or panic, she thought as Chuck disappeared into the mansion. The door closed behind him, leaving Lola alone with Nicole, who was intently studying her with her vulture gaze. Lola shifted uncomfortably under Nicole's unsettling gaze.

"So what did you want to speak about?" Lola demanded. Let's get this over with quickly. Lola wanted to go inside and find Chuck and hug him. Yep, hug him, not kiss him, or anything, but she just wanted to be in his arms. That wouldn't complicate things; friends hugged, so she wouldn't be violating her own rule. A thank-you hug; there was nothing wrong with that, she argued.

"You know Chuck?" Nicole asked Lola.

"Yes," Lola replied suspiciously, gazing at Nicole. "You know him, too?" Lola added.

"Oh, yes, I *know* him," Nicole said, emphasizing know meaningfully. If Lola had been furious before, now she was burning with fury. She ignored the fearful squeeze against her chest. She took a step closer. Even though she knew when Nicole was lying, doubt

175

had been planted.

Before she could respond or do anything, Nicole straightened herself up and said, "I'm sorry to inform you, your work at Vance Decorates is terminated, effective immediately." Her voice resonated with authority.

What? WHAT! Wha— "WHAT?!" Lola staggered, fisting her hands. Had she been fired? Had Nicole just fired her? Nicole? Her? Of all people? Now?

Nicole sighed, annoyed, like it was a simple thing to grasp. "You are fi-r-ed," she said, enunciating all the syllables, annoyed, rolling her eyes.

That did it. The audacity of the woman! Lola saw, breathed, smelled and felt red. "Fired! You're firing me? Me? After you broke up my relationship with David! After you s***** his d***! You're firing me!" she yelled, outraged, balling her hands into fists again. She couldn't believe it! Was this really happening? On what grounds could Nicole fire her? Letting her suck David's d***? How was that a crime?

"On what grounds are you firing me?!" Lola fumed.

"Ah, wa…, wel…, aah, hm," Nicole stuttered incoherently, stumbling a step backwards.

"Ah, wa…, wel…, aah, hm? What? Huh? What grounds?" Lola snapped, irritated, taking a step closer, towering over Nicole.

෴ ♥ ෴

Chuck should have connected the dots. Nicole Vance was the woman he had hired to do the interior design for his chalet, after

Elena had insisted that Vance Decorates was the best place to go for an interior designer—which everyone needed, according to her. He should have known that Elena had been talking about Lola, who worked for Nicole—who was her boss who had cheated with David. Chuck had met Nicole before, but their encounters had always been professional. Not once had she looked at him like she did today. Nicole had been what he could only describe as flirtatious with him. He had liked it when Nicole had gazed at him flirtatiously, but for the wrong reason.

When Nicole had glanced at him with her dull brown eyes, Lola had stepped in front of him like she was blocking Nicole from him, protecting him from Nicole's advances. He had fought the biggest smile. He didn't like Nicole. Never had, and much less with her sudden change in attitude towards him. The way she batted her lashes, looking up through them—and how her voice sounded like sweet poison. He wouldn't be surprised if she was the one who had initiated things with David.

When he entered the mansion, Chuck had found Elena and Mack gazing out the window, half hiding behind a heavy red floral embroidered curtain.

"And now, she wants to talk to Lola," Elena whispered to Mack.

"About what?" Mack asked. Elena shrugged, unsure.

At the sound of footsteps entering, Elena glanced up. She waved Chuck over. "Come, we are spying on them," she invited him in a loud whisper, like it was a big secret.

Chuck nodded, walking over to the window and gazing out as well. It was hard to see through the decorative beige cement railing of the back terrace, but by raising his head a little and squinting, he could see Lola and Nicole standing there. He couldn't see their lips move, but he guessed they were talking. Lola suddenly turned pale and in the same second, bright red. Her hands fisted, and her body shook with anger.

"Uh-oh" Elena sang, shaking her head. "What?" Chuck asked, curious.

"Nicole might die today," Elena stated calmly.

"Or get seriously injured," Mack added, eyeing the situation with more care. Elena turned, grimacing, toward her friend. Mack smiled, his eyes lighting up, but Chuck barely registered it as he began turning towards the door.

"Wait! Where are you going?" Elena stopped him. "To stop whatever's happening outside," he said. "Why?" she inquired, tilting her head.

"I don't want Lola to get hurt."

Elena's face softened. "Trust me, Lola won't hurt herself. Her dad taught her extremely well how to fight. I'd worry about Nicole, but honestly, don't waste your worries on her. She's not worth it."

Chuck was shocked. Elena was the definition of sweet and pure; she liked everyone. Or, at least, he had thought that. As if reading his mind, Mack said, "Nicole is the one person she can't stand." Chuck nodded. He had kind of figured that one out.

"I don't like Nicole because she's always gone out of her way to make Lola's life a living hell, ever since college." Elena paused, gazing intently at Chuck. "Be careful around Nicole," she warned.

"Why?" It was his turn to inquire with curiosity.

"Just be. Please," she demanded softly. He nodded. Of course he would be careful around Nicole. He didn't trust the woman at all.

"Uh, I think maybe we should stop them. I actually think Lola's about to hit Nicole," Mack said, heading towards the door. Chuck's gaze flickered outside, and he saw Lola towering over Nicole with her hands fisted at her sides.

In no time, he overtook Mack, who was already on the lawn, and stepped between Lola and Nicole, his back to Nicole.

With one hand, Chuck cupped Lola's face, forcing her look at him. He gently whispered, gazing into her sparkly brown eyes, "Ssshhh, it's okay. Breathe. She's not worth it." He wrapped his other arm around her slender body. Lola nodded, closing her eyes, and began taking deep breaths. Chuck felt Lola's arms wrap around him as she laid her head on his chest, and then she lifted her head to look up at him. Her face was red. Her beautiful brown eyes gazing at him, he wanted to kiss her, but he couldn't do it. Not to his heart. Lola had made it clear this morning that she didn't love him or anything close to it, if even at that.

Still, he brushed Lola's straight blond hair off her cheek, but instead of kissing her, he contented himself with brushing his thumb over her bottom lip. She closed her eyes and breathed in. She held her breath for a second or two before releasing it with a shaky laugh. Lola stepped out of his embrace. The air might be warm, the sun might prick his skin, but Chuck couldn't feel anything other than the emptiness in his arms.

"I'm better now," she said and then added "calm" to convince him.

"Good," Elena said from behind him. Chuck turned, stepping beside Lola. In the distance, he saw Mack walking with Nicole back into the mansion, as some other guests were beginning to come out. "Because it's time for the boat ride!" Elena clapped her hands excitedly and jumped in place.

In unison, Lola and Chuck glanced at each other, bursting into laughter, remembering that morning in his apartment. Elena studied them closely, like she had earlier. What was the woman seeing? Chuck wondered.

Chapter Sixteen

Puppies. Baseball. Soccer. Food.

Nothing.

Absolutely nothing was helping. Nothing Chuck thought of helped ease his erection. It sat hard between his legs as he tried to row the white canoe on the little lake. There were a dozen boats floating on the lake, with couples sighing, giggling and even giving sobs of happiness. The other couples were on the large lawn, playing little mindless games, waiting their turn. Lola and Chuck were the third wave of a dozen couples on the lake, reading poetry to one another. But neither Lola nor he was in the mood to talk. But since they didn't want to be completely anti-romantic, they decided to each recite their favorite love quotes to one another, instead of babbling out a ridiculously long love poem to one another. Elena could have chosen shorter poems, Chuck thought as he eyed the papers in the middle of the boat, rowing aimlessly on the lake. Lola had volunteered to go first, quoting H. Jackson Brown: "Sometimes the heart sees what is invisible to the eye."

"Nice," he commented, nodding his appreciation. But the heart was often blind and poor at choosing the right people to love, he noted to himself, suppressing a sigh as Lola said, "Your turn."

'Doubt thou the stars are fire;

Doubt that the sun doth move;

Doubt truth to be a liar;

But never doubt I love.' Shakespeare," he recited.

"Hamlet?"

"Read it in school, always remembered that verse," he briefly explained.

"Mmm, very nice." She nodded her approval and smiled. Her brown eyes and golden hair shimmered in the sunshine. Chuck had looked away, knowing for now that their pretending part was over. Unless it was required, Chuck wasn't going to go out of his way to talk with the woman. The woman who had tried to make conversation with him. He had just nodded.

Giving up, Lola had lain back on the end of the boat. Chuck watched her out of the corner of his eye. She closed her eyes, enjoying the sun. It had been all good until then. A few seconds later, a light, cool breeze blew, making Lola not only shiver but also making her nipples stand out through the thin cotton fabric. It didn't help that her dress was the same coral shade as her nipples. They teased him, reminding him how delightful they had been in his mouth, reminding him how delicious Lola tasted, how he would nearly lose it every time she moaned. Her perked up nipples were so much of a temptation, he had to actively refrain from jumping across the boat and onto her, like a savage, and making her moan and gasp like he had last night.

Oh, last night… Her sweaty body against his sweaty body—His erection jerked at the memory. Oh, god. He wanted her. No, needed her. Now.

Puppies. Baseball. Soccer. Food. It didn't help him, like it hadn't earlier.

He groaned softly, swearing under his breath. Or, at least, he thought he had groaned quietly. Lola sat up, staring at him questioningly at first. Then, her expression changed when she gazed into his eyes—craving eyes. Lola's gaze soon burned with passion; then her gaze dropped down to his lips and back up to his eyes. Chuck could feel himself about to lose it. He had stopped rowing; the boat stood still as they sat motionless, gazing at each other. The air between them became thicker and thicker with longing. Lola's chest lifted up and down as she breathed more heavily, her nipples still erect underneath her dress.

Now it was his turn. He gazed down at her mouth, then at her neck and finally at her perked fabric peaks and back up again to her face. He craved the feel of her soft skin on his mouth, trailing his tongue lightly over her body. He gazed at her with scorching desire. His breathing became heavier and heavier—like hers.

Lola's fervent gaze slid down to his mouth and then to his shoulders and farther down, to his chest. It traveled lower and lower, until it met his bulging hardness. A small whimper escaped her perfect lips, her bottom lip trembling. She gazed back into his eyes. Chuck groaned. It was too much; her gaze held the same desire as his. She wanted him, too. There was no mistaking it. He didn't care;

he was going to take her right here.

He stared at her firm nipples, longing to feel them. He lightly licked his bottom lip. He heard her moan as her legs involuntarily shifted slightly open. In response, his erection jerked in his pants.

DING! DONG!

The bell announced that the activity was over. Unmoving, they stayed as the other boats dutifully passed them with quiet murmurs and giggles. Lola and Chuck needed to get back to the lawn and do the other activities.

Lola stared at him with desperate hunger and said, her voice thick with need, "We, um, we should get back," and swallowed hard.

Chuck nodded and let his gaze wander up and down her body one last time, making her bite back a moan.

Pushing back his desire, he rowed them to the edge of the lake, where the last wave of couples were waiting to get on the lake and read poetry to one other in romantic, white canoes. Chuck needed to get a grip on himself. Before, he had almost let his temper reveal how much Lola had hurt him with her rejection. And now this?

He had some dignity. He couldn't let her get in his mind, no matter how much he wanted her. Or how much he wanted to hear her babble away or hear her laugh, or watch her eyes gleam every time she got a new idea, a new thought, and chatted away about it in the same second.

How could he love her? he asked his heart.

Waiting on the lawn was a set of volunteers handing out sheets to each couple. Lola reached out to receive the sheet, but the woman ignored her outstretched hand and handed it to Chuck. He glanced down. The very soft, pink, sweet-smelling sheet was the itinerary for the rest of the day. At the top, in bold letters, was his name with a plus sign adding Lola's. A longing for it to be true burned in Chuck.

It was just a crush. Like it had always been. He hadn't fallen in love with Lola, he assured himself. There was nothing different about the way he felt about Lola since he had first met her. The only difference was that he knew a little bit more about her. She was less of a mystery now. Even though, in reality— if Chuck was being honest—she had become more of a mystery. She was no longer his neighbor who gazed at him with her brown eyes. No, now she was Lola Moss, a woman of excitement and endless conversation about sports and colors. She was also a woman who had caused him pain with her rejection... Of course.

He hadn't been hurt by her rejection, he now realized. What he felt was not pain, but disillusionment about a woman he had thought was different. He had been caught up in the whole pretend situation with Lola. He wanted to laugh to think that for one second, he had actually thought he was in love with Lola. Silly. Really silly. Weight lifted off his shoulders. Sure, Lola was great, and sure, he still had a crush on her, but crushes came and went. And they were mostly felt when in the presence of the other person. But out of sight, out of mind was truer than ever, he thought.

With a smile, he eyed the itinerary, before passing it to Lola, and headed towards the mansion. They had an hour before heading towards the drawing room, where they would have to cook a romantic lunch as a couple. Until then, they had free time.

"Hey, where are you going?" Lola asked as he headed towards the mansion—specifically with the library in mind. He planned to finish that book he'd started the day before, while Lola had worked.

Lola was right beside him, trying to keep up with his determined step. Chuck didn't exactly ignore the question, but when he looked pointedly at the mansion, Lola decided to look at the itinerary.

"Oh, look!" She pointed at the sheet. "It has our names on it." She smiled up at him. He nodded. Silence. "Don't you think it was rude of her to hand you the itinerary? My hand was out there waiting for it." She stretched out her hand, reenacting the moment. He shrugged.

"Do think it's because you're a man and I'm woman? Because, I mean, look. It says 'Chuck and Lola.' Not 'Lola and Chuck.' Why? I mean, 'Lola and Chuck' sounds better, don't you think?"

He shrugged, uncaring.

"Of course not. You probably like 'Chuck and Lola' better. Of course you do. It probably validates you as a man," Lola muttered.

Chuck's head snapped to the side as he raised a half-surprised, half-questioning eyebrow at her.

"It's true, isn't it?" she taunted. Chuck stopped, forcing her to stop, too. "Well? Is it? Yes? No?" Chuck shook his head. "Do you like 'Lola and Chuck' better?" He nodded. Lola nodded, too. "Are you going to talk to me?" Lola asked. "Say anything." She searched his face.

Chuck thought about it and shook his head.

Lola's jaw clenched, her eyes narrowed. He could see those thinking wheels turn. He found himself holding his breath, as if he was awaiting a verdict. It came in a spark of a challenge. It was clear in the way her posture changed and became more upright, her eyes suddenly glittering with determination.

Chuck battled the smile threatening his lips. Only Lola, he thought, would turn this into a game. One which he found himself also accepting, taunting her with his gaze, promising she wasn't going to win.

Her chin jutted out, accepting the challenge.

"So what do you want to do for the next hour?" she asked.

He hoped she didn't think it was going to be that easy. He glanced over at her and gave her a half smile, before continuing his way to the library. Would she follow? he wondered as the sound of her following footsteps reached him. Chuck smiled, feeling anticipation simmer in his gut.

"The library?" She raised an eyebrow, gazing at the sign that asked for silence. Chuck smiled, knowing he was already winning. "Alright, if that's how you wanna play it. Fine." She straightened herself up, pushed the door open and marched into the library. Looking over her shoulder, she asked, "Aren't you coming?"

Oh, he was coming, alright.

The library was probably one of the biggest rooms in the whole mansion. Mahogany wood bookshelves formed row after row, stacked one on top of the other on the wall under the high ceiling. There were two large windows, one on the left side and the other at the back. About five other couples were in the room, two absorbed in their books, one man looking out the window, clearly bored, while his partner concentrated on the book in her hands. The two others walked around, looking at the books with no real intention of reading any. And in the middle stood a large mahogany desk with an old fashioned globe and a telescope sitting beside a reading loupe. The book Chuck had been reading the previous day still lay on the desk where he had left it.

Lola marched to the very end of the library, near the back window, where there were two armchairs facing each other with a table between them. Should he join her? Chuck grabbed the book off the desk. It would make it easier for her if he did. Did he want to make it easier? No. He wanted to have fun. Chuck sat down at the desk and opened his book to page seventy-two, where he had left off.

By the time he had read the second page, the hair on the back of his neck had risen, warning him that Lola was behind him.

"Are you really going to sit at the desk?" she whispered. He nodded. "Fine." Momentary silence followed by the sound of her footsteps retreating echoed in the library.

If anyone had asked what page seventy-five of his book talked about, Chuck wouldn't have been able to answer for the life of him. He was concentrating too hard on tracing Lola's wandering footsteps through the library. Half a page later, Lola was beside him, announcing in a whisper, "I want to sit at the desk, too." Chuck raised an eyebrow. He narrowed his eyes. She wasn't going to sit on him. Like he was going to move away from the desk to give her room to sit on him. She smiled knowingly. Before he registered what she was doing, Lola wiggled her way into his lap. Her hair brushed against his nose as it crushed into her neck. He could feel the pressure of her whole body squishing against him, and he could also feel her determination to sit on him. He had to forcefully pull the chair back a few inches, to give them enough space to breathe.

"Thanks."

He didn't nod. Lola pursed her lips, studying his face, her

body half twisted on him, half looking over her shoulder. She glanced around the room before settling her attention on the book in his hands. The action confused Chuck, but he followed suit, returning his attention to his book.

"Wow! Look at this. Don't you think it's pretty?" Lola pointed to an illustration in the book. He briefly glanced and shrugged. A page later: "Oh, look at this one. So intricate, don't you think?" He looked again and then returned his attention to his book. Lola sighed, frustrated.

"What's the capital of Canada?" she asked in a whisper. He didn't look up. Of course he wasn't going to fall for that question.

"I killed someone," she announced. The bored man sitting by the window looked up, startled by the announcement. The man glanced at his date, who also heard Lola's words. Pale and unsure whether she was kidding, they glanced at one another. They nodded and walked out of the library. Lola noticed and shrugged, embarrassed.

"Oops. I didn't mean to say it so loud," she whispered. Lucky for her, the two wandering couples who could have heard her had already left, as Chuck had predicted. "Do you think they really think I killed someone?" Lola asked, horrified by the idea. She looked over her shoulder, waiting for the answer. A quick glance his way, and she muttered, "Right. If you tell me what you think they thought, I'll have sex with you," she bargained.

Chuck raised a tempted eyebrow. Lola smiled, awaiting the words. He smiled and shook his head. Did she think he was that easy?

"No, I don't." She read his thoughts. And thus began a series of elaborate, made-up stories, wild accusations and just plain non-sense. Lola's leg bounced uncontrollably as she got more and more desperate for him to say at least one word. Nothing worked. It wasn't that her stories weren't entertaining, nor did her random accusations set his teeth on edge, but there was something missing. Chuck didn't have the need to reply with words. His body's reaction did the job perfectly.

Lola got more and more agitated—so much so that she jumped off of him and began wandering around the library. Every other paragraph, she would whisper something new in his ear; she was a pirate. An heiress to a vast fortune, looking for a talking man to give her fortune away to. He was no better than a wall.

Every time Lola started a phrase with "you," Chuck involuntarily held his breath, awaiting an accusation related to his past. But to his relief, it was always utterly childish—like he smelled and whatnot. It dawned on Chuck, as the hour came nearer to a close, that Lola's insults and threats became more and more silly, like she had lost the purpose of the game and was having too much fun whispering things.

"I faked my orgasm last night."

Chuck raised an eyebrow, seeing right through her bluff. It wasn't male ego, but he knew that last night, she hadn't been faking. Last night couldn't be faked.

"Fine." She stomped her foot and marched away. Chuck shook his head, chuckling. He could hear her pacing behind him. Glancing around the room, he noticed that they were the only couple left. In that short period, Lola had managed to drive away the two absolutely absorbed reading couples.

"Grr! What do I have to say that will make you talk?" she said, out of the blue.

Chuck shrugged his shoulders, not bothering to turn around. He smiled. He was getting to her. For some reason, he liked being able to fluster her so.

"Smile all you like, but mark my words. Before dinner, I will have you talking," she vowed and stalked out of the library. How had she known he was smiling?

A deadline. He liked it. He put down the book and walked after Lola.

Chapter Seventeen

Cooking? They expected her to cook? Lunch? Wasn't dealing with a stubborn, silent Chuck enough? Now they had to inflict this on her?

Lola pouted. It was going to be a disaster. She glanced down at the measuring cups and spoons—at least she knew what they were. Then there were bowls filled with different ingredients which she had to measure and mix together. Of course they handed her a recipe but hm, it wasn't reassuring. Each step was a hundred-word paragraph, saying things like "jelly roll pan" and "kneading."

Who knew making brownies looked so difficult? Not to mention bread. "Every home should be blessed with bread," was written on the recipe. Sure, it should, but Lola felt that her bread was more blessed when it came mass-produced and in a package with an Italian flag. Alongside smeared peanut butter and good old straw—raspberry jelly.

Lola glanced at everything at their little cooking station in the drawing room. Another couple was there, and Mikaella and Mack were also supposed to be there, but they were nowhere to be seen. Lola noted that she hadn't seen Mikaella in a while, either. She'd ask Elena about her later. For now, Lola was starting to get hungry, and she had to bake her own bread and brownies and make a salad and dressing from scratch.

Was she worried? Oh, please, her? Yes. Yes. YES. She didn't cook. Cooking wasn't part of her repertoire of talents. Keeping her eyes open for a long time? Yes. This, no. Oh, it was going to be a disaster; she could feel it.

Lola glanced at Chuck. He looked too at ease around all the tools and ingredients. Almost as at ease as he was without talking. She'd make him talk, she vowed again to herself, for the hundredth time. Patience. She needed patience. Something she really didn't have.

"Have you ever baked your own bread?" she asked Chuck. He shook his head. Lola relaxed a little. Good, she thought Then she caught sight of Chuck's amused smile.

"Why are you smiling?" she prompted him. He winked at her and turned his attention to the four recipes.

In the past hour, Lola had learned that he could reply to every single question with a nod, shake his head or give that stare. The one where he made her feel like he was seeing right through her and that only challenged her to be more creative, more conniving.

Lola glanced back at the raw ingredients. Alright. Time to man up. Hundreds and hundreds of people cooked every single day; it couldn't be that hard. She had a recipe with "easy-to-understand" instructions, and best of all, she had Chuck, who knew how to make

193

pancakes from scratch. He must know the ins and outs of cooking better than she did—like she knew the ins and outs of Mycroft, her microwave.

As she eyed what she believed was cocoa powder, a tall man entered the room wearing a white padded coat jacket and a low version of a chef 's hat. He had dark brown hair, and his olive complexion was covered in seasoned wrinkles. He greeted them in an Italian-accented voice. He was a handsome man, Lola thought as she gazed at the chef. He was slender and looked anything but frail. His wrinkles were tight against hard-edged features, but most of all, he had a melodic way of speaking which enchanted Lola and the other women in the room.

Snapping her out of her thoughts was the all-too-prominent presence behind her back. Lola shivered, knowing that if she moved an inch backward, she would be pressed against Chuck. How she longed to be in his arms again, to not have to think about anything but his warmth. Not think about cooking, or the fact that she was jobless and had no prospects. Lola pushed back the thought. She would think about it when the weekend was over. For now, she slid back the inch and leaned lightly against Chuck. She glanced up as the chef finished explaining the recipes.

What? He was done? No come-back? She hadn't been paying attention.

"Well, I think it's going to be so easy," the other woman drawled out. She was dressed in crisp, clean designer clothes, and she had manicured hands and salon-sleek hair. "Who do you think will be first to finish?" She looked down her nose at Lola and Chuck and stuck out her chest, already knowing that she would win.

Lola's competitive side kicked in, and she glanced at Chuck, who nodded, reading her gaze.

At once, both couples turned to their makeshift cooking stations and began the competition. Lola found herself in front of the baking goods, while Chuck was already starting on the salad and dressing.

"Er, don't you think maybe you should bake and I make the salad?" she wondered out loud. Chuck raised an eyebrow, and his gaze asked if she didn't think she was capable of the challenge.

"Can't make bread?" the woman mocked. "I make the best bread, don't I, darling?" she asked her partner, who nodded, reassuring her. She smiled at him knowingly and went back to measuring the ingredients.

Lola's nostrils flared. Throwing away the years of saying she didn't know how to cook, Lola turned, grabbing the recipe sheet in one hand and the half-cup measure in the other. She could do this.

Alright. Dry active yeast. Honey. All-purpose flour. Salt. Canola oil. Cornmeal. Ice cubes? Lola frowned. Whatever. She had all her ingredients, and thankfully, the bowls came with labels, making it easier on Lola. She could do this, she thought determinedly.

She read the instructions. Simple enough. Ooh, she got to punch the dough. Lola smiled, excited to get to that part. She rushed through the steps—first, because she wanted to win the un- announced competition and second, because she was dying to try out kneading.

Smiling, she turned out the dough onto a floured surface. The yellowy-beige dough morphed into all her troubles, fear and doubts. Lola punched it once, then again and then another time, as a smile spread across her lips. She imagined that she was a world-class boxer, beating away all her troubles, fears and doubts. She was winning. Take that, doubt she could find a new job. She punched the dough. Take that, fear of getting hurt, attaching herself to someone who could hurt her for a lifetime. She punched with her other hand. Take that, pain of hearing the sobs in the house that was supposed to be empty. Take that, doubts of not being enough for a man. Take that, cheating men in her life. Take it all. She punched, alternating one hand with the other, with little more than a nanosecond between each punch. She huffed, supporting herself on the table. She shook the thoughts out, but she smiled, feeling a weight lift off her chest.

From the corner of her eyes, she saw Chuck raise a concerned eyebrow at her.

"Didn't I tell you I also box?" she winked at him. He shook his head, chuckling at their inside joke. They smiled at each other, remembering the time in the bathroom, but Lola was no fool. She could feel Chuck trying to see right through her. This time, he couldn't. Both satisfaction and disappointment washed through her. Lola refrained from frowning at her disappointment. Did she want him to know what she was going on in her head? She never wanted anyone to know. Not even herself.

Interrupting their moment, the nasal voice said, "Oh, you guys are a set-up couple?" The woman said it as if they were a mixed breed, instead of the pure breed they were.

"No," Lola lied, hating the way the woman's superiority grew in front of her eyes. "We've been together a year." She smiled. Chuck nodded beside her, wrapping an arm around her waist and shrugging.

"Oh." The woman gave her a tight smile, "Then why didn't

he know that you box?" she asked pointedly.

"I was joking," Lola pointed out, like it was obvious. The woman narrowed her eyes and scanned Lola's body. "Of course, you don't look like you box. I would know, since I do."

Lola wanted to roll her eyes, but she resisted just enough for the woman to return to her bread. Chuck raised both his eyebrows, saying with his gaze, "She's crazy." Lola giggled and nodded, getting back to the bread.

Next step: "If the surface of the dough is smooth, let it rest for twenty-five to thirty minutes," Lola read. Lola glanced at the beige lump and confirmed that it was smooth. While it rested, she started on the brownies.

As Lola measured the ingredients, she noted that she liked cooking. There was something comforting in having exact measurements and steps to achieve a result. All her worries eased. The power of the mind—all this time, she hadn't known how to cook because she had thought that she couldn't, after a few disasters. But she could, and she was.

Beside her, Chuck was already done. A large bowl of neatly cut-up, multicolored vegetables sat on the table with a creamy dressing. He leaned on the table and watched Lola as she measured the ingredients. After a few seconds, he moved to help her out with the dry ingredients. He reached for the bowl.

"No." She snapped the bowl away before he could grab it. "If you talk, then I'll let you help."

Chuck narrowed his eyes but shrugged, saying, "Your loss" with his dark black eyes. No, it was his loss, because cooking was fun. If only he would talk… GRR! When was he finally going to talk?!

Deep breaths, Lola, deep breaths. She blew out her breath. But it was strangely fun, she had to admit.

Okay, back to baking. Melted butter. Done. Cocoa powder measured and in bowl. Done. Alright, pour and mix butter and cocoa. Alright. Lola grabbed the butter off the portable mini stove top and poured it into the chocolatey powder. There seemed to be a lot more liquid than powder, she noted. Of course, it was the wet ingredients, she assured herself. Now mix. First, she tried with a wooden spoon, but as she struggled with mixing the ingredients that seemed too wet, she eyed the electric mixer. Grabbing the electric mixer, Lola placed the tip of the whisk into the bowl as her thumb hovered over the start button.

"Done!" exclaimed her competitor out of the blue, scaring Lola half to death. In her sudden panic, her thumb pressed down on the start button. Chocolatey, buttery liquid flew onto the wall, covering Lola and splashing Chuck along the way. In her panic, Lola dropped the electric machine, causing an even bigger mess. Thank goodness for Chuck, who quickly unplugged the turning whisks.

The room was silent for a heartbeat. Lola gazed at Chuck, wide-eyed, and Chuck gazed at Lola, mirroring her expression. Lola burst into hard-hitting laughter, buckling over from the impact of her own laugh. The room was filled with her laugh, intertwined with Chuck's.

Then came the scream of the other woman in the room, sobering them right up. Lola took a step back as Chuck took a step in front of her, blocking her from the puffy, chocolate-covered woman. A string of profanities followed, and the woman's partner tried to calm her down. Lola stood, half-scared and half-amused, behind

Chuck. She watched closely as the man whispered many things, trying to calm to the soon-to-be murderess. After several attempts, he managed to calm her with one of his whispers. The woman's hazel eyes snapped up to Lola's face, and that air of superiority burned through Lola. The woman's chin lifted, her gaze the same as that of Lola's third grade teacher, calculating superiority and looking to hurt. Lola braced herself, pushing back the laughter of a room filled with kids.

"I guess I shouldn't expect much from an ignorant woman and her brute of a man." Chuck flinched, and Lola's blood boiled. Brute? How dare she call her Chuck a brute? The woman was the brute. She was so brutish that she was even more ignorant than the most ignorant person alive!

"Either way, I knew I was going to win, and I guess it's fair for the loser to eat a half-meal."

Lola tilted her head, giving the woman a large smile. "You're right. Chuck and I will have to eat salad, but you enjoy your carbs—I mean, bread and sugar. Sorry. I meant brownie. Please enjoy all those calories for us."

If a glare could kill, Lola would have died a second before the woman stalked off, her partner following.

"Well, that went well," Lola nodded before bursting into laughter. Chuck joined her, and a thought popped into her mind. "Does laughing count as talking?" she wondered out loud. Chuck smiled and shook his head.

"Fine," she allowed for now. "We really made a mess, didn't we?" she asked him, eyeing the splattered wall. Chuck raised an eyebrow at her, and with his eyes said, "We?"

"Alright. I made I mess. Don't you think Elena will be mad?" Chuck shrugged. Lola bit her lip, praying that the walls were salvageable.

Lola shouldn't have been surprised to see Elena waiting for them in the hallway with a wicker basket in her hands.

"I know, I know. I'm sorry. I'll take full responsibility," Lola said before Elena said anything.

Elena held back a smile. "You better," she threatened, but the smile got the better of her. "Oh, Lola, you should have seen Edith's face," she giggled and then covered her mouth, feeling bad she had. "She was so mad, but oh, she has been a pain since she arrived. Nothing is up to her standards. Not the food, not the activities. Not even the mansion!" Elena exclaimed.

Lola relaxed. "Oh, I'm not sorry about her. I'm sorry about the room," Lola clarified.

"Don't worry about the room. I hired the best of the best cleaning companies to clean after the weekend is over. I had planned for a few disasters. Especially with you around," Elena teased.

"Ha. Ha. Ha. Very funny."

Elena gave her wide, toothy grin. Lola shook her head, laughing. "Just one thing, though. She asked me to tell you not to talk to her."

"Oh, I hadn't planned on talking to the woman."

"Good." Elena smiled. "Now that that's settled, here." She passed Lola the basket in her hands. "I had a feeling you might need a backup plan for lunch." Lola grimaced. "Everyone is outside for a picnic. By the way, was there an explosion last night?" Elena asked.

"Oh, many explosions." Lola nodded seriously.

Elena's eyes widened in horror. She glanced at both Lola and Chuck, checking if they were hurt. Lola winked at her, and Elena frowned, confused.

Elena gasped, catching on, and blushed a deep shade of pink. "Okay, then," she laughed nervously. "I'll let you go on your picnic." She turned to leave, in the opposite direction.

"Wait." Lola stopped her friend.

"Yes?"

"Have you seen Mikaella?"

Elena shook her head. "No, I haven't even seen Mack. But when I do, I'll ask him."

Lola nodded, grateful for the reassurance, and walked outside with Chuck.

Outside, Lola sat in between his legs, leaning her head back on his shoulder on the red gingham picnic sheet. A beautiful spread of cheeses and olives lay in front of them. Lola enjoyed each bite, loving the comfortable silence between herself and Chuck.

"So what will it take to get you to talk?" Lola mused out loud.

❧ ♥ ❧

Honesty.

That's all he wanted from her. If she was honest—said something completely honest—then and only then, would he talk. It wasn't that she wasn't honest, but it wasn't ever the truth, either. If he hadn't known that Lola would say the first thing that popped into her mind, then he would have thought she was a liar, instead of someone with a highly active mind.

"After we eat, I think we should take a shower," Lola said.

201

We? He liked that. "It can be we, if you ask." Lola wiggled her eyebrows, reading his gaze. Chuck shook his head, pushing back his fantasy. He'd settle on living his fantasy in his mind a little longer.

After they were done, they quietly made their way to their room. Chuck watched from the corner of his eyes as Lola's brows trembled as she thought.

Honesty, he reminded himself. Only if she was honest would he talk. When and if she was, he would ask her about what haunted her brain right now. But only then. Lola showered first, and Chuck had to leave the room, because his fantasy was too much to take. He found relief in the ice-cold shower he took.

Chuck walked out of the bathroom wrapped in a towel and found Lola still wrapped in her towel, sitting on the bed. Her head rested hard on her hands, and her eyes were lost in deep worry and contemplation.

At the sound of his approach, she looked up. Her brown eyes had glazed tears over them. She tried to smile, but it was obvious to both of them that she was faking it.

"Will you lay with me?" she asked in a small voice.

He nodded.

In the process of climbing farther onto the bed, Lola's towel slipped off. Chuck refrained from acting like a mad man and cuddled beside Lola, his towel falling as he climbed onto the bed. She rested her head on his chest, and he let silence settle. After a while, Lola turned her back to him and looked over her shoulders, saying with her gaze, "Cuddle."

Chuck cuddled beside her as she played absentmindedly with a bump in the sheets.

"Nicole fired me," she said softly. Chuck closed his eyes and hugged Lola tighter against him. No wonder she looked so worried. "And I'm scared," she announced, honesty trembling in her voice. "What if I don't find a job? What will I do? I mean, I ended up working with Nicole because she sabotaged my other opportunities."

"Don't worry. Everything will be fine. I'm here for you," he assured her.

Lola was quiet and still for a second.

"What do you mean?" she asked him.

"Worst-case scenario, you can work for me."

"I don't think I should be left around sharp, heavy, potentially very dangerous objects."

Chuck smiled into her hair. "I meant more of a partnership. I could build a house, and you could decorate it."

"I like the idea." She relaxed. "For a worst-case scenario," she teased.

"Just know I'll be there for you," he vowed, realizing the truth of his own words.

Lola was silent for a few heartbeats and then she turned to face him. "You talked," she smiled, her eyes no longer tormented.

Chuck shrugged. He had wanted honesty. He had learned how hard it was for her to admit such a thing to him. Lola snuggled closer to him and pressed a soft kiss on his lips. He savored the freshness of her kisses and held her tighter against his naked body. Lola rested her head on his shoulder.

They were silent for a while. Chuck listened to Lola's breathing and realized it had become steady and deep. He smiled, realizing she had fallen asleep.

Chuck had never paid much attention to love. He didn't know a crush from true love, but with Lola in his arms, with the need to tell her he loved her, he knew it was love—love. The kind that happened only once and lasted for a lifetime. He didn't make a habit of showing his love, if he felt any for the woman he liked. But with Lola, all he wanted to do was show her a million ways that he loved her and only her.

A truth truer than the sun's warm shine.

Chapter Eighteen

Lola sat in a room decorated in soft blue. It had a large window seat, a couple of chairs and a strategically placed long white sofa. Lola sat on the window seat, hugging her knees as she rested her chin on top of them. She gazed onto the front yard. The night sky matted the darkness with navy blue light. Wind blew in the tree nearby, filling the air with a soft, shushing sound. She gazed into the darkness of the night, into the darkness of her memories. The wind no longer shushed but wailed with pain-filled sobs.

There, in the middle of the front yard, a little blond girl was running, yelling "Daddy!" A familiar silhouette turned around towards the little girl, opening his arms and lifting the girl into a giant hug. Booming laughter erupted from the very back of his throat. He whispered into the girl's ears, saying how much he loved her, how much he had missed her. The little girl smiled, but her brown eyes searched her father's face. The man's eyes were glittering with happiness. The sadness the little girl had seen two weeks before, when he'd sent her away, was gone.

Lola closed her eyes. The memory was gone. She opened her eyes again. The man sat on a bed, looking out the window, longing for something in the sky. He wasn't aware that his little girl was standing by the half-open door. He sighed, hunching in pain, before looking up again. Sensing that he wasn't alone anymore, the man turned and found the little girl gazing up at him with confused, wide brown eyes.

"Hey, kiddo!" The easy smile appeared, and he unfolded his long body off the bed. "I thought I was picking you up at three."

The girl nodded, searching for answers in his face. "Jo's mom drove me. Practice finished early."

Her father nodded understandingly. "Are you hungry?" he smiled, picking up his little girl and carrying her down the stairs.

"Really hungry. We ran a lot today. I scored two goals in practice."

The man's chest puffed out proudly, and the little girl launched into a detailed description of her soccer practice.

Lola looked away and closed her eyes, hoping the tug in her heart would go away.

She glanced back outside. The little girl was older now, eating ice cream with her father. They sat around a tiny metal table near the ice cream stand. The day was one of those days where everyone was in a good mood. Good things were happening and joyous memories being created. The girl licked her peach ice cream as she watched a family made up of a mother, a father and a girl around her age walk to the ice cream stand. While they waited for their order, the mother suddenly hugged the girl, causing her to squirm and squeal in delight. The laughing mother then stood and gazed lovingly into her husband's eyes. The man's smile was beyond any words that could describe love. He wrapped an arm around her, pulling her in for a kiss, then pulled the little girl into a hug.

The girl's gaze flickered to her father, who was also watching the family.

"Dad are we abnormal?" the girl asked.

"Why would you ask that? Of course not."

"Well, because I don't have a mother," the girl stated, remembering how they teased her at school. "Normal kids have both parents. Normal dads have a wife."

"Lola, answer me this: do you love me?" he asked seriously.

"Yes, I love you."

"And I love you more than anyone. Nothing else matters. As long as there is love, we are as normal as that family over there." He pointed to the hugging, laughing family.

The girl nodded and smiled as she listened to her father launch into a frivolous, made-up tale to entertain his little girl.

A week later, in the small kitchen, the girl was doing her homework while her father cleaned up. Out of nowhere, she asked him, "Was my mom a nice person?"

A shock went through the man. "She was the nicest person alive."

"What did she do?"

"She was amazing at everything. She was an architect who stole my heart."

"But if she stole your heart, then that makes her a bad person, right? Because stealing is bad."

Her father chuckled, shaking his head. "No, she didn't steal my heart; I gave it to her completely," he clarified. The girl nodded.

"So she was an architect?" She mispronounced the word. "What is that?" the girl asked.

"An architect is someone who designs buildings." The little girl nodded, tilting her head as she thought.

"I want to be an architect," she announced, determined about her decision. Her father smiled, and his eyes gleamed with joy or, perhaps, sadness; she couldn't tell anymore. The man gazed at the girl, seeing hints of his late wife.

"Hey, want to help me out at the store this evening?" he asked. The girl's eyes widened, and she nodded excitedly. "Alright, go get ready and meet me out front. I'm going to throw out the garbage."

The girl waited out front for several minutes. Anxious to get going, she went back in, searching for her father. He wasn't anywhere to be found. Then, a familiar figure caught her eye through the little half-open kitchen window. Her father stood holding a half-empty garbage bag in one hand and the garbage can lid in the other while he gazed into nothingness, hunching over in pain. Slowly, the girl made her way back to the front and waited for her father, also looking into nothingness herself. In the car, the little girl and her father laughed and joked.

Lola's jaw clenched as she swallowed back the ball of questions in her throat. The wind blowing through the trees now blew harder as it blew into dust the girl and her father laughing in the car. And blew in the dark toward the girl, now seventeen, sneaking into the house after midnight. She wiggled her way through the window that was always half-open.

The house was quiet, and she tiptoed, knowing her father would be asleep. She didn't want to wake him up. He thought she was staying over at her friend's house, but the teenager had a sudden need to be in her room, to be home on Friday night. She was smiling, anticipating the surprised look on her father's face in the morning— when she banged into the table. Papers fell from the impact; she quickly bent over to pick them up. They weren't papers; they were photos, she realized. Old photographs of a young version of her father with an arm around a woman. In was too dark to see clearly, but it was a picture of her mother and father. She laid it back on the table carefully.

Tiptoeing, she walked up the stairs ever so quietly. Each step she took brought her closer to the sound of pain. The upper floor shook with the sobs coming from her father's bedroom. She couldn't tell how long she stood gazing at the door. An eternity, it had felt like, while her heart beat against the tiny pricking needles of pain in her chest.

Taking a deep breath, she opened the door as quietly as she could and looked inside. Her father lay in a fetal position, clutching a dress in his fisted hands. She stood there, feeling her heart ache as she gazed at her father. She didn't know what to do. The full moon shone on her through the curtainless window. Sobs and small cries of torture filled the hollow air. Her father lifted his head. All was silent for a split-second. Brown eyes squinted through tears.

"Lo- Lolicia!" came the relieved cry, and her father rushed off the bed and swept her up in a tight bear hug. "I missed you so much, Lolicia. I love you. I love you so much," he choked out in a sob. "You have to see Lola." Lola froze in his arms. "She is so big now. Talking about boys with a dreamy look. Do you remember how you used to dream about talking about boys with her?" he asked his wife. "You'll love Lola. She's so much like you. Oh, god! How I have missed you." He hugged her tighter.

"Dad," Lola said softly, holding back her tears. Her dad froze and slowly pulled back. He searched her face in the darkness.

"Lola?" he asked, confused. She nodded, her chin trembling. Holding her at arm's length, he looked down. She could see the moon glint in his tears, despite the darkness. Another eternity passed. "I'm sorry," her father's voice trembled into a whisper. "I thought you were your mother."

Fat tears rolled down Lola's cheeks. "Yes." She was both stating that she knew and asking.

"Yes, you look so much like your mother."

Lola shattered into tears. Her father's arms were around her once again. She clutched at his shirt, which smelled faintly of peaches. Like all her mother's clothes did. The scent of peaches, intertwined with the sound of her crying along with her father, rocked Lola to sleep on the cold floor, in the trembling warmth of her father's arms, wondering about love.

The next morning, a soft kiss on her forehead woke her. The sun was shining brightly, promising a glorious day.

"Good morning," her father greeted her.

"Good morning." She managed to smile through her aching cheeks.

"Are you hungry?" he asked her. She nodded, not really feeling hungry. "How about grilled cheeses for breakfast," he offered, grinning, knowing they were her favorite. Now her smile was genuine.

Lifting her off the floor, her father guided her back downstairs. He began preparing the meal. Lola sat hugging herself at the small kitchen table. The pictures that had been there last night were gone, almost like she had imagined them, but a quick look at her father's new attire confirmed that they had been there.

"Did you love my mother?" Lola asked.

"Yes."

"Do you still love her?"

He glanced over his shoulder. Pain like she had never seen before—never knew was possible—trembled in her father's features. "Yes, I do."

Lola nodded.

It was all that was said on the topic. After that, conversation about her mother became more scarce than before. They never talked about that night, either. It was never acknowledged.

As Lola watched her father flip the golden sandwich, as he talked about his plans for the summer, Lola confirmed her thoughts from the night before.

To love meant to hurt.

The wind quieted outside; the trees stood still in the night. Her memory faded into darkness. Lola hugged herself, wishing she could somehow hug her feelings. She blew out a shaky laugh, pushing back all those years of memories. How long had it been since she'd allowed herself to remember them? Lola shrugged at her own questions.

The little blond girl had grown into a woman. A woman who was hiding away from the world because confusion mingled in her every breath. Thanks to no other than Chuck. In his presence, more than once he had pushed her to remember those memories. More than once she had to swallow back her memories. Tonight she had been too tired, too confused.

She had woken up this morning feeling confused, and by the looks of it, she would end the day confused. She glanced up at the brightest star in the sky and whispered, "Mom, if you can hear me, please help me. I'm scared and confused. Please don't leave my side. Please guide me."

Glancing at her hands, she sighed, taking matters into her own hands. Confusion came from a lack of coherent knowledge. The only way she could beat it was to put things in order.

When had it all started? Last night. Why? Because she had spent the most amazing night of her life—not to mention had the best sex ever—with an amazing man who had trusted her. A man who confided in her about his past.

Then this morning had been surreal. In the boat, he had managed to soak her panties without a single touch. And without saying a single word, she was able to communicate with him—read his answers, his replies, through those eyes, through his body. To understand him so easily was concerning. Then, she'd fallen asleep in Chuck's arms and napped.

They had napped. Together. Napped! Naked! In each other's arms! Lola had never done that. She had never napped with a boyfriend, let alone naked. Naps weren't a part of her relationships;

they were a mere myth to her. But it had felt so right, so natural. So unconcernedly intimate. Worst of all, it felt like she belonged in his arms, that it didn't matter where she was as long as it was in his arms.

Lola shook her head, hugging herself.

When they woke up, Lola had smiled and kissed Chuck and then they had made love. They had *made love*. Not sex, not a quickie or anything she was used to, but made love. The slow and tender kind of love. The one in the movies, where dust played in the warm sunlight, and everything was in slow motion. Yep, that kind of love. Chuck had kissed every inch of her body, savoring her completely. The sun had glowed, filtered by the silk curtains, on their naked bodies. She had set out to discover his body, taking note of how he reacted and what he liked. They had kissed so tenderly and moved together as one until, in perfect unison, they had reached their climax. Lola had never known it was possible; people always told her it was a romantic, silly notion but that in reality, it never, ever happened. A legend, they liked to tell her. She wondered if with Chuck, there would be any other kind of climax.

Afterwards, they had lain with their bodies interlaced and talked about everything and nothing. She had never felt more connected with a man before. It unsettled her. She wasn't sure how to react or what to say. *Hey, I'm starting to like you more than physically? I'm starting to wonder what it would be like to date you?* No, she couldn't say that.

Lola sighed, glancing down at her phone, checking if she'd received any messages. Wanting to distract herself from her train of thought. Instead, she concentrated on the worry pinching her gut as she waited for Mikaella to text her back. Lola had found out that

Chadwick had left abruptly, dragging Mikaella with him.

Apparently, he needed Mikaella to do some work for him. Lola texted Mikaella to make sure she was alright. She didn't like Chadwick and if by the time Lola went to bed, Mikaella still hadn't texted her back, she'd call her every second for a good hour. If she didn't pick up, then the police would be alerted of kidnapping. According to Chuck, Chadwick was a good guy, but she wasn't convinced. Lola kept remembering the way Chadwick had gazed at Mikaella; she just didn't like it.

The thought of Mikaella reminded her of dinner. Another confusing moment, if not the most confusing of all. At the start of dinner, Larry had left to take some international calls for work—surprise. Lola had rolled her eyes. Leaving only Elena and Mack and Lola and Chuck at the table. In other words, the people who mattered to her were sharing an intimate dinner with the man she liked. Lola had swallowed the lump in her throat. The dinner had disconcerted Lola because it had been so perfect. She had sat beside Chuck, their legs touching, and whenever both hands weren't required to eat, she had laced hers with his. Chuck had laughed and joked with Mack and Elena while Elena and Mack had taken it upon themselves to tell embarrassing stories about her. And although she was blushing from head to toe with embarrassment, Lola had joined in their laughter, loving the quick complicity the three had developed. Lola could see that Elena and Mack approved of Chuck. They treated him like he was her real boyfriend.

But he wasn't, she reminded herself. Just because they had sex, it had changed nothing; it didn't mean he loved her, or anything. No doubt he was pleased with the arrangement. He was a man, and men liked to have sex with no emotional attachments.

Yeah, but did men make love like he did?

She didn't know. It could be that she had just had rotten luck before Chuck. It was very plausible. Or Chuck could be one of those rare, amazing lovers. Another plausible explanation. She had many explanations, but she decided to draw from experience. And in her experience, a man could have sex multiple times and never feel one ounce of attachment. Which was why she liked them so much. Chuck was a man, and he was also pretending to be her boyfriend. He was pretending—Lola gave a small in involuntary gasp. She… she was starting to believe that she was his real girlfriend.

Did she want to actually be his girlfriend? She shouldn't. They hadn't been on a real date.

In fact, they had "met" each other, what—Lola counted—Thursday, Friday, and Saturday. Three days! They had only known each other for three days. She could fall in lust after three days, not in love. Yes, whispered a small voice inside her. In love? What? No. She could care… *deeply*? No, no, no, no, that voice was wrong. She couldn't. It made absolutely no sense. No. Uh-uh. *I need time and commitment to fall in love.* A solid foundation. Like she had with David. Now with David, it had been the time to fall in love with him. They had gone through all the logical steps. But obviously, that had failed.

Just then, David walked in. Ha! Lola laughed inwardly; this was just too perfect. Now he decided to speak with her? Lola searched for the anger she should have felt, gazing at David as he came closer. But she felt surprisingly calm in his immediate presence.

"Hey," David greeted her. "Can I join you?"

Lola nodded.

Wait a second. Lola realized she was starting to nod rather than answer. So Chuck was rubbing off on her. Huh. David sat down opposite her, taking hold of her wrist in one hand and holding his spread knees in the angle his elbows formed.

"So what's up?" Lola raised her eyebrows.

"I'm worried about you," David replied.

Lola couldn't help grimacing. David grinned.

"Why did you suddenly leave, after dinner?"

"Keeping track of me? Stalk much?" Lola avoided answering his question. David rolled his eyes and waited. Lola nodded. She hadn't realized that her departure had been so obvious. At dinner, she had felt so overwhelmed by all of her mixed feelings and thoughts, she had just disappeared to find a quiet place to think.

"I'm okay. Don't worry," she replied automatically. David wasn't convinced. "What? It's true. I am okay," she said slowly, to prove her point. David still looked unconvinced.

"Lola, you do realize I've lived with you for the past year. I know when you're not okay. And right now, you're not okay."

Oh, yeah, he knew her. Pff. Sure, and he also hadn't cheated on her. Please, Lola thought sarcastically. It annoyed her that David had a point. She wasn't okay, which contradicted the part of her that felt okay. Quiet fabulous, actually.

"Lola, I need to tell you something."

"What? That you cheated on me? Yeah, I know." She couldn't help it; it just snapped out.

"Do you really want to go there again? I thought we had already screamed it out, got it out of our system." He asked seriously, searching her eyes.

"You cheated on me! After everything we've been through, after living together. How could you not expect me to go there? Especially when you state that you know me. Didn't you think cheating on me would hurt?" Lola said, outraged. She wanted to talk about it even if she had moved on. Anything to avoid the real topic at hand. She watched David sigh, looking down as he gave up.

"Look, I'm not proud of myself," he began saying. "I didn't want to end our relationship like that, but it just happened. Lola, you and I have drifted apart. We never have sex—"

"We had sex," Lola interrupted him.

"*Had*, in the past, in the beginning of our relationship, but when was the last time we had sex?" Lola thought about it. Christmas. No, no they were going to, but then something had happened. Burning cookies. Right. Let's see… Halloween. That was four months ago… He had another point.

"Halloween. Okay, you have a point, but that doesn't excuse you for cheating."

"No, it doesn't, but we had sex on Halloween, and the time before had been at the beginning of summer." He had another point.

"Okay, you have a point with the whole sex thing," she snapped, getting really annoyed.

"My point is that we haven't been a couple for the last four months. You have work, and I have my work. Then we spend our time with friends, and then there is no time for us. Lola, what I want to tell you is, we have been more like roommates or friends who lived together. And we kind of have always been."

"What do you mean?"

David studied Lola intently.

"You're not okay because of him, right?" he asked her. The room began spinning. Talk about a sudden change in topic. Where had that come from? What did one thing have to do with the other? Instead of answering the sudden question, Lola asked him, "Why?"

"Lola, you and I have been more like friends than anything else. Sure, the sex was good. Do you remember the day you met Chuck?" he asked her.

Whoa. She was getting disoriented. Lola nodded. Of course she remembered. They had met in the mailroom of the building. She remembered being mesmerized by how manly he looked and how he had made her heart flutter with his unreadable black gaze. As well as that magnetic pull she felt in her core, filling an empty void she didn't know she had. It had also been the day David had decided they should move in together.

"You remember how we had taken a "break," and that day, I was going over so we could talk about us and whether or not we should continue dating?" Lola nodded. "Well, I saw you that day, talking with Chuck. You looked at him like you never did at me, with your eyes sparkling. I remember I was going to just break up with you that day, but after seeing you look at him like that, smiling at him with so much warmth, I got jealous and wanted you just for me. I wanted you to look at me like you had at Chuck." Suddenly passionate about the subject, he continued. "Lola, what I'm trying to say is when you're with Chuck, you're a completely different person, a better person. You've changed. You glow and smile, and you seem full of life."

He had what?! How dare he?! He had wanted to break up with her?! She was the one who had wanted to end things with him—

Wait. He was jealous of Chuck? Why? Had she looked at Chuck with sparkling eyes, like he put it?

She ignored the question and sharply snapped, "It's all pretend. Chuck and I, it's all pretend. He's only pretending to be my boyfriend and all it entails," she added softly, realizing her own game was turning against her. "He doesn't love me or care for me." She shrugged the feeling off. "Anyway, it doesn't matter, because I can't love him. I mean, there was no 'courtship,' no time for me to like him, let alone love him." Courtship? Really? She asked herself. What was she, in the fifties? In the nineteenth century? Like she had ever been courted.

Why was she trying to come up with excuses? What was so wrong about liking Chuck? When she had liked David, she hadn't overthought it like this. Then again, David had never made her feel the way Chuck did.

David smiled knowingly at her. *What?* She leaned away suspiciously, eyeing his amused smile.

"Lola, I care for you. I have and always will, but I've seen how Chuck is with you, how he looks at you. Chuck not only cares for you, but he loves you. He does. I can tell, like I can tell you're not listening to your heart."

David cared for her? Why wasn't her heart swelling up? Why had it swelled up when David had said Chuck loved her? And for the record, she was listening to her heart... wasn't she? No, she was. Of course she was. At times like this, she was listening to her heart. Like everyone was supposed to. And her heart was confused.

"I think you're wrong—" Lola began.

But David interrupted her by sighing and saying, "Just listen to your heart, not your logic. Don't confuse them." He got up and kissed her forehead. Before she knew what she was doing, she grabbed David's arm and pulled herself up, crushing a kiss on David's lips.

Except, she didn't make it to his lips. An inch away, she stopped, unable to close the distance.

"Why me? Why date me for two years?" she asked instead, searching into his oceanic blue eyes.

David pushed her hair back off her shoulder, saying, "Because we wanted the same thing, Lola. We wanted to be in a relationship, but we didn't want to commit. We didn't want any attachments. We just wanted to have fun. But now, you can't run away from love. Especially, true love."

"And you?"

David gave her that charming smile. "As for me, I've still got a few years left." He winked. Lola rolled her eyes, laughing.

"It would never have worked out …. between you and me… but I want you to be happy. After everything we've been through, I just can't not—not care for you." He stroked her cheek. "Listen to your heart," he advised softly, and kissed her cheek. She gave him a faint smile as he walked out the door.

Click.

The soft sound of the door closing reached Lola's ear. The same sound she had heard a few days before. Except this time, she found solace in the sound. This time, she saw the door close.

Beep. Beep.

Her phone announced a message. "I am alright. I love you." Lola read the text from Mika. She relaxed and sat back down, but unease still simmered through her.

Chuck… Oh, Chuck, what have you done to me? She gazed out the window.

Chapter Nineteen

David Anderson closed the door behind him and headed towards the back yard. It was so clear that Lola was in love with Chuck, he would have thought she had already figured it out.

Actually, it didn't surprise him that Lola hadn't figured it out yet. Knowing her, she would be trying to make sense of everything. How many times had they talked about something making sense or not? He knew she was trying to understand her feelings, instead of just feeling them. It had always been a mystery to him—the importance of finding logic in everything. She could say all she liked that she was a go-with-the-flow kind of gal, but deep down, she was ruled by logic and solid foundations.

For the last two days, David had caught small glimpses of Lola and Chuck. They looked so in love; they looked so right for each other. David had never seen Lola so happy before. No, he had—the day Lola had met Chuck. David had been so jealous. He was used to women—all women—looking at him like Lola had looked at Chuck that day. But Lola had never looked at him like that. He knew the moment Lola told him she was with Chuck at the Valentine Weekend—he knew his pride and ego had stepped in on something real and big.

He also realized that he did care for Lola, in a way he couldn't describe other than as a good friend—maybe in a brotherly way—and he wanted to see her happy. Chuck made her happy. So David felt he had to step in again this time. Only this time, to help the couple, rather than to break them up.

David smiled. Sooner or later, Lola would realize she loved Chuck. David wanted to pat himself on the back. He'd done a good deed.

The full moon stood still in the dark sky, among millions of stars. In the moonlight, David walked outside towards the bench near the little lake. He needed to think about his future; he needed to make some decisions. As he neared the bench, he saw a female silhouette, sitting still under the pale moonlight, on the bench.

From where David was walking, he could see her profile. She had her hair in a high bun. She had a long neck, and her nose was straight and tilted upwards at the tip. She turned her head as he reached the bench. In the darkness, David was barely able to see her features, but from the little he did see, he knew she was beautiful.

Not wanting to miss this opportunity, he squared his shoulders and licked his lips.

"Do you mind if I sit here?" he asked the woman.

She shook her head, saying "Not at all" and gesturing with her hand to the empty area beside her.

"Such a nice night," David commented as he sat down. "Yeah, it's nice and tranquil. It lets you think," she said. Her
voice sounded like bells.

"It does. It's why I came out," he informed her conversationally.

"Me, too," she informed him.

"I'm David," he introduced himself, his voice saturated with promise.

"I'm Gabriella," she returned.

David gave her his charming smile, promising to rock her world. She tilted her head, enjoying his smile.

Oh, darling, you won't know what hit you.

Chapter Twenty

10 pm.

Lola had been gone for two hours. Chuck had searched the whole mansion, trying to find her, but damn, this place was huge. He had decided it was best to wait for her in their bedroom.

Worry bounced his knee up and down as he waited, checking the clock every five minutes. What if she was hurt? What if she was in trouble? Maybe he should go and look for her again. Had he done something wrong? This question repeated itself over and over again. But he knew he hadn't—to his knowledge, at least. Because everything was better than perfect.

His knee stopped bouncing, and his body sighed, relieved, as Lola entered the room. Her blond hair was in a ponytail, and she held her elbows as she walked towards him.

"Hi." She gave him a weak wave, looking nervous. He nodded. "I'm sorry I took off. I needed to think."

"About?" He worried. Lola shrugged and stopped a few feet from him, her gaze asking, wondering if she could come closer. He opened his arms. She smiled, letting go of her elbows, and sat on him, snuggling her nose into his neck.

"Chuck?"

"Yes?"

"Are you tired?"

"No."

"Do you want to go to the pool?" She straightened herself off him, offering her hand.

Chuck rose, taking her hand. He was a patient man. Soon he'd get her to talk. They walked out of the bedroom.

"Wait." He stopped them, realizing they did not have their swimsuits. "Our bathing suits."

"Well, if you want to wear yours, you can," Lola stated, "although I would prefer it if you didn't." She winked him and let her gaze drop to his pants. "I was planning on wearing my birthday suit. I hope you don't mind." She smiled sweetly.

Mind? He had already started walking towards the pool with speed in his step. Lola noticed and giggled, trying to keep up with him.

The sound of her giggle eased the tension in his body. He knew everything was alright.

"Last one in the pool is a stinky monkey," Lola yelled, breaking into a run.

Lola was fast. But he used his strength to propel him faster. They ran through the maze of the mansion until they reached the pool at the same time.

The pool was in a semi-isolated room, with a window as its back wall. The full moon shone through and reflected onto the pool. The room was dark, except for the light coming from the moon and the small blue electric lights every half-meter inside the pool. The water glinted, inviting them with its smooth calmness.

"Last one in the pool is the loser," Lola said, already slipping out of her dress. Chuck knew he was going to lose, because there was no way he was going to miss a chance to see Lola undressing. She wore a satin bra which she was slipping off with too much ease. Her hands rested for a second on her matching panties, a smile teasing her lips. Chuck hand's faltered as Lola turned around, showcasing her bare bottom in a thong. Knowing he was watching, she slowly slid the satin fabric down with little movements of her hips. Chuck swallowed hard. She flicked the panties off with her foot and dove into the pool.

The splash of Lola diving in head-first brought Chuck back to reality. In as little time as possible, Chuck was diving in head-first, too. The eerie silence mutated into a profound, bubbling silence which Chuck enjoyed for a few seconds before resurfacing. The water was cool with subtle hints of warmth to come.

Lola was nowhere to be seen; she was swimming under the water behind him.

They swam a few laps, warming up.

Chuck was regaining his breath, holding onto the edge of the pool at the deep end, with both hands. He heard Lola splashing around, and seconds later, she was between his arms. She tried to control her out-of-control breath, as he was doing. She was smiling and trying her best not to laugh. She wrapped her legs around him, so she didn't have to fight against the natural pull, urging her to sink into the water.

The room quieted.

"Tell me something about you," she said.

"You already know everything."

Lola raised an eyebrow and shook her head. "I don't know about your past girlfriends."

"Because they're the past."

"But don't you think it's unfair that you know about David, and I know nothing about your ex?"

"You really want to know?"

Lola nodded and smiled, assuring him she did. But he could see a gleam of doubt in her eyes. "Please, I just want to know."

"Why?"

"Because I'm curious. And I guess it will also tell me more about you."

Chuck raised an eyebrow, unsure, but if she wanted to know him, he was all for it. Especially if it meant because she was thinking perhaps, just perhaps, that she wanted more than this weekend. He could only hope.

"What do you want to know?"

"What's her name? What did she do? Why did you guys break up?"

"Silvia." The name no longer held resentment. Lola nodded. "She was a social worker, and we broke up because she got tired of trying to fix me."

"Fix you?" Lola asked, confused. Chuck nodded. "What do you mean?"

"She thought I was broken."

"Why?" He gazed at her meaningfully. "Oh. Because of your past?" He nodded. "Your past can break you?" Lola asked, more to herself than to him. He nodded, but Lola didn't notice, as she was lost momentarily in her thoughts.

"Were you—are you broken?"

"No." He shook his head. "But she was convinced I was."

"I don't think you're broken. I actually think the opposite. I never met anyone stronger than you. And not just physically," she winked. Chuck laughed, taking the moment to steal a kiss from her.

"So she left you?" Lola asked.

He nodded. "Left" was rather a nice way to put it. Silvia had made him leave, with an unceremonious kick in the butt. He could still remember coming home from work, his bags all packed by the door while she sat drinking wine at the table. She never drank wine unless it was at a dinner party. His second major clue after seeing the bags he had thought were filled with her things.

Her brown hair had been tied tightly in a ponytail, and she was dressed in her casual wear. A silk blouse and black pants. She had sat him down and announced that she didn't want to be with him anymore. She was tired of trying to help him; a wall was easier to help, according to her.

Silvia had dreamed of having a family, of having Sunday brunches with the whole family, including grandparents. But she didn't want her kids to have people like his parents as grandparents. She told him that at first, she had thought that if she could fix him, then perhaps his parents wouldn't be that bad. Him, his parents and that sister. Chuck could still remember how hard it had been not to

229

glare at Silvia for the disgusted way she always talked about his sister. Gabriella was a million times better a person than Silvia was. Sure, she bounced from job to job, but she would soon settle down. After a whole insulting hour, Silvia had finally finished with, "Your things are packed. Please leave and never come back."

"Her loss." Lola broke through his memory, tightening her legs around him.

"And my win," he grinned.

Lola giggled and said, "So you don't miss her?"

Chuck shook his head. He had stopped missing her the moment he had walked out of his house. He had stopped loving her the second he had reached his car. And by the time she met Lola in the mailroom, she was forgotten.

"You said she didn't want to be with you because you were broken, right?"

He nodded. Lola also gave a nod. She twisted around, leaning her back on his chest while her legs pressed against the pool wall. He could feel the small waves she made as she fiddled with her fingers underneath the water. She lay her head on his shoulder and took a deep breath and blew it out. Chuck waited for her to say something, but she remained quiet, fiddling away. He wondered if it had anything to do with why she had abruptly left, after dinner was barely done.

"Would you date someone who was broken?" Lola wondered out loud. The question sent a shock of surprise through his system. "I mean would you date someone who was haunted by memories? No, I mean, broken—like, perhaps, you might have been. I don't know. Never mind." Lola laughed. The sound was too light, giving away the fact that it was a fake laugh.

Holding himself with one hand on the edge of the pool, Chuck twisted Lola around. He lowered his head, trying to get her to look at him, but she was determined to gaze at the water.

"Are you broken?"

"I don't know. Perhaps I am, but I'm also content with my life. I'm happy most of the time, and for the most part, I only have happy or embarrassing moments, but both make me smile and laugh. Can I be broken if I can feel all that?"

"The question isn't if it's possible but whether you feel broken."

"I didn't, but now…" She sighed, pausing. "Now, I don't know. Now, I'm aware my life isn't complete. I don't want to be broken. To be broken is wrong. It's weak."

"Is the forest weak?" he asked her. He'd spent years thinking he was weak because he was broken, until he'd stumbled upon the little lake where he was building his chalet. There, gazing around, contemplating life, he finally understood.

Lola glanced up, gazing at him, confused. She shook her head.

"Do you want to know why I chose to build my chalet in the forest, in the middle of nowhere?"

Lola frowned, confused by the change of subject, but she nodded. Her mind was always curious. He caressed her cheek with his thumb before continuing. "Because the forest is beautiful."

Lola's frown deepened. She nodded. "Why?"

"The forest is beautiful, because it's filled with broken trees, branches, plants. They lie on the ground, dying. But instead of weeping, feeling sorry for themselves, they let new life flourish on them. They become the essential foundation to life around them."

He stroked her cheek with his thumb, pausing, enjoying the way her eyes were here, yet imagining the forest.

"They connect the strong, standing tress to one another. They complete the beauty of the forest. Without them, the forest would be a bunch of strong standing trees, looking beautiful but feeling empty, cold and devoid of life."

Lola gaped at him and then looked down. "Is the forest a metaphor for life? And I'm the broken tree?" she asked.

He lifted her chin and gazed hard into her eyes, making sure she would hear, understand what he was going to say. "You are the forest. The broken trees, branches and plants are the things that hurt you. The past, memories—things you have no control over but that affect you. But without them, you wouldn't be Lola."

Lola's eyes glittered with the moon, with joy and with sadness. "So you think I'm beautiful, like the forest?" Lola asked, changing the mood.

"Well, depends on the view."

Lola gasped, and he threw his head back, laughing.

"The forest can sometimes reach a fraction of your beauty," he continued.

Lola giggled, rolling her eyes. Her eyes then found his, and she was thoughtful for a while. He couldn't look anywhere other than her brown eyes.

"Tell me who broke you," he demanded softly, needing to know.

"It wasn't a who but a what."

"What broke you?"

"A compass."

"Compass?"

"My compass was missing north. The love of a mother."

"Do you miss her?"

"Can I miss someone I never met?"

He nodded.

"Then you have your answer," she said lightly. "Do you love your mother? Even if she was so horrible? Would you have preferred not to have a mother?"

"I don't know," he answered truthfully. "Would you rather have had a mother like mine than none at all?"

Lola shrugged. "I think I— You know what? I don't want to think anymore. I just want to feel." She searched his eyes for his answer. He didn't want to think, either. Lola smiled, reading his eyes. "I just want to feel."

"You mean like this?" He slid his finger into her folds. Lola's breath caught, nodding as she bit her lip. He kissed her hard, savoring the taste of her lips mixed with the chlorine of the pool water. Lola smiled, enjoying the feeling along her folds. She gazed into his eyes and pushed further into the pool. Reaching the middle of the pool, she kissed him, bringing him underneath the water.

He twirled around Lola as she swirled around him while they kissed each other, trying to defy the pressure pushing them upward. Their lips never unlocked while their hands found each other and got lost in the dark water, and then his found the smooth round-ness of Lola's bare bottom. Every now and then, one would pull the other up for air, but as soon as they were breathing, they were back down underneath, in the pressurized, empty silence. The only sound Chuck heard was that of his own heart, the only feeling was Lola. He could feel more intensely than if they were the same person. If she was him and he was her. Each touch was more potent than any they had felt to this point, more meaningful than the last.

Pulling each other out of the water, Chuck gazed into Lola's eyes. Gently, he guided her back to the pool wall and pressed her against it. He began kissing her with fever.

Chuck pressed Lola harder against the pool wall, and she pulled back. With serious gleam in her eyes, she debated something, he could tell.

"Just for tonight, I want to feel you."

Chuck knew she didn't mean him—his lower brain—but him as a man, as a human being.

"No pretending?" he hoped.

"No," she agreed. "But just for tonight," she warned. He nodded, his heartbeat picking up. He couldn't believe it; this was what he wanted. Lola wanting him for him. Knowing everything she did and still wanting to be real with him. It was just—oh. Wait. He didn't have a condom. What if by the time they reached their room, she had changed her mind? He hoped not.

"Hey, where are you going?" Lola asked as he pulled away.

"Back to our room."

Lola smiled knowingly and urged him to came back. He was within reach of her long legs, and she wrapped them around him, securing him close to her.

"I trust you." She gazed into his eyes. The word "trust" weighing more than kilograms of gold. "To pull out." She winked at him, lightening the mood like she knew how to. She slid onto him, stretching around his hardness.

Do not blurt out you love her. Not now. Do not blurt it out.

"I hope they have a good pool filter," Chuck said, trying not to laugh as they sneaked out of the pool like a pair of delinquents. Lola whispered her giggle, nodding.

"Hey, last one to the room will be on the bottom." She winked at him and burst into a run. Chuck jogged behind, wanting to be on the bottom.

Don't not blurt out you love her.

Chapter Twenty-One

Lola's nostrils flared wide open, Chuck noticed as he placed a plate of pancakes underneath her nose. The corner of her mouth started watering at the warm smell of fresh, buttery pancakes. He gazed at her waking-up features.

Chuck had woken up early, with Lola nestled beside him, fast asleep. After a night like last night, he would let her sleep, he had decided. Chuck tried to move inch by inch out of her embrace, but then he made the mistake of looking down at her sleeping face. She was so beautiful to him, with her golden hair sprawled on the pillow, her mouth halfway open while her cheek rested on her palm.

"Chuck," Lola had mumbled, smiling and hugging him tightly for a brief moment, and then she had rolled over. His heart lifted at the sound of his name. Was she dreaming of him? He enjoyed the idea. Immensely. Almost as much as he loved her. Ever since he had realized the depth of his love for her, it had been hard not to blurt it out, almost next to impossible. As he gazed at her beautiful sleeping features, he decided he would tell her he loved her. He needed to tell her.

What will happen if she doesn't return my love? Or worse, doesn't care for me at all?

He knew there was a ninety percent chance she didn't love him, but he hoped she felt something for him. She had to, right? After a night like last night? Just a little something? He could work with a little something.

If she didn't care for him at all… well … the weekend was almost over, and as far as both were concerned, they had no obligation to see each other after the weekend. He could forget about her, Chuck assured himself. His heart tightened at the thought.

Although he knew he would eventually see her coming in or out of her apartment, he could handle it. Even if his lower brain reminded him of her moans intertwined with the sound of her laughter… her legs wrapped around him, the feeling of her soft breasts in his hands. He felt himself harden at the thought. He ignored it.

Chuck would tell her, he had concluded with finality. It was perfect today, with Valentine's Day in the air, and he could make her some breakfast and take it to bed to surprise her. Then he would tell her, he had decided.

You'll scare her. True. Damn. Well, he could just tell her he wanted to make their relationship official. Official? Really? What was he, in the fourth grade, asking Sally to go steady?

He could tell her he wanted to stop pretending, but last night hadn't been pretend. Something they had both agreed on. They had also agreed it was only for one night. Did that mean that today, they were back to pretending? Knowing Lola, it most certainly did.

But surely, if he told her he wanted to continue things, he wouldn't scare her, right? Or at least, he would scare her less than he would if he blurted out that he loved her and wanted to spend the rest of his days with her.

Chuck had decided to make her a pile of pancakes with a small square of butter placed on top and a cup of chamomile tea, which he knew was her favorite, to help his case. He hoped it was working as he slid it underneath her nose once again.

Lola slowly opened her eyes and zeroed in on the warm pancakes with the butter melting on top. A little drool rolled down her chin. She licked her lips and looked at him, wonderfully surprised. He smiled, encouraging her smile.

"Happy Valentine's Day." He kissed her forehead.

"Happy Valentine's Day." She smiled, sitting up and looking at the pancakes, her eyes glittering with anticipation. Biting back a smile, he placed an empty plate in her lap, put some pancakes on it and poured some syrup on top the little stack of two pancakes. Lola smiled hugely as she cut a piece and brought it to her mouth. She closed her eyes as she chewed, humming her appreciation with a face-stretching smile.

She opened her eyes and announced, "My favorite food is your pancakes." He nodded his thanks, beyond pleased. *I would cook you pancakes every day,* his heart thought.

"Aren't you going to eat?" asked him, looking down at the empty plate in his hands and back up at his eyes, searching for the answer. He nodded and served himself, sitting in front of her.

They ate in silence.

"Wow. I can't believe you did this for me," Lola said after she had finished her last bite of the buttery pancakes.

"I am glad you liked it." He smiled.

Lola nodded and then bit her lip, looking embarrassed as she asked, "Um, do you think I could have more?" and pointed at the small pile of pancakes left.

He smiled, serving her the rest of the pancakes. As Lola ate her second round, Chuck enumerated the activities they had to choose from today. While he had been making pancakes, Elena had gone into the kitchen for some breakfast, too. He found out that she was a happy early riser. She sort of reminded him of Lola, when she went into a bubbly rant, alive with more energy than was humanly possible. Elena become even more alive when he had told her about his plan to make Lola some breakfast, and she had squealed with joy, saying it was so romantic.

"I talked with Elena this morning, and she told me we have a choice of activities we might want to do this morning." He paused, remembering. "At ten, we can build a small wooden toy house of to represent our love, or we could bake heart-shaped cookies in the kitchen—she suggested we don't," he warned her, and Lola giggled, not feeling guilty. "Or write each other poetry in the library or watch a romance movie in the basement home theater," he said before adding, "What would you like to do?"

Lola thought it over and said, "How about building a house? That seems like fun." She paused. "Can we decorate it?" Lola's eyes widened at the possibility.

"I don't know," he replied honestly. The idea appealed to him greatly, more than the others, which seemed too... too... too romantic and girly for his taste. He was glad Lola had chosen building the toy house. "But I do like the idea of building the house." He agreed with her choice.

Lola stuck out her tongue in a grimace, rolled her eyes and said, "Of course you would." She popped the last piece of pancake into her mouth.

He smiled and continued telling her the schedule. "After lunch, which is served outside," he said as an aside, "there will be a scavenger hunt through the woods."

"I can't wait! I know it's going to be so much fun. It's the masterpiece of the weekend. Did you know that she individualized all the clues for each couple? It's going to be amazing!" Lola squealed and leaned forward, pressing a pancake-tasting kiss on his lips. She pulled back, smiling gratefully. "Thanks for breakfast. I can't believe you did it for me. It was really delicious." And then she added, "Oh, and thanks for the tea."

Chuck nodded. Lola lay back and sighed contently with a hand on her belly.

This is the perfect time. Tell her.

Chuck took a deep breath as Lola rolled over and looked at the time on her phone, which was on the night stand beside the bed.

"Oh, my god! It's fifteen to ten!" She jumped off the bed.

He let go of his breath. It's okay. *I'll tell her later,* he thought.

Five minutes later, Lola came out with her hair wet and a towel wrapped around her body. All he could think as she grabbed her clothes and went back into the bathroom, shutting the door, was that she was naked underneath. His imagination ran wild. He wondered once again what it would be like to shower with Lola, watching the water drip down her body, her hair wet and pulled back. He could lick the water off her breasts. They could stand beneath her shower and let the water fall on them as they kissed. He could turn her around and press his hardness against her bottom. Maybe… no, definitely play with her nipples and hopefully hear her moan. Along with the water, he could slide his hand down and slip one finger into her—

Puppies! Cute puppies, small puppies, big puppies.

Chucked sighed in relief as he felt his arousal die. *Good.* And right on time, Lola came out, wearing slim, fitted jeans and a grey t-shirt with a huge red heart that clung to her breasts. Her shoulder-length golden-blond hair was pulled back into a high ponytail. She wore no makeup, as usual, he noted. She didn't need any makeup, he thought; she was beautiful as she was.

Chuck watched as Lola frantically searched through her large bag. She moved, tossed and turned everything inside her bag. Her hands never rested, always moving through what seemed like a black hole. Her hand suddenly stood still, a flash of sorrow passed over her face, and she gently caressed something inside her bag. She sighed regretfully and continued looking through the bag.

"Ah-ha! Found them," she exclaimed a few seconds later, holding a pair of gold earrings. Afraid she might lose them again, she hurried to put them on. The change was subtle, but the earrings made her somehow more beautiful. Little gold balls.

"I'm ready." She looked at Chuck with her glittering brown eyes.

Chuck nodded, getting off the bed. He would tell her later, he thought. Now, wasn't the time.

Chuck's large hands struggled to glue down the small red heart on the front door. The door was tinier than he thought he had built it. Good thing they were decorating first, because Chuck had a feeling he would end up destroying the toy house. Lola had suggested that it would be best if they built the walls and roof and door separately and decorated each separately. That way, the end result would look prettier, according to Lola. He had agreed, mainly because he could tell Lola was itching to get her hands on the bottle of paint.

Lola was painting the house walls and roof red, pink, white and purple. She mixed the colors together, making them overlap one another, creating an abstract swirling pattern. It was stunning.

Chuck's job was to paint the door white and then glue a small red glitter heart on it. It was easier said than done.

His large hands wouldn't cooperate. He put the small heart on the tip of his finger and put a glob of glue on it. He ended up getting glue all over the tip of his finger, which caused his finger to stick to the door when he went to place the heart on the upper middle part of it. He tried again and again and again to glue the damn heart on the door, but every time, his large finger would end up sticking to the door instead.

Frustrated, he pulled the door from his finger for the fifth time and saw his fingerprint smudge on it. He sighed. He had one simple job, and he couldn't do it. No. He could. He was Chuck Moran; he could do anything he set his mind to. He tried again. And again. And again until Lola's giggle broke through his determination. He looked up, confused.

"Here. Let me help you," she offered, giggling, and she

grabbed the door from his hands. Chuck let her. He closely watched how she did it. Lola picked up a new red heart, placing it on the tip her finger. He had done that. She delicately put a dab of glue on it—on only the heart, not on her finger. He hadn't done that. Then, with the help of a toothpick, she transferred the heart from her finger to the door. He hadn't done that, either. Then, she was done.

Lola looked up from the glued, glittered door, lips pressing hard against one another. She was holding back a smile, he realized. She lifted her hand and placed one finger between his smashed eyebrows, easing back his half-confused, half-frustrated eyebrows. The smile got the better of Lola. She grinned. Sunlight came from behind her, as if she was glowing.

Now.

His heart began beating faster and faster, louder and louder in his chest. He took in a deep breath. "Lola, I—"

"Sorry, but could we borrow some pink paint?" Chuck heard a raspy female voice ask behind him. He growled inwardly. He was about to turn and glare at whoever had asked for more pink paint, but Lola was smiling cheerfully and saying, "Of course." She passed them the pink bottle of paint.

"Oh, we only need a little," the woman clarified with guilt in her voice.

"It's okay, we're done with it," Lola assured the woman with a warm smile.

"You sure?"

Lola nodded, smiling reassuringly.

"Thanks," the woman sighed, grateful.

Lola turned her attention back to Chuck and asked him, "So

what were you saying?"

A cloud passed in front of the sun, glooming everything. The moment was gone. Chuck cleared his throat and proposed, "I think we should hot glue everything."

"I think so, too," Lola agreed, reaching for the glue gun as she gazed intently at him for a brief moment, as if sensing that wasn't what he had wanted to say. Thankfully, she didn't press the issue. He thanked her mentally. He'd tell her when the moment was right.

By eleven, they had finished the house. It looked good. It looked like a hippie might live there, but still, the house was beautiful, with Lola's painting and his construction. It was simple and nice. A cabin more than a house, with a square foundation, a door and two windows. A classic style. Sturdy and solid, just like the love he desired.

They both gazed at the house on the craft table between them. "We did good." Lola admired their work.

"We did," Chuck agreed, leaning over and kissing her cheek. Lola's half-smile quivered with joy. They tidied up all the materials momentarily, arranging them against the edge of the table.

"It does look good, doesn't it?" Lola gazed at the toy house, pleased, after a few minutes of silence.

Chuck nodded.

"I would live there," she announced. "Except maybe paint the house a normal color," she added, laughing

"Me, too," Chuck agreed, smiling.

"You know, I would much rather live in a place like that," she said, pointing at the house, "than a place like this," she said and pointed around the mansion. He understood her completely.

He found the mansion stunning and well-constructed, but he also preferred to live in a home like the one they had built or in his chalet.

"Me, too. I like the simplicity."

"Like your chalet?" Lola asked.

Chuck nodded.

"Me, too," Lola said. "It's what I love about my apartment. It's simple and not too big or small. Just right," she said.

Chuck smiled, remembering that he thought the same about his apartment. One more reason why Lola was perfect to him.

"So are you going to move out of our building when your chalet is done?" he heard her ask him. Her voice held true curiosity and... Fear?

"I don't know." He shrugged his uncertainty. She nodded, avoiding his gaze.

Since they had finished earlier than everyone else, with an hour and a half left before lunch, Lola proposed that they sneak into the basement home theater to watch the romantic movie. Chuck thought they might as well go. The moment was long gone, and he felt the looming presence of his failure.

Walking out of the room, Chuck knew that Lola was up to something. Her steps became lighter, and she kept looking over her shoulder. Worst of all, he started mirroring her movements without realizing it.

Echoing footsteps in the distance had both of them pressing back against the wall. Lola grinned with amusement, anxiously biting her lip while the footsteps echoed until they disappeared behind a door.

"Alright, Moran. This is a dangerous mission. We have three minutes to sneak into the home theater. Now, I warn you, it's at your own risk. The movie has started, and we may not completely understand it." She looked at him seriously.

Chuck was still taken aback by her calling him Moran, and an amused smiled lingered on his lips as he watched Lola seriously go into spy mode. "Are you in?" she asked. He nodded and saluted her.

"On my count to three, we go. Three, two, one." Lola dove into a somersault, crossing to the other side of the hallway. She looked both ways before waving him over. Chuck looked both ways in the empty hallway, turning around slowly as he made his way to Lola. In this manner, they reached the home theater.

The "home theater" was rather like a real theater. There were rows of identical chairs, and a huge screen covered the back wall. As they entered, one of the house servants offered them a large bag of popcorn in a red-and-white striped bag. Lola was excited about the bag. "Isn't it so cool?" she whispered as they sat down at the back.

"Yeah," he whispered back and popped some popcorn into his mouth.

The movie was a romantic comedy with some hard-hitting action. Chuck guessed that Elena had chosen one with a little action for the boys. Twenty minutes into the movie, Lola rested her head on his shoulder and intertwined her fingers with his.

Now?

No. Now wasn't the time. Later he would tell her, he promised himself.

After the movie had ended, with a happily-ever-after ending, everyone headed outside for lunch. A long table was filled with food, buffet-style. Everything was a Valentine cut-out or a Valentine color or theme. One by one, they filled their own plates with heart-shaped sandwiches and color-coordinated food. Chuck and Lola sat down to eat with Elena and Larry.

"Everything is so amazing," Lola congratulated Elena, who beamed, pleased.

"Thanks, and wait until the scavenger hunt. It's going to be so much fun!" Elena said eagerly, clapping her hands.

"I can't wait. By the way, the food is simply and utterly delicious. Who did you finally hire?"

"I actually didn't hire anyone. I got an email saying I didn't have to worry about the cooking for the weekend. The mansion had a chef who was more than happy to cook for everyone. Isn't that nice?"

"Wow. Really?" Chuck heard Lola ask, mirroring his surprise.

"Yep. And for free, on top of everything else."

"Free?" Lola stammered, almost choking on her heart-shaped cucumber sandwich.

"Can you imagine? I'm so grateful for everything this person is doing. I wish I could send them a thank-you gift, but I have no idea who she or he is," said Elena. Her small face fell as she thought. Turning to her boyfriend, she stated, "I think we should try to find out who this person is."

"Anything you want, darling," Larry replied and leaned in to kiss her.

"Great! I think I want to give them a basket. Or is that too impersonal?"

"What's too impersonal?" Mack asked, joining the group.

247

"I want to give a gift to whomever let me use the mansion."

"No! Don't!" Mack said, almost in a panic. Calming himself, he said, "I mean, I'm sure if you leave a thank-you note lying around, they'll find it. No need to look for them."

"Them? Do you think it's more than one person?" Elena asked, completely ignoring Mack's sudden fear-stricken features.

"I don't know, but look. I just think if they went through all that trouble to be anonymous, we should respect that." Mack convinced Elena, with softness ringing his tone. Elena didn't like it. Chuck could tell by the way she set her lips in a straight line. But she nodded.

The way Mack's shoulders dropped in desperate relief had Chuck raising an eyebrow. Mack sat down beside Elena, cupping her cheek in his hand and stroking it with his thumb as he leaned in to kiss her forehead. Chuck couldn't help but flicker his gaze toward Larry, anticipating the worst. Larry didn't catch the kiss, but he caught Mack with his hand still cupping Elena's cheek. Larry's eyes settled on the hand with accustomed dislike, mingled with hints of powerlessness.

"I have news from Mikaella," Mack announced as he dropped his hand from Elena's cheek. As soon as he did, Larry's gaze became normal again, like nothing had happened. Lola and Elena's heads snapped at once towards Mack.

"Is she alright? Is she okay?" both women asked at the same time.

Mack nodded, saying, "She is as fine as you can expect her to be."

"What's that supposed to mean?" Lola demanded, not feeling reassured like Mack had intended.

"Well, how do you feel when you have to work on a weekend?"

"Work? Mika's working?" Lola asked, unconvinced.

"Mika's doing some research for Chadwick. Apparently, he hired someone from the library to help him with this research. And the library picked Mika about a week or so ago," Mack informed his worried friends. Elena also looked unconvinced about the explanation for Mikaella and Chadwick's sudden departure.

"Wait. She said a little more than a week ago?" Lola asked, getting onto something.

"Yes," Mack nodded. Understanding dawned on Lola's face. A mischievous grin played on her lips. Chuck frowned, confused.

"Why did Mika tell you all this?" Elena asked Mack, offended.

"She sent me a long message this morning, explaining and apologizing for leaving without saying goodbye. And she really wished she could be here today. She would do anything to be here, she actually said. Anyways, she told me to tell you," he replied.

"She texted me last night, telling me she was okay and not to worry. Why didn't she tell me everything she told you?" Lola asked, offended, too.

"Yeah." Elena jerked her chin up.

Mack sighed. "Because you guys react like this," he said, pointing at both offended, defiant but worried friends. "And would fail to see the point." He paused, muttering under his breath, "Like you have." Even more offended, Lola and Elena narrowed their gazes at Mack. "She knows both of you and knows how much you guys worry. Plus, she feels horrible for leaving so abruptly."

They both nodded understandingly. Suddenly, Elena exclaimed, "We could rescue her!" Lola agreed eagerly, and both plunged into planning ways to rescue their best friend.

Mack rolled his eyes and pointed out, "This is why she told me and not you directly. She's working. You can't rescue her from work. She needs it." He looked at both, transmitting a silent message.

They both nodded, understanding. Mack then enchanted them with a nonsensical story he had lived the week before. The group of friends continued talking and talking, while Larry sent some texts here and there or briefly listened to the trio's conversation and ate.

As Chuck watched Lola interact with her friends, he noted that Lola especially enjoyed the heart-shaped cucumber tea sandwiches. She didn't notice as he transferred his to her plate. Or, at least, he thought she didn't notice, but as she reached for more food and found two cucumber tea sandwiches, her gazed flicked to his plate and then to his face. Her gaze was unreadable. He felt some color rise up his neck and into his face, embarrassed by his show of emotion. She'd laugh at him. But Lola leaned in and kissed him tenderly. She gazed briefly into his eyes before picking up a heart-shaped sandwich and turning her attention back to her friends, who hadn't missed their exchange. Mack winked at Chuck, giving him a thumb's up when Lola and Elena weren't looking. Chuck quietly chuckled, shaking his head as he rested his arm on top of Lola's chair. Lola shifted her body slightly, so she could lean on him.

This was happiness.

Chapter Twenty-Two

The scavenger hunt started at one thirty. Each couple had to start in their room, where they would find their first clue. Sitting on the bed was a soft pink piece of paper. Lola picked it up and read out loud, "Twenty-one questions underneath the stars."

"The camp," they said unison, remembering the campsite where they had spent their first night together, underneath the stars, and had asked each other questions. They both walked down the path, as they had the other day. It seemed like tradition to walk down the path in silence. But for once, though, Chuck was happy as he walked it. He wasn't thinking about his parents or trying to figure out why Lola had reacted the way she had after their first night together. This time, Chuck was simply enjoying the warmth of Lola's hand in his. As well as deciding if after they found whatever they were scavenging, he would tell Lola that he wanted things to be more than they were. He wanted things to be real between them.

Soon they reached the campsite, where another soft pink paper lay in the middle of the camping spot. It had a little white bow on top. This time, Chuck picked up the piece of paper and read it out loud. "Every romance should have the hottest weather." And he added, "And then there's a winky face."

"What's that supposed to mean?" Lola asked, coming up beside him and peering over his shoulder to look at the pink sheet. He handed her the soft pink piece of paper, and she read and reread it. Her eyes moved across the paper like a laser.

Hottest weather? What did that mean? Hottest weather... weather.... Hottest... Hot... warm... south! He got it! They had to head south from here. He turned in a small circle, trying to locate which direction was south. They had come from the east, so that would mean— He turned again... Here— He stopped a quarter of the way into the circle. He realized that there was a tree with a broken branch pointing into the woods, and he saw that someone had walked there before—no doubt making it easier for them to walk through.

He turned his attention back to Lola and found her still gazing intently at the piece of paper. Although Chuck had already figured it out, he wanted to know what Lola thought it meant. As if reading his mind, Lola looked up and turned to him, squaring her shoulders.

"I think it means we *have* to have sex, and then a new clue will appear," she said in a matter-of-fact way.

He staggered. What? How had she come up with that logic? Not that he disapproved of it. Lola smiled at him, reading his mind again.

"It says, 'Every romance should have the hottest weather,' with a winky face." To prove her point, she pointed at the smiling drawing. "In other words, it says every romance should have hot sex," she explained, as if it was obvious.

"Or it means we should head south," Chuck blurted out, wanting to kick himself. Damn. He could have milked her logic.

"Oh." Lola blushed "… Yeah… You're probably right… That makes sense…" Lola smiled sheepishly.

"But I like your explanation better," he offered with all the sincerity in the world. Lola's gaze flickered up at him, liking his words.

Lola's smiled teased him as she closed the space between them with deliberate slowness. She placed her palms on his chest, letting them travel over to his shoulders and back down his chest. Her bottom lip jutted out in a fake sad pout, and she seductively teased, "Yeah, me too," her eyes sparkling with mischief. She tilted her head, giving him better access to her lips. Then, she began inching forward to meet his lips. She grazed his lips ever so slightly with a satisfied moan and pulled back. "So which direction is south?" she asked abruptly, in her normal voice.

It took Chuck a few seconds to remember. He finally pointed at the tree with the broken branch behind him. Lola nodded and passed close by him—too close, making him turn as she walked by. She looked over her shoulder provocatively and then disappeared into the woods. Chuck's breath caught, and he followed behind her. He took a few seconds to enjoy the view of her hips swaying as she walked, then in three steps he was walking beside her.

They walked in silence. The kind of silence which screamed with whatever tension two people could have. In their case, sexual tension. It got stronger and stronger with every new clue. Her hand patting his butt. Lola randomly stopping in front of him, forcing him to bump into her bottom. With every clue, Lola always found some way to turn it sexual and tease him.

Finally, they reached their treasure: a thick tree with a tie around it, in the same soft pink as the pieces of paper. The tree stood in a small clearing. On the tree was carved a huge symmetrical heart with one last note sticking to it, and beside it on the ground was a pink bucket with tools inside it.

Lola entered the clearing first. The moment Chuck set foot in the tiny clearing, Lola turned and jumped on him, wrapping her legs around his waist as she kissed him. Chuck caught her by her bottom, widening his fingers to get a better hold of her. As well as enjoying the feel of her derriere in his hands. Lola deepened the kiss, and he let her, more than willingly. He moved one hand up to Lola's back and slid the other one down into her jeans. His fingers felt the soft barrier of her skin. He froze. The kiss was slightly broken. She smiled against his lips and said through uneven breaths, "I couldn't find my underwear this morning." She informed him like it wasn't the greatest news ever. He growled, and his hardness jerked up, strong and willing. He pulled her a bit lower, letting her get a good feel of how hard she made him. A hungry moan fleeted her lips, and she began kissing him hungrily.

Chuck lowered himself to the ground, Lola straddled on top of him. "Condom," Lola whispered urgently. He let go of her and reached for the condom he had put in his front pocket that morning. He didn't trust himself around Lola and thought it best to be prepared. And oh, was he glad he was. Because feeling the heat radiate from between Lola's legs was driving him insane with need. As he reached for the condom, he "accidentally" touched Lola between her legs, making her shudder and gasp. They both stood quickly and slid down their pants. She bit her lip, wanting him. Chuck groaned; the blessed woman was actually not wearing any underwear. He quickly slid on the condom and sat down on the ground. Lola followed, sitting on top of him. Chuck gently pushed between her folds; she was already soaking wet and hot. Lola gasped and pressed her lips against his. She slid her hands underneath his dark blue, long-sleeved shirt and pulled it over his head. He did the same with her shirt, unhooked her bra and sucked her left nipple as his hand toyed with her right. Chuck felt Lola tighten; a growl escaped under his breath. He pushed upwards, and Lola moaned, tightening more. Her lips met his, and her movement also met his. His pushed up as she pushed down. They started slowly, letting the moment build, then slowly going faster and faster until they were both gasping and moaning. She came, gasping his name; a split second later, he groaned with finality.

They stayed unmoving, regaining their breaths. He pressed a kiss in the hollow of her neck. Lola squirmed, laughing lightly and gazed at him.

Recognition flashed through her brown eyes. They slightly widening, and she looked down. Chuck caressed her cheek until she looked at him. When she did, her gaze was unreadable. She smiled at Chuck and kissed him affectionately. *Everything is okay.* Chuck was relieved but refused to acknowledge his relieve. He feared that she would become cold and distant like she had the first time. It was a worry he had that wouldn't go away. Soon, he would tell her, and he would know if he should really worry or not.

After reading the sticky note indicating their instructions, Lola and Chuck carved their initials onto the tree.

"So tell me about you," Chuck said as he started chipping a curved line.

"Well, I…" Lola began talking about her childhood and growing up with only her father. She told him, "People tend to pity my situation. They feel like I missed out on something." She shrugged. "But I don't feel like I have." She paused. "I'm lying. I do. Sometimes, I wish I had a mother to talk about girl stuff with. My dad has been everything I need. I can discuss anything I like with him… but we both agreed early on, some girl stuff was off-limits, like peri—" She cut herself off, making a face. "… You know what? You don't need to know that. Anyways," she sounded out every syllable. "Don't get me wrong. I know people mean well, and it's not pity but sympathy they feel, but to me it is pity. And I hated it, but then it's better they react that way, I guess."

"I know what you mean."

"You do?"

He nodded, looking at her pointedly.

"Oh, right. People pity you for that. I mean, I guess they would. People thrive on it. It gives them a sense of superiority. But still, who would pity you?"

"You."

"What? Me?"

He nodded, remembering how their first night together had only been out of pity.

Lola struggled to choke out her words. "What makes you think that?'" she demanded, insulted.

"Our first time."

Lola was about to argue and then she thought about it. Seconds ticked by, increasing Chuck's nerves. "But what makes you think that?"

"The way you reacted in the morning."

"Oh," Lola breathed it out in a long breath. "No. It wasn't pity. I was just confused about the night before."

"Confused?" He raised an eyebrow.

Lola looked down, realizing she had said something she hadn't wanted to say. "Er, yeah, confused. But anyways, back to pity. I hate it, therefore, I don't do it."

"Why were you confused?" Chuck already knew this little trick and wasn't going to fall for it. He wanted to know.

Lola pursed her lips, narrowing her eyes on him, not amused. "Fine," she grumbled. "I was confused, because I... It happened so soon. I wasn't expecting it to actually happen. You know what I mean?"

He cocked his head to the side, gazing into Lola's brown eyes, which glittered with anxiety as she waited for his answer. He had been a fool. A real hard-ass fool. Lola wasn't like any girl he had met. He knew it. He shouldn't have ever doubted it. "Do you want it to happen again?" Chuck winked at her and grabbed her by the waist, pressing down a longing kiss. Lola giggled into the kiss, pushing him back down on the ground.

He just kissed Lola, and she just kissed him. Their hands wandered every now and then, but neither went further, neither wanted to stop the passionate kiss. An infinity could have passed, for all Chuck cared, but eventually, they both needed to breathe.

257

"Initials?" he said through raggedy breaths. Lola nodded, smiling. "So tell me something no one knows."

Lola raised an eyebrow. "If no one knows, what makes you think I'll tell you?"

"Fair." He gave her a nod.

Chuck worked silently on his initials beside Lola, who worked on her "L."

"When I was little," Lola said after a few minutes, "in the third grade, we had to do a presentation on our mother for Mother's Day. Mine was short and to-the-point. I didn't have a mother, because she had died in childbirth." Lola paused and shrugged off a thought. "Anyways, one kid shouted at the end that I had killed my mother. After that, no one wanted to talk to me. There's something no one knows. Not even my father. I think I may have mentioned it to Mika or Elena. I'm not sure." She smiled up at him.

"Stupid kids," Chuck said through clenched teeth. If he got his hands on that little— Chuck took a deep breath. Wrapping Lola into his arms, wanting to shelter her from the pain she could feel just remembering it. Lola stroked his beard, smiling.

"Now, your turn," she grinned, winking at him. Chuck couldn't help laughing. He should have wondered why she had suddenly told him. Getting back to work, he told her about the time he thought he had gotten his girlfriend pregnant. He had panicked for a whole day, only to realize at nightfall that for her to get pregnant meant they had to have sex. Something she was stubborn about not doing. And not to mention, it was April Fool's Day.

Lola guffawed for several minutes, bending over as she held her stomach. Chuck also laughed along with her, remembering how naïve he had been. Once Lola was finally able to control her laughter, they continued working on their initials as they talked animatedly.

Chuck loved learning more about Lola. He slowly started to realize as she talked that Lola was giving him more and more information about herself and what mattered to her. She could talk a lot about many things that seemed like they mattered, and sure, on some level they did, but not like what she was talking about now. She was really opening up to him. *It's a sign. It's now or never.* He was going to tell her he wanted her more than some weekend thing, more than pretending; he wanted something real. Yeah, that sounded good.

They finished carving their initials, Lola's on top and Chuck's on the bottom:

L. M.

+

C. M.

Now.

Chuck cupped Lola's face with one hand and kissed her sweetly. He pulled back and stroked his thumb on her cheek. He took a moment to enjoy the sight of the shallow depth of her profound eyes. "Lola, I ha—"

"Oh, look. Here, they are." Elena's excited voice shrilly interrupted him. Chuck snarled inwardly. His eyes twitched to glare at the small woman, but he refrained. First, Elena was like a sister to Lola, so glaring at the woman would backfire on him. Second, Larry was with Elena—not that Chuck was scared of the man. He could take Larry in his sleep. But he wasn't in the mood to face a boyfriend who was offended for his girlfriend. Third, it wasn't Elena's fault that every time Chuck wanted to tell Lola, the weather, time, or someone would interrupt him.

"I have been looking all over the place for you. I would have thought you guys would have finished two hours ago." Elena smiled as her gaze darted around the small clearing. Her gaze zeroed in on something on the ground behind Chuck. He didn't need to turn to know that it was the discarded condom. Her cheeks turned red. "Again?" Elena gazed, surprised, at Lola with astonishment thickly coating her voice.

Lola smiled unrepentantly, shrugging her slender shoulders. "What? I like explosions." Lola winked.

Elena rolled her eyes, a smile playing on her lips. "Come on, we have to get ready for the ball. We have to do our hair, nails and make-up." She practically danced as she informed them, delighted with the plan. Elena turned towards Chuck. "Mack has set up a room for you guys to watch some sports before getting ready," she informed him. Chuck nodded, gazing back into her searching gaze. He noticed that her gaze and behavior were always more serious and studious when her eyes lay on him.

The group of four headed back to the mansion together. Chuck felt Lola's wondering gaze flick towards him more than a few times as they walked back. Her gaze was unreadable. It was quick and almost seemed afraid that he would be able to read or guess her thoughts through her eyes. He gave her credit, because he did try.

What was she thinking?

Mack, Larry and Chuck stood in front of a large full-length mirror in the room where they tied their black bow ties. Chuck stood to the left; Larry stood in the middle and Mack on the right. They were almost identical, all dressed in black suits. Chuck had spent the rest of the afternoon wondering what Lola had been thinking, or more, what she was doing right that second. He thought just of her; he barely paid attention to the tennis match that had been on. All he wanted was to tie his bow tie as quickly as possible and go find Lola. But the girls had instructed the men that they had to stand below the stairs at six and wait until their girls descended. Mack told Chuck that Elena had been inspired by *Titanic*, the movie by James Cameron.

Larry had been surprised when Mack had mentioned it; he hadn't known. Larry, whose hands trembled slightly as he tied his bow tie.

"You seem nervous," Chuck noted.

Larry laughed nervously. "Yes, I am."

"Big night," Mack teased him.

"Yes." Larry gazed at himself, with serious features, in the mirror. "I'm proposing to Elena." Anxiousness returned to his face.

Mack's blood drained completely from his face. He stood dumbfounded, staring at Larry in the mirror. Chuck found himself surprised, too, gazing at Larry, who was pale and trembling, his hand needing to be in motion.

"Y-y-y you are?" Mack stuttered, white as a sheet.

"Yeah," Larry croaked. He cleared his throat. "Elena kept hinting about a proposal. She would constantly say, 'Wouldn't it be nice if someone got engaged during this Valentine Weekend?' I got the hint." He gazed seriously into the mirror again. "So here I am." He glanced nervously at his feet in the mirror.

"You love her?" Mack asked, with urgency trembling in his voice.

261

"Sure." Larry shrugged like it wasn't important. Mack looked down and mumbled something about excusing him and fled the room.

Larry turned to Chuck, waiting for him to say something.

"Good luck," Chuck said to the nervous man. Although he wasn't sure if he meant it. Mack had asked him if he loved Elena, and Larry had said "sure." Sure? If anyone had asked if Chuck loved Lola, he would have said something along the lines of "Hell, yeah!" *Sure?* ... To each his own, he shrugged... *Sure?* ... Chuck shook his head.

Standing at the bottom of the staircase, Chuck watched Lola descend the stairs. His heart stopped for a second at the sight of his angel. She was gorgeous. Chuck smiled.

Sure? No.

Hell, yeah, he loved her.

Chapter Twenty-Three

Damn. David was right.

She loved him.

Lola Moss loved Chuck Moran.

She loved him!

She couldn't believe it. Like loved, *loved* him. There she was, loving him after a weekend. How could it be possible? Lola shook her head, not caring as she smiled. She loved him! Ha!

Wait. But… What if… What if he didn't love her back? What if David was wrong about that? She had fallen in love with him the day she had met him. The way he made her feel then and every single time they had talked. And even now, it was love. It was her heart trying to tell her she loved him. Fear gripped her.

It had taken a scavenger hunt, teasing him, loving his reactions and then sex on the ground with her jeans still around her ankles and in her favorite sneakers to realize she loved him. It made absolutely no sense to her.

Was there something wrong with her? Don't go there.

She didn't care; she was happy. Should she tell him? No, it might scare him off. Men got scared of stuff like that... Oh! Maybe she could tell him she wanted a real relationship with him—not just pretend or something for a weekend—a real relationship. They could date after the weekend was over. She liked the idea. Fear eased away. She'd test the water for a little longer. She hoped he liked the idea, too. Tonight she would tell him, she promised herself.

Lola neared the stairs, slowed down and nervously twisted her fingers together. What if he didn't want anything other than this weekend? What if this was just a fun weekend for him? What if he was involved with someone? If he was, then he wouldn't have come to the Valentine Weekend with her. She chided herself for her stupidity. What if she told him and he didn't return her feelings? Then she'd be embarrassed and would have to face him whenever they saw each other in the building. She'd pretend they had never made love or that he could make her moist by only using his profound gaze if he wanted to. Lola could try to forget, or at least believe she had forgotten, everything in case he told her he had just been pretending all this time.

Oh, god. Maybe it was too soon to say anything. Maybe she wasn't even in love with him. Maybe she was in lust with him... No. She would tell him. If not, she would live for the rest of her life wondering "what if " she had told him. Better to face the rejection than go insane with more "what-ifs." A rejection, she could handle. Her own wondering mind? No. It drove her insane.

No, actually, she could live with wondering "what if." *Really?*

Sure. Of course. Why not? Yes... *yeah? Urgh. Brain, thank you. I'll make sure to send you a Christmas card this year.* Lola rolled her eyes.

Elena's sweet voice broke into her thought process.

"Lola? Lo-ola? Are you okay?"

"Yeah, I'm good. Just nervous," she reassured her friend.

Thinking that she was nervous about her gown, Elena reassured her. "You look amazing. I feel bad for Chuck. He won't know what hit him." She smiled mischievously.

Lola grinned and gestured at Elena's petit body, covered in a champagne-colored gown. "You look like a queen. Larry is a fool to think any less." They grinned at each other, laughing as they hugged one another.

"I wish Mika was here," they said in unison, pulling back. Both women sighed. Lola hoped Mikaella was happy, wherever she was right now.

Lola felt pretty in her gown. It was royal blue and strapless. It was made out of chiffon and had a simple beaded pattern along the straight neckline. It cinched at her waist and flowed out over hips, down to the floor. Along her right leg was a long slit up to her mid-thigh, making her feel powerful and sexy. She found herself sticking out her leg with attitude, to match her mood.

Lola took a deep breath. Everything was going to be okay. *Just be normal. Be yourself.* Chuck won't know as long as you act normal. Okay, she was ready. Holding hands with Elena, they walked the last few steps and turned, each taking a deep breath.

Chuck was waiting at the bottom of the staircase. He looked up as Lola began walking down the stairs. She purposely started with her right leg, sticking it out more than she should, to give Chuck a good view. Lola watched as Chuck's admiring gaze slid down her body and then her long naked leg. His breath seemed to catch. She smiled, pleased she had that effect on him.

At the bottom of the stairs, Chuck extended his hands and helped her down the last steps and murmured in her ear, "You look gorgeous." Lola bit her lip, smiling. She felt gorgeous. She felt like the world was hers.

"Thank you," she purred and then teased, "By the way, still couldn't find my underwear. Oh, well."

Chuck tightened his hold on her and swore under his breath. Lola beamed and placed a kiss on his cheek as he led the way to the backyard. Lola realized they were the same height with her heels on. It could make things easier—better placement, she thought, grinning mischievously.

The backyard was stunning. There were fifty small tables with white cloths covering them, candles burning and a single rose in a clear vase in the middle of each. On opposite sides were white plates and crystal wine glasses. On the green grass, placed randomly all over the ground, were fake lit candles. Lola admired everything.

Lola and Chuck were guided to a white-covered table near the edge of the lake. It was beautiful. The very few trees surrounding the lake were decorated with hearts and fake hanging candles. Lola couldn't wait until the sun set, so she could see all the candles lit, illuminating the place. They had a seven-course meal. Lola hadn't thought she could eat so much, but everything was so delicious and well-decorated, it was impossible not to eat everything. Lola noticed after the fourth course that the chef had deliberately put a small portion on each plate but had decorated everything around the plate, making it seem like a lot of food. Each plate was a work of art—the colors, the shapes, everything was romantic and inviting. Could the chef cook for her every day? Lola wished. But she would gladly settle for Chuck's pancakes every day. It was seriously the best meal she'd ever eaten. She would choose Chuck's pancakes over the artful work of a chef who had studied at the Cordon Bleu any day. Maybe she was more in love with Chuck's pancakes than she was with him, she hoped. No. She loved him. For him. Nothing to be scared about, she assured her panicking heart.

On that thought, Lola wondered if it was the time to tell him. Yes. No. Yes. No. Yes. The ambiance was romantic, they were having a delightful dinner with great red wine, and the conversation had been stimulating as well as a turn-on. Every now and then, Lola or Chuck would say something with a double meaning, loving the re-action the other had. Yes, now was the perfect time. *But what if I ruin the good mood if he rejects me?* Because it would feel like a rejection, then she would ruin the night for both of them. The night was going too well. Maybe she'd wait. Her fear eased. Who knew? A better moment would come, Lola hoped.

"Wonderful food," Lola commented, grinning as they waited for their desserts. Chuck nodded and smiled at her... affectionately? Was she starting to become delusional?

"Lola, I want to tell you something," he told her after a few seconds of silence. The sky was dark now. All the candles were a lit; it was beautiful, more so than Lola had imagined. It was very romantic.

Lola nodded, gazing at Chuck. His gaze was unreadable; his thick black eyebrows were knitted together and moving faintly as he thought. Lola waited for him to speak again and watched as Chuck took a deep breath and said, "I want to tell you, that, um… I would like it if w—"

"Chocolate soufflé covered in an almond sauce. And a pyramid of aphrodisiac chocolates." The waiter interrupted Chuck with a trained, professionally friendly voice. Lola saw Chuck look up at the sky and sigh, frustrated. She was about to ask him what was wrong, but then the waiter placed the chocolate soufflé in front of her. Lola's mouth watered. Then he placed a small chocolate pyramid between her and Chuck, and Lola was sure she was drooling. Casually, she wiped off the edge of her mouth to make sure.

Chocolate was heaven's way of saying I love you, Lola thought, gazing at the chocolate soufflé. She licked her lips and looked up at Chuck, who smiled at her. Lola smiled back, waiting.

He reached over to caress her face. "Dig in," he urged.

Not needing more of an invitation, she dug in. She moaned. Yep. It was that good—even better than yesterday's patisseries. Chuck closed his eyes briefly when he took his first bite.

"It's really good," he commented his obvious approval.

"Good? It's heaven!" Lola exclaimed, offended for the soufflé.

After they finished eating their dessert, Lola asked Chuck what he wanted to tell her, but he gazed at her and then said it hadn't been important. He said he had, in fact, forgotten. Chuck then picked up a chocolate ball and fed it to her. Lola's curiosity was piqued at his attempt to distract her. She remembered he had wanted to tell her something. And it was something important—the chocolate ball dissolved in her mouth as did her curiosity, silky hazelnut cream spread across her tongue.

Chuck lifted another chocolate to her mouth. This time, Lola licked his fingers and lightly sucked them as she gazed at him inno- cently, suggesting something else. Chuck went pale; his breathing got heavier.

"What?" she asked him innocently, knowing her eyes were suggesting mountains of mischief. She loved how hungry he looked. It never failed to make her feel desirable. *Now?* Definitely not. Now wasn't the moment to tell him. The atmosphere was playful—not the time to be serious.

"Would you like to dance?" Chuck asked her. They were inside, in the grand living room. Everyone stood around, talking to one another. The men all wore black suits, white shirts and black ties, while the women wore gowns of every color of the rainbow and every shade in between. A live band played soft, romantic music.

"Yes," she replied, smiling nervously. Chuck led the way to the dance floor, where couples were gently swaying together to the music, gazing into each other's eyes. Chuck hesitated before stepping onto the dance floor. "What's wrong?" Lola asked.

"I don't know how to dance," he confessed. Lola sighed in relief. Neither did she. Unless it was the foolish, acting-crazy type of dancing.

"Me, either," she told him. Chuck whipped his head around, surprised at her words.

"But you move your hips so well," he said, his eyes sparkling at the memory. Lola felt herself blush and mumbled something she herself couldn't understand, looking away. Chuck gently stroked her lips with his and then grabbed her hand, twirling her before pressing her against himself, with one hand on the small of her back. They swayed gently together, barely moving their feet. Dancing wasn't that hard, Lola thought to herself; she could move her hips.

Lola glanced around at the people in the room and caught sight of Elena and Larry talking with a couple. Elena was looking around for something. Or rather, someone, Lola knew. She would bet Elena was looking for Mack. Lola hadn't seen him either since the morning. Elena had told her that Mack would be eating in the kitchen, since Mikaella had left and he was left partner-less. He must still be eating, Lola concluded. Elena looked beautiful; her champagne-colored gown had a sweetheart neckline and hugged her tiny waist. She had her hair down, curled and swept to one side.

Elena had been nervous getting ready, saying that Larry was perfect and that he was perfect for her. She had been like a broken cassette. In the end, she asked it, rather than affirming it, like she had at first. Lola worried about her, but Elena just brushed off her concerns and then went into a detailed description of what she thought of Chuck. She liked him. Lola smiled and turned her attention back to Chuck.

Lola danced, gazing into his raven-black eyes. The world around her disappeared, and all she could see was Chuck, feel his heartbeat against her, feel his warm breath tickling her neck. She smiled happily, resting her head lightly against Chuck's head. They swayed together; every now and then they would kiss tenderly and gaze into each other's eyes. Now. Now was the time. Lola took a deep breath.

"Chuck," she started. "I want to—"

The music stopped, and a male voice apologized. Lola gazed

over at the band, and standing in front of them was Larry, holding a microphone. He looked nervous, Lola noticed. Larry began speaking with a slight tremble in his voice. He apologizing for interrupting the music, and he thanked everyone who had come. He announced that he wanted to share this moment with them and asked Elena to join him on the low, black stage. Larry slid down on one knee.

Oh! My! God! Larry was going to propose!

❧ ♥ ❧

Okay. This is it. *This is what you've wanted*. It's happening, Elena thought to herself. Over the last two months, Elena had hinted time after time to Larry that this weekend would be perfect for a proposal. It was a romantic weekend, although she had barely spent time with Larry. He always had an important call to make or an urgent email to send to his colleagues.

It didn't matter; he was proposing to her right then. He had picked up on her hints. And she loved that about him. She loved him. Yes. She loved him…

Elena looked around the room, wanting to share this special moment with Mack. She hadn't seen him all night, and it was starting to get a little worrying.

She gazed back down at Larry on his one knee. She smiled *This is what I want*. Why wasn't she happy? Why did her smile feel forced? It was just nerves, she assured herself. She knew this was what she wanted. Larry was the man she wanted to marry.

"Elena, I love you. Will you marry me?"

"Yes," Elena grinned with a shaky laugh. She barely noticed

271

Larry's shoulders drop in relief as she looked far behind him and saw Mack, standing by the door, gazing intently at her, still as a rock.

Elena's heart squeezed.

Mack.

❧ ♥ ❧

"**C**ongratulations!" Lola squealed, excited, hugging Elena. Lola couldn't believe it. Elena was engaged! Lola was happy for her—but to Larry? It didn't matter. Elena had chosen Larry; that meant she loved Larry. They had been together for years. And if she loved Larry, then Lola would stand by her and be happy for her friend.

Understanding dawned on Lola. No wonder Elena had kept repeating that Larry was perfect, that he was the man she loved, so many times. Elena must have intuitively known that Larry was going to propose.

"Congratulations," Chuck said to Elena, shaking Larry's hand. He briefly eyed Larry. Whatever Chuck had been looking for, he found it and relaxed beside Lola.

"Thank you." Larry grinned like the happiest man alive. "Next is you guys," he teased Chuck lightly, pushing back his shoulder. Lola's blood turned ice-cold, freezing her in place as her eyes stared wide into Chuck's wide raven-black eyes. Each searching for the other's reaction to Larry's words. Was Chuck worried that Lola might enjoy the idea because he didn't feel that way about her? He should. Lola adored the idea more than she should, she guiltily admitted. Her heart expanded with joy as she envisioned Chuck on one knee, declaring his undying love to her. It was a priceless image. Or maybe he liked the idea just like she did but was scared of her reaction. Or maybe he didn't like her and was scared that Larry had put ideas into her head—and possibilities. Or maybe he loved her like she did him, and he wanted to propose to her.

Or maybe I'm overthinking things. He doesn't want to propose. He just met me. Lola scowled. Would he like her but propose? No. Let's not blow things out of proportion.

"Congratulations," someone behind them said. Lola and Chuck moved out of their way. Chuck led Lola back to the dance floor; he pulled her into his arms, resting his cheek against hers. They moved slowly with the music. Lola relaxed in his arms and closed her eyes. Chuck's hand held her firmly by the small of her back, pressing her close to him. Lola felt like a string connected her to Chuck. She wondered if he could also feel it. A blissful infinity seemed to pass by before the song ended and another even slower song started.

Lola opened her eyes and shifted her head to gaze into Chuck's black eyes, and without thinking, she blurted out, "You know Larry was joking, right?"

What? Really? Of all the things she could tell him, she had asked him that? She should have told him she wanted their relationship to continue beyond this weekend... But it was a defense mechanism, she argued. She had asked because before she made of fool of herself, she needed to know what he thought about them, and Larry's comment had given her something to start with. If Chuck said something along the lines of "Yes, thank goodness," then she would swallow up her feelings and not tell him.

"Lola, about that..." Chuck began in a grave voice. *Oh God, start swallowing.* "All day, I've been trying to tell you this." *Gulp.* "I want us to be mo—" Chuck's phone rang, interrupting him. *"Us to be mo what?" "Mo friends?" "Mo lovers?" "Mo what?" Did "mo" mean more?* Lola searched his face.

Chuck growled and yanked his phone out of his pocket and glared at the screen. He frowned, confused and worried, at the caller's flashing name.

"Sorry. I have to take this," he apologized, answering his phone. Lola nodded, concerned about whatever was happening. Chuck stepped out of the grand living room, leaving Lola alone. Lola wandered to the window, accepting a glass of champagne from the waiter. She gazed out into the darkness. Mo what?

What did Chuck want them to be mo? Mo of what? Lola took a sip. The bubbles in the champagne glided down her throat. Lola hoped he wanted to tell her that he wanted them to be more than a pretend couple. Lola wanted to be his girlfriend; she wanted to fall asleep in his arms and wake up in them. She wanted to be with him and maybe eventually marry him. Lola could see herself living with Chuck for the rest of her life. Could she be lucky enough that Chuck wanted the same thing as she did? Lola hoped.

Chapter Twenty-Four

Great.

Chuck sighed. A house they were almost done building had been burnt down to the ground by a drunken group of kids. As if he needed another reason to hate drunk people. All his crew was booked until next year, on other jobs. He'd have to hire a new crew, and fast.

So much work to do when he arrived back in the city. Here he had been hoping to prolong his vacation for a week and spend every waking and sleeping moment with Lola.

"Having work trouble?"

The hair on his arms rose. *Run.* He turned, and standing there in a skin-tight red dress was Nicole. A smirk outlined her lips, and her gaze was cold and calculating. She took two long steps closer to him as her smile turned sweet and she cocked her head to the side. "I hate it when that happens to me, too, but I guess that's the price of running your own business."

Chuck nodded, taking a step back, hoping she would understand. She did and didn't look discouraged. On the contrary, her smile widened at the challenge, and she took two steps, closing enough space for her to comfortably lay her hand on his chest.

"Oh." She bit her lip. "So strong." She trailed her hand across his chest. In one swift movement, he gripped her hand. Her hand stilled, and she glanced up. Her gaze revealed deep intelligence, as well as an ego which he had just offended.

"Trying to steal this boyfriend?" Lola's calm voice drifted down the hall. Lola marched towards Chuck and stepped in front of him. He knew it wasn't the time to smile, but he did, just a little. How could he not, when Lola was acting like his bodyguard?

"What? Steal your pretend boyfriend?" Nicole asked, incredulous.

"Wha-how?"

"Please. Everyone knows it. It's so obvious." Nicole rolled her eyes. "And even if he was your boyfriend, I'd never want to be with a brute of man." She turned, disgusted at him. "Everyone knows his family is a bunch of alcoholics."

Chuck froze. How did she…? Chuck searched her face with ferocity. She smirked. "I get what I want. I wanted to know all about you. Now I do, which is why I don't want you." She turned to Lola. "But I think he's exactly what you deserve. A nobody for a nobody."

Chuck winced. No. Lola didn't deserve the shame burning in him, burning in Gabriella.

"Who told you?" Chuck demanded.

"I have a friend who works in the police force. Tragic. Both parents in the hospital, but at least it was the laugh of the department."

"A friend or a fuck friend?"

"Darling, it's the same thing. Just ask David." Nicole winked at Lola and walked away.

"Pff. Coward. How dare she say you're a nobody? She's the nobody. Like, really? If it wasn't for her parents, she wouldn't have a company—unlike you, who actually built it from nothing." Lola shook her head.

"But she's right," Chuck admitted.

"What? No!"

"I am, Lola. And it's why we shouldn't be together." He nodded. "Lola, I think after this weekend, we should never see each other again."

Lola stumbled back. "Why?"

"Because you shouldn't be with someone like me."

"Don't you think I should be the one to decide that?"

"Lola, it's the reason I'm single. The same reason my seven-year relationship with Silvia ended. It's why it will never work between us."

"How do you know? I don't care about your past. I don't care if your parents are saints or drunks."

He cared. "Are you telling me you would like to invite my parents to brunch? Spend a day with them? Call them your family?"

"What does that have to do with anything? I thought you didn't want to have anything to do with your parents."

"They're still my parents."

The world stopped. It blurred out his vision as understanding took over. They were still his parents. Whether he liked it or not, he cared for them. He didn't hate them; he loved him. And because he did, that was why it hurt so much. There was nothing he could do but accept that he'd been hurt, with a lifelong shame and constant judgment. Resentment lifted off his shoulders. He couldn't change what had happened. No point in fighting something already long gone. He had to accept the shame. But Lola didn't. "You don't deserve the shame."

"Let me decide!"

"NO!"

"But I lov—" Lola stopped herself.

Lov? Did she mean love? Because he loved her. Chuck tried gazing into Lola's brown eyes, but she dropped her gaze to the floor. Shit. A real hard-ass fool didn't even begin to express how stupid he was. She didn't care if his parents were drunks, and if she didn't care, then he shouldn't, either. Shit. Shit. Shit. He'd ruined every- thing. Chuck opened his mouth to apologize and once and for all tell her he loved her, but Lola blew out a shaky laugh that resonated through the hall.

"Oh, god." She laughed again. A laugh coming from deep in her throat. She shook her head. "I think we got carried away with this whole pretend relationship."

No. No they hadn't. Chuck tried to spit out the words, but he couldn't.

Lola took his silence as a confirmation. "Well, I guess that says it all, huh?" Lola bit her lip, looking away. "You know, these shoes are really hurting me."

Lola bent over as she hid the tears streaming down her cheeks. A distraction. She needed a distraction "Lola." Chuck's voice was urgent as he began. But Lola didn't want to hear it. She didn't want to hear her name on his lips ever again. She didn't want to ever again hear him at all. She wanted to cover her ears and sing at the top of her lungs, "La! La! La! La!"

But since she was a mature woman, she simply kicked off her high heels and sprinted down the hall in the opposite direction. She ignored Chuck shouting her name. The sound of his pursuit pumped adrenaline through her. At the first corner, she turned into the first room, not wanting to risk Chuck catching her.

Lola tripped over something and fell flat on her face. Tears rolled down her face, and she began sobbing. She couldn't hold it in anymore.

"Lola?" She heard Mack's familiar voice ask in astonishment. Lola lifted her head and saw Mack lying on the floor beneath her legs.

"Mack," she said through a sob. In one swift motion, Mack sat them both up, hugging her.

"What's wrong?" he demanded.

"Chuck," she sobbed, "doesn't..." She wailed, unable to finish the sentence.

Mack let go, outrage puffing his face. "What?! Chuck?! Did he hurt you?! Because I swear—"

"No, he didn't" Not physically. He had been much crueler than that. He had made her love him. LOVE HIM. To love is to hurt. How stupid was she? Lola noticed that Mack's eyes were red and a bit puffy. Instead of answering, since Lola believed that if she

279

could ignore the truth, the pain would eventually go away, she asked Mack, "Why are you here? And on the floor, I may add." She sniffed her sob.

"El— I don't know," he said. Yes, he did, Lola thought. She'd been so caught up in the excitement of Elena getting engaged, she hadn't thought how Mack would take the news.

"Do you want to leave? The mansion tonight?" Mack asked abruptly.

"Yes." Lola began nodding instead of answering, just like Chuck. She stopped herself. Lola didn't want to be anything like Chuck or be anything of his.

"Meet me out front in fifteen minutes."

"Okay," she nodded and kicked herself for nodding. What? Was she really going to go through her life without ever nodding, she asked herself ? Yep, pretty much, she replied stubbornly.

Fifteen minutes later, Lola and Mack sped down towards the highway. In less than ten minutes, Lola had packed her bags and run down to Mack's car, relieved that he was already there. Lola had been so scared to run into Chuck. She knew she couldn't face him. At least not as a mature woman. She would have either stuck her tongue out at Chuck or burst into tears in front of him. Lola hated to admit it, but she would most likely have burst into tears.

Tears were still running down her face as she closed her apartment door. Lola looked around her apartment, throwing her bags on the floor. She didn't know what to do. She could go out to a bar, get really drunk and forget about Chuck. Or she might end up only remembering Chuck while she told everyone everything they had done. No, she didn't want to do that. An image of what Chuck must have endured with his mother made her shudder and vow for real this time never to drink again. This time, she was going to stick to her decisions. Plus, chocolate and a huge bucket of ice cream appealed to her.

Lola took her time changing out of her blue gown and into comfy sweatpants and a t-shirt. She headed towards her kitchen for some ice cream. She hoped she had some left, but she stopped in front of her door.

"Lola!" a breathless voice shouted through the door.

Knock! Knock! Knock!

Lola stared wide-eyed at the door and stood still.

Chuck! Chuck was here! He had followed her. Lola's heart began beating faster and faster. Why was he here? He had made it clear with his silence that they'd taken things too far. In other words, she meant nothing to him. She hadn't expected him to come after her. Did that mean he did care for her?

She should be happy. She should feel ecstatic that Chuck was on the other side of the door, calling her name in an anxious voice. But Lola found herself furious and miserable. She didn't want to hear what he wanted to say to defend himself.

"Lola, I know you're in there. Please, Lola, let me in. It's not what you think. Please let me in, let me explain," Chuck pleaded from the other side of the door. Lola remained silent.

"Lola, I can feel you there. Please let me in, let's talk," he said.

Oh! He could feel her there? *Oh, really*? She could feel him, too, but that didn't change the fact that she still wouldn't open the door. What did him feeling her, on the other side of the door, have to do with anything? Was she supposed to open the door now? Like that would happen. And why did her heart lift a tiny bit, knowing he was aware of her? Of course he was aware of her; he was standing on the other side of the door. He could probably see the light coming from her apartment.

Light!

Lola turned off all her lights and went back in front of the door and waited silently in the dark. She heard Chuck sigh and the gentle thumb as he pressed his hands against the door and softly say, "Lola, I don't want to do this like this, but since you won't let me in..." He took a deep breath. "Here goes. All day, I've been trying to tell you I want us—"

Lola pressed her palms hard against her ears and ran into her bathroom. She shut the bathroom door, collapsing on the floor, sobbing. The word "us" electrified every memory of him, flashing it across her brain—his handsome face, his neatly trimmed black beard, his black eyes and eyebrows, his stylish black hair, his caresses, his kisses—everything about him, about them, their time together. She couldn't handle it. It was painful. Then she remembered Chuck pulling away from Nicole's lips. Smiling lips, her memory reminded her. And that brought a whole new set of tears and sobs.

Chuck didn't love her or care for her, Lola thought to herself. He was just having fun with her; it meant nothing to him. She meant nothing to him. A part of her brain argued that Chuck and Nicole did know each other already, and apparently Nicole had been with Chuck before. But Lola wasn't sure; she never asked Chuck, out of fear it might be true. But it was. Why else had they been kissing? It made sense to Lola.

Lying on the hard, cold bathroom floor, Lola whispered into

the darkness, "Sorry, Dad, but I'm not a smart woman. I fell for someone without building the relationship on a solid foundation like I should have—like you always taught me. I'm sorry," she sobbed.

Lola couldn't stop crying. Even if she wanted to stop crying, tears rolled down her cheeks and onto the bathroom floor without her consent. She needed to get up and do something—anything other than cry over a man, but it felt good. *No, get up, Lola. Do something.*

Obediently, she got up and turned on the lights and stood there, tears silently coming down her face. Lola wanted to talk to someone, but Mack was in no mood to talk. Poor him. Elena's engagement had hit him hard. Lola suspected Mack secretly loved Elena, and his reaction all but confirmed it today. There was no way Lola could call Elena and say love was stupid, after leaving the night of her engagement to cry over some guy. So that left Mikaella. Lola would text her and ask her to call her when she had time. Lola looked around her bathroom one last time before stepping out and getting her phone. Her gaze fixed on her shampoo for her blond hair. Wendy!

Running out of her bathroom, Lola got her phone and texted Mikaella and then called Wendy. She glanced at her microwave as the phone rang. 2:30 am. *Oops!* Wendy would be sleeping, or maybe she was with a guy. Lola was about to hang up, but it was too late; Wendy picked up.

"Hello." Lola heard Wendy's soft voice answer. Lola sighed in relief. It didn't sound sleepy.

"I'm so sorry. I didn't realize how late it is," Lola apologized.

"Lola?" the woman asked.

"Yes, I'm sorry. I just needed to talk to someone, but I didn't realize how late it was," Lola explained, feeling guilty.

"It's okay, don't worry. I'm really sorry, but I can't talk right now. But do you want to meet tomorrow for coffee?" Wendy asked.

"Yeah," Lola sighed in relief. "I'd like that."

"Meet me at Gruau Coffee, at three, tomorrow?"

"Okay, see you tomorrow," Lola agreed. "I'm sorry," she apologized one last time.

"It's okay, don't worry. Sorry. I have to go. See you tomorrow. Bye." Wendy seemed to hurry to hang up.

Lola grimaced, feeling bad. She must be with a date. Oops. Lola sighed. She gazed at her phone, wanting to talk with someone. She pursed her lips, thinking as she let herself cry. There was only one person who she really wanted to talk to. Her father.

He picked up on the third ring.

"Hello?" said her father's sleepy, croaking voice. With age, it had acquired a croak that Lola liked.

"Hi, Dad," she sniffed.

"Lola?" There was a pause. "Everything okay? It's six in the morning here."

"I know. I'm sorry. I just wanted to say happy Valentine's Day. Well, late happy Valentine's Day." Lola swallowed back a sob.

"Oh, darling, happy Valentine's Day." He smiled the words and paused, listening to Lola sob. "Everything alright?"

"No," Lola whimpered and sniffed.

"What happened?"

"I fell in love." She broke into a sob-fest.

On the other end of phone, she heard her father chuckle. "Darling, shouldn't you be laughing with utter joy?"

"No. I don't want to love. To love is to hurt. Who wants to hurt?"

"What makes you think that?" her father asked, disconcerted.

"You."

"What do you mean?"

"Well, you spent all your life hurting because you love Mom."

There was a silence on the other end.

"Oh, Lola. Love didn't hurt me. Love made me able to raise a beautiful daughter. Love made me strong. Love made it easier for me to breathe, to laugh. Love is what woke me up every day with a smile and the joy of wanting to live." He paused. "I know I'm not perfect, Lola. I'm sorry if I hurt you with my pain, but understand that my pain was fleeting compared to the love I felt for your mother. And for you." His compassionate voice paused again. "I don't regret it, you know. I don't regret my life with your mother—never remarrying—but most of all, I don't regret my life with you." He paused again.

"This will sound selfish, but Lola, you are so special, I don't think I would have been able to share you with your mother."

Lola laughed through her tears. "Dad," she sniffed, smiling. She shook her head, still laughing.

"It's true," her father said, dignified.

"I love you, Dad."

"I love you too, Sweetheart. Now tell me about this man. Hey, don't think because I'm pushing seventy, I can't beat his ass."

Now Lola really lost it laughing.

"Oh, Dad," she sniffed, "he's unlike anyone I ever met. He's my next-door neighbor."

"Is it that fellow you have a crush on?"

"What—how did you know?"

"Mika told me when I visited you six months ago. He's a burly man, isn't he?"

The moment she had Mikaella on the phone, the woman would have a lot of explaining to do. "Yeah, I guess." Lola shrugged.

"Darling, do you mind if I don't beat this one up? I don't want to break my new hip."

Lola smiled, assuring her father it was quite fine and she could take care of herself.

"I know you can, kiddo. Hard for a father to admit it, but you're grown up. A woman." It was her father's turn to sniff.

"I miss you so much."

"I miss you, too. Come visit me soon. Promise?"

"I promise, Daddy."

"I love you, Darling. Call me whenever, okay? Even if it's six in the morning," he grumbled, teasing her.

"Dutifully noted. I love you, too. Bye."

They hung up, and Lola gazed into nothingness, with her cell phone resting on her lip as she thought.

If love didn't hurt, then why did she want to hug herself into a ball and cry herself to sleep?

Love. Love? What was love? Chuck.

Chapter Twenty-Five

Lola caressed her yellow teacup, feeling the warmth of the hot tea caress her fingers in return. She looked down at her jasmine tea and finished telling Wendy what had happened at the Valentine Weekend. They sat across from one another by the large window in the neighborhood café, Gruau.

Gruau Coffee had been decorated by Lola—well, Vance Decorates, but still. It had been she who had made the designs, and everything. She had been told the owner wanted French décor with a twist of "home-sweet-home." Meaning warm colors—colors that helped people relax—with an elegant, simple touch. Lola had worked hard on this project; she had even asked Elena to sculpt some things for her and Mikaella to paint a couple of paintings to integrate and balance out the place. Gruau Coffee was soft orange with slashes of brown and sprinkles of blue. Lola was proud of herself; it looked good. Even better now, with all the furniture broken in.

"And then he came after me, but…" Lola paused. "I don't know. I didn't want to play anymore," Lola finished saying.

Wendy grabbed her hand and gave her an understanding and supportive smile with a gentle squeeze.

"Men." She shook her head. "They really know how to get you, huh?"

"Yeah, they do." Lola pouted.

Lola noted that they both looked—putting it nicely—horrible. Lola's eyes were red and hideously puffy from crying so much. Wendy looked exhausted; she had dark, heavy bags under her green eyes, weighing down on her rosy cheeks. Her light brown hair was in a messy, frizzy bun on top of her head. They wore almost identical outfits, worn-out jeans and comfy hoodies. The only difference was that Lola's hoodie was grey and Wendy's was black. Wendy looked like she would collapse any minute from fatigue as she sipped her green tea.

Must have had some night, Lola thought mischievously and grinned. A night she could have had. Perhaps many nights. She sighed inwardly.

"So what's going to happen with Nicole? Are you going to quit?" Wendy asked after some thought.

"I wish I could," Lola said longingly, "but Nicole fired me on Saturday." How she wished she could walk into work tomorrow and quit in front of everyone—maybe make a little… big scene. It seemed like fun, and she could release some of her pent-up frustration. But nope, she wasn't that lucky.

Now Wendy really gasped in shock. She gasped so loud that people around turned to stare at her, alert.

"No! I can't believe it! Nicole is a…" Wendy looked pointedly at her, with significance. Lola got it. "I mean I can't believe her." Wendy shook her head. "What a friend." She rolled her eyes.

Lola began nodding, agreeing with Wendy, but she stopped in mid-action.

Oh, my god! Just nod already. It's not the end of the world.

"Yes," Lola said, ignoring her thoughts and stubbornly holding her head still. Maybe too still, since Wendy was studying her with open curiosity.

"What?" Lola asked, feeling undressed.

"Every time you start nodding, you always stop yourself and then a look of exasperation flashes across your face," Wendy explained.

Damn. She was quick.

"Chuck nods more than he talks." Lola shrugged, not wanting to deny it.

"You really love him," Wendy said tenderly, her tired eyes softening.

No, she didn't. Lola had spent most of the night thinking everything over. She had come to a conclusion she liked and that had finally let her sleep: she wasn't in love with Chuck. Cared for him, yes, but love? No, she lied to herself again.

"Don't fight it," Wendy simply said, breaking into her thoughts and touching her arms affectionately.

Lola sighed. "You have experience with this?" Lola asked, curious.

"Not exactly, but I see it all the time at the store."

"So the man you were with last night isn't the one?" Lola

couldn't help asking.

Wendy scoffed, and laughing good-naturedly, she said, "I wish! I wasn't with a man last night, not that way. Believe me."

"But you were with a man last night?"

"Yes, unfortunately," Wendy said, and her expression was completely priceless. It was somewhere between sour and exasperated as she rolled her eyes. Lola held back a giggle and settled for an amused smile. "But enough about me. What are you going to do about work?"

"I don't know. Send out resumes to any and every job available."

"What is it you do?" Wendy inquired, curious.

"Interior design."

"Why don't you start your own company?" Wendy's eyes opened wide, liking the idea.

Lola looked unsure. Start her own company? A one-person company? She didn't think it would be much of a success.

"I don't think I'm cut out to start my own company."

Wendy pursed her lips and narrowed her gaze on Lola. "Answer me these questions, and we'll find out," she proposed.

"Alright," Lola said, thinking that was fair. She straightened in her chair and waited for the questions.

"Are you disciplined? Is your job your passion? Would you be willing to work more than forty hours on a project? Are you organized? Do you have tenacity and willpower?"

"Yes. Absolutely. I already do. Depends on the mood, but for the most part, yes. A messy place isn't pleasing to the eye. And, yes." Lola answered question by question.

"Well, there you have it. You have a start as an independent worker."

"You mean self-employed?" Lola read between the lines.

"What do you think all start-up owners are?"

Wendy had her at that point. Lola smiled.

The half hour that followed was spent on the same topic, as Wendy wrote down on a napkin list after list of things for her to do before registering her company. Market research, including demographics, and a whole lot of other statistics. Marketing strategies— and look up an accounting/budgeting crash course. Even if Lola wasn't the one who would do her own finances, it was best that she knew what they were doing with her money. During the whole half hour, Wendy was relentless as she encouraged Lola to start her own company and take charge of her own life.

Lola was still unsure, but the good part was that her rent was covered for at least four months, and she would still have some cash in her savings to start up a small, very small, tiny business. Lola knew her friends would help her find some clients. Lola knew the world of décor in and out. She also enjoyed the idea of being in charge of a team. That was going to be her ultimate goal.

"You really should just think abou—" Wendy broke off, her face turning pale, all the blood draining from her face. She gazed over Lola's shoulder at the entrance. She looked almost sick. Before Lola could ask her anything, Wendy suddenly stood up, mumbling, "I forgot, I left the, ah, the stove on at my apartment. I'll talk to you later. I'm sorry. Bye." And she disappeared through the back of the café.

Lola gazed around, confused, wondering why Wendy hadn't

used the front door. Lola looked behind her at the entrance. There stood a man who looked dangerous, but not like Chuck did.

This man was dangerous—dangerous compared to Chuck, whose dangerousness was more of an attractive male air, kind of like an accessory or perfume. The man standing by the entrance was star- ing after Wendy, his eyes cold and hard. A shiver ran through Lola. She prayed nothing would happen to Wendy. This man looked like he could hurt her and then have some ice cream afterwards.

She would also have taken the back way out, to avoid being close to a man like that.

As Lola finished her tea, Wendy texted her, apologizing and saying that they should meet up again soon. Lola relaxed, not real- izing that she had been worried about her new friend. Sitting in the café, she thought about Wendy's words to take charge of her own life. And Lola decided she would.

Feeling the same empowerment, she felt every new year, she decided to start a journal to document her progress. When she had her successful company, she could read the journal to give her moti- vation and show herself how far she'd gone.

Tuesday February 16th

Dear Diary,

I woke up late today. Very late. So late I thought, why make breakfast when premade caramel chocolate bars exist? The chocolate helped with all the crying I've been doing. I can't seem to get Chuck out of my mind. The worst is, I think of him and then cry. Or cry and think of him. It's the same thing, really. I just cry and cry, thinking about the man. So I did what I had to and bribed myself into thinking about something else. If I worked on my new business, then

I would be allowed to watch sports in the evening. I worked so hard, I skipped lunch and ended up ordering an extra-large cheese pizza at ten, with the intention of eating the whole thing.

Lola passed out, thinking about Chuck as a smile traced her lips, after eating the second slice.

Wednesday February 17th

Dear Diary,

I woke up at 8:00 this glorious morning. Without giving it much thought, I made myself—I burnt myself—two pieces of toast and ate it over the sink, while in my mind, I reviewed and prioritized my to-do list for the day. First, write a short description of a project and then, the number-one priority for the day was the market research. I barely thought about Chuck today. Every now and then, I would have a random memory pop up, like his handsome face or his throaty voice. But it never lasted, never enough for me to remember the pain I felt every time I thought of him. I feel proud of myself. Yesterday, I didn't think of him in the afternoon, and today all day, which means I get to watch sports. Yay! I ate some leftover pizza and sat down to watch my favorite team win its hockey match. Woohoo! Yes!

Lola fell asleep with the memory of Chuck on her brain. A grin spread as she swore she could feel Chuck beside her.

Thursday February 18th

Dear Diary,

So I'm officially out of food. I woke up this morning, and the single edible thing in the house was a burnt piece of toast. I thought about not toasting it, but since it was the last piece—meaning the outside slice— it never tastes good unless it's toasted.

293

My fridge is empty. My cupboards are so empty, I don't think there is even any air left in there. Anyway, I showered and got dressed in clean, decent clothes, not holey sweatpants and the dirty old t-shirt that I have been wearing for the past two days.

Never have I ever done groceries so fast. I was practically sprinting along the aisles and running with my hands full of white plastic bags with the red grocery store logo. People must have thought I was stealing them, from the fugitive glances I kept giving. Not my fault. I feared bumping into Chuck. I still can't face him. I was so paranoid I would see him. I literally sprinted up the stairs. And let me tell you this, it is no easy task. Food is heavy. It can knock you off-balance if you keep looking back.

I know. I know. At some point, I'll have to see Chuck, but I just don't want it to be now. I want to look my best—hopefully, with a celebrity boyfriend by my side and not with dark, heavy bags under my eyes and an air of utter loneliness about me.

But good news! I have food now. Yay… It doesn't seem worth the bruised knee I got from falling down the stairs. Either way, I concentrated on my market research. Demographics were still my goal today. So many statistics to go through. I ate a sandwich with an apple for dinner and vegged out in front of the TV to watch some sports.

I'd definitely rather have a hockey player by my side than a pretty Hollywood star when I next meet Chuck. I have to confess, the thought doesn't bring much solace. Damn Chuck. Making me love him.

Lola fell asleep thinking about Chuck once again with a smile playing on her lips as she dreamt of him.

Friday February 19th
Dear Diary,

This morning, I woke up realizing that Chuck is most likely not fall-ing asleep thinking about me. It wasn't a great start to the day. I ate like a nor-mal person, though, some cereal and tea. Then I worked a little on my business. But I felt restless and decided to clean my apartment. I threw out everything I had from working with Nicole. Except the last design I did. It was too beautiful to throw out.

After my apartment was sparkling clean, I sat down and watched a marathon of romantic movies because there was nothing better to do. Big mistake.

Lola passed out in front of the TV, crying her eyes out.

Saturday February 20th

Dear Diary,

I must be a masochist to force myself to endure all those movies with happy endings, with those ridiculously handsome actors. But they had nothing on ~~my Chuck.~~ Chuck. Those drop-dead gorgeous actors were too pretty—not manly enough, like my Chuck. He was natural— unpretentious and unrehearsed... Urgh... I want to scream. Why won't he leave my thoughts?

Two words. Ice cream. Yes. For breakfast. Now I'm calling Elena.

Just came back from an exhausting day of shopping with Elena. I bought way too much clothing I really don't need. Even a pair of stilettoes. I can't walk in those. But it felt good to be out with Elena. She wasn't her chirpy self, which was great because we both spent the day whining about men. Me, of course, Chuck and Elena, Mack. The man still hasn't called Elena.

Anyway, I'm exhausted. I think I'm going to call it a night.

Lola fell asleep without a thought passing through her sleepy brain.

Sunday February 21st

Dear Diary,

Something big happened today.

I woke up this morning to a knock on my door. I panicked. At first I froze, thinking it was Chuck. I thought of staying in bed, but curiosity got the better of me, and I tiptoed to the door as silently as I could. I peeped through the peephole, wondering if Chuck looked as ruggedly handsome as ever, or if he looked miserable, like I feel. I hoped the latter and was disappointed. David stood there, looking charming and handsome. Not Chuck. I opened the door and walked back to my bed, where David followed me. He sat beside me, hugging me. "He's a jerk," he said, releasing me. I half smiled.

"That's what everyone keeps saying," I admitted. "But it doesn't really help, because every time someone says it, I have to bite my tongue so I don't defend Chuck. He isn't a jerk."

Chuck really isn't a jerk, I know that. He just makes poor decisions. I know him, and Chuck isn't mean by nature, like a jerk is.

David made a not-surprised face. Without thinking, I asked "Why Nicole?" David sighed and said, "She was always throwing herself at me. Every chance she had, she would try something on me, and every time, I wouldn't let her but that time, my desire won out, but it wasn't her. It could have been anyone, really—or just a mouth, for all I cared."

David had come by to pack his things. It was weird, but I felt the same things I had felt when I saw David and Nicole together. Relief. I am relieved. I feel like that part of me is truly gone. Now is the time to start my life. The way I want it, how I want it and being who I truly am. Broken or not broken. With commitment issues or not. I am me. And I love me for me.

Monday February 22nd

Dear Diary,

Another big thing happened today.

I woke up quite hungry this morning. I made myself three sunny-side up eggs and two pieces of toast smeared with peanut butter and jelly and a hot chocolate. And, may I add, not burnt. Yep. Didn't burn them. Woohoo. It felt good to eat a hearty breakfast, because it gave me all the energy I needed to work. I immersed myself in planning my new business, "Sunset."

Today I am on a roll. I found a name. Finally, as you can see.

On top of everything, I realized I could live without Chuck. I could nod, and it wouldn't kill me. It gave me the extra push to work hard on my new business, Sunset. I was working and concentrating when I heard a knock on the door. Thinking it was David, I opened the door.

Nope. Not David.

Gabriella. Yeah, Chuck's sister. Oh, god, she is going kill me, was the first thought I had. Gabriella walked in without an invitation and sat down on my couch. Wanting to run away, I followed slowly, frightened for my life. I hesitated before sitting down beside her.

"Look, I'll make this quick, okay? I'm not here to kill you, or anything," Gabriella assured me. I let my shoulders drop in relief. "I know you didn't do anything wrong, so you're off the hook." Gabriella grabbed my hand and looked into my eyes. Big event number two. "I am here to tell you I have never seen my brother so happy before. You make him happy. And I believe you were happy with him. I think you guys should be together, but that's not my choice, I know. Anyways, Chuck is going to visit our parents at the hospital tomorrow. He asked me to ask you if you could go with him."

I didn't give her an answer.

Tuesday February 23rd

Lola was too preoccupied to write in her journal and discarded it. There really wasn't anything to think about. She had to feel. And what she felt was love for Chuck. And Chuck needed her. She had promised him that if he needed her to go with him, she would. She'd never broken a promise.

She was going. Even if she was terrified. What would he say when he saw her? How would she react when she saw him?

Thirty minutes later, Lola stared at her closed door, dressed in her new blue jeans and a new soft pink long-sleeved peplum top. She held her keys in one hand while the other ran through her loose hair as she blew air out of her mouth. She stared at the closed door like it was an impossible challenge. She could do this…

You can do this. I can do this. I can do this. Lola Moss, you can do this!
With that thought, she flung the door open and walked out.
I can do this.

Gabriella had informed her that Chuck would meet her at the entrance to the hospital at four, so there was Lola, standing awkwardly outside the entrance. It was three fifty-five; Lola was just five minutes early, but every minute was torture. Twice, she almost bolted, but instead, she took deep breaths and remained standing in front, fidgeting. She turned her back to the parking lot; she didn't want to see him arrive in his shiny, black four-door truck.

"Lola?" asked a surprised, deep, throaty voice behind her.

Lola gulped. Her heart stilled in her chest for a second and then went into overdrive. She turned slightly and saw Chuck standing a few feet away. He looked horrible, she noted. He had dark bags under his eyes; his beard had grown and wasn't neat or groomed. But he still looked good to her. He was wearing worn-out jeans with a white t-shirt. Lola refrained from jumping on him and kissing him.

As Lola gazed at Chuck, she felt the same pull—a magnetic pull connecting her to Chuck—she had the day they had first met. "Chuck." She greeted him nervously.

"What are you doing here?" he asked, surprise still heavy in his voice. What? What did he mean, what was she doing here? Hadn't he asked his sister to ask her? He closed the distance between them, leaving a foot between them. Out of respect, Lola guessed.

"Your sister said you wanted me to be with you today, when you visited your parents," Lola said, confused, as panic gradually settled in. What if he didn't want her here? What if he had changed his mind?

"My sister?" he repeated, shocked, and paused, closing his eyes. His face hardened, and his jaw flexed.

He looks mad. Run, Lola, run.

But when he opened his eyes, his gaze was tender, and he said, "Sorry. I didn't have anything to do with what my sister said." Gabriella had played a prank on her. Instead of killing her, she had humiliated her. And here Lola thought Gabriella was on her side. *Nice.* Chuck was going to apologize for his sister's behavior and tell her he didn't want her there. Lola held her breath.

"But I'm glad you're here. I would like it if you came in with me." Lola stopped mid-inhale. Weight evaporated from her shoulders. Wait. What? He wanted her? He wanted her to come with him, to visit his parents? Lola's heart began expanding with joy.

"If you want to," Chuck added after Lola didn't reply. He looked nervous; it endeared him to her. "It's your decision. Not mine," he added, looking into her eyes to reinforce that it was her choice, just like she had said it was a week before.

She smiled, letting go of her half-breath. "I would love to," she told him honestly. Chuck nodded, with a smile almost breaking out on his bearded lips, and guided her into the hospital without saying anything else.

As they walked to Chuck's parents' room, Chuck walked beside her and gently slid his hand in hers. Lola smiled happily.

Chuck's parents were on the sixth floor—the third room to the right of the elevator, as Myriam, the jovial nurse, indicated to them.

Lola was nervous about meeting Chuck's parents. And she was scared of meeting his mother. She had never met a woman who could beat up her husband. Nor had she met a man who would beat up his wife; the mere idea scared her. Somehow, the idea of a woman beating her husband scared her more. She guessed it was because people talked more about men who beat up women; the news covered it constantly; she was more used to the idea. Women were the victims, never the predators. But every human was both, Lola liked to think.

There was also another thing she was nervous about: how was Chuck going to introduce her? Was he going to say, "An acquaintance of mine, a friend, or a girlfriend?" "A friend," she concluded. They were no longer pretending.

"You okay?" Chuck broke into her thoughts as they exited the elevator.

"Yeah... Um... I'm just nervous," she admitted. Chuck stopped and turned towards her. He gazed into her eyes and caressed her face with his free hand.

"I won't let anyone hurt you," he reassured her. *Hurt me? Who would hurt me? There's a possibility I can get hurt?* So much for reassurance.

"Don't worry," he said, smoothing out her frown with his gentle touch.

Lola took a deep breath. "Okay, I'm good as long as I am with you." *Oops.* She had just wanted to say "I'm good", not "I'm good as long as I am with you." She wasn't even sure how he felt about her, or if he wanted to be with her in that way.

"Me, too," he said, gazing into her eyes with a black gaze. He began leaning down to kiss her. Lola tilted her head to meet his lips while her heart hammered happily. He did want her! Yay! .... Or... That was at least what she thought it meant... Let's stay positive, she urged herself.

The kiss was soft and supple. Lola pulled back to gaze briefly into his raven eyes before kissing him again. Chuck smiled. So did she.

"Lola?" David's familiar voice reached her ears. Shock jolted through Lola, paralyzing her puckered lips. She turned towards the familiar voice, Chuck mirroring her, down to the puckered lips.

David stood in the hospital hallway. A second later, Gabriella walked out of a room.

"Hey, you guys made it," Gabriella said at the sight of them, a large smile painting her lips. She turned her attention to Chuck and commanded him, "You have to get in there. She is driving me insane, and she keeps asking and asking about you."

Chuck nodded and pressed a quick kiss on Lola's cheek before disappearing into the hospital room alone, his features serious, leaving Lola with Gabriella and David.

Gabriella looked like Chuck. She had the same raven-black hair and eyes, with fair skin and plump lips. While Chuck was well-built and muscular—very—and filled-out, Gabriella was skele- ton-like skinny. She was a little taller than the average woman. She stood in front of Lola, smiling triumphantly in a "You're welcome" way. Lola tried to be mad at her, but she just felt happy that Gabriella had meddled between her and Chuck's relationship.

They all stood in the hospital hallway, silently gazing at each other. David broke the silence. "What are you doing here?" he asked Lola.

"What are you doing here?" Lola returned the question.

"It's complicated." He shrugged.

"Same." Lola copied him. They both grinned at each other, sticking out their tongues in grimaces.

"But really, why are you here? I thought you never wanted to see Chuck again," David persisted.

Lola gazed at Gabriella. David followed her gaze. Gabriella smiled sheepishly at both of them, shrugging her shoulders.

"Yesterday, I went see her and told her Chuck needed her," Gabriella explained to David.

"How did you know where she lived?" David inquired suspiciously. "I thought you said you didn't know where your brother lived."

"I don't. I didn't. I followed you the other day."

"You followed me?" David asked, shocked, his blue eyes almost popping out. He eyed her suspiciously.

"I needed to know where she lived," Gabriella explained. "Don't flatter yourself," she added, exasperated as she saw David's expression. He smirked a half-charming, knowing smile at her. The kind of smirk that had always made Lola go weak in the knees. Gabriella rolled her eyes, shaking her head, unaffected.

Lola gazed from David to Gabriella and back, confused.

Chapter Twenty-Six

Chuck couldn't think of a time when he had been so surprised or so happy to see someone as he had when he had seen Lola standing and fidgeting in front of the hospital entrance. He wanted to run up to her and grab her and never let her go. He missed her every night went he went to bed and every morning when he woke up without her. Every second that passed during the day. He was sure he was dreaming. He had to be. Why would Lola be there? Maybe she did care for him. His feelings had hoped.

Over the last week, Chuck had time to think. Too much time to think, while he did nothing else but continue building his chalet. In all, he had realized it wasn't his parents' fault—his past or the shame he carried that had broken his relationships. It was him. He had given his past too much importance. He was the one still caught up in his pain to realize that Lola didn't care. She actually didn't care if he came from a family of saints or of drunks, as she had put it. He couldn't blame her for not wanting to be with him. And this time, he knew it wasn't because of his past but because he was a presuming ass.

Even if it did hurt, pouring his heart out to Lola—well, Lola's apartment door was closed, and he could only hear silence. Despite that, he waited until the sun rose from the dark sky. Every minute waiting outside her door was a like a painful slap of reality. He had messed up big time. Everything he had achieved with Lola in a weekend, he had blown because of his old patterns of thinking. Old. Not anymore. He wasn't going to mess up now. To think he almost hadn't come today.

If he had known Lola would be standing in front of the hospital, wearing sculpting jeans and a pink shirt, looking beautiful with her blond hair down, he would have given in to Gabriella's pleading without hesitation, without thinking twice.

Gabriella had called him the day before, early in morning, begging and begging for him to go that day to visit his parents. He hadn't wanted to hear it. But Gabriella had persisted, even after he kept hanging up on her. On her third call in a row, Chuck finally agreed. He knew he had to at some point, he argued. It was better to get it over with and accept the idea of visiting his parents.

Chuck had seen Lola standing there, and he felt a pull towards her, a magnetic pull. It was the same pull he had felt the first time he had seen her in the mailroom where they met. The magnetic pull he now knew was love. He had loved Lola since first laying eyes on her.

He almost broke into a dance when Lola had let him hold her hand as they walked around the hospital while they searched for his parents' room. He had almost begun singing when Lola had said, "I'm good as long as I am with you." Chuck's heart sang. She did love him. Or at least she cared. He could work with "cared." Hell, he would take a "sort of like you." Anything that meant he could be close to her, he would take.

But first things first, he thought, squaring his shoulders and walking into his parents' hospital room.

The room was empty except for single beds on either side of the large room, facing the little corridor they formed. The beds were all separated by light blue curtains, creating alcoves with identical furniture and spaces. His parents were at the back of the room, by the windows, facing each other. Chuck walked toward them, noting that there were three beds on each side. He walked to the window and turned, facing the entrance. From the corner of his eyes, he could see both his parents lying in bed.

"Chuck, I'm so happy to see you," his mother cooed at the sight of him. Reluctantly, he turned to face her and nodded. His mother still had a fading black eye and stitches in her lip from the fight. She was hooked up to a monitor and had some tubes and many needles in her. She looked the way he remembered her—black hair and eyes just like his, her thin mouth chapped, hollow cheeks. And she looked tired and desperate. But not as desperate as he thought she might have looked. How long had it been since she last drank? He knew she couldn't go a day without drinking, and when money was tight and she had to wait a day, she looked completely desperate, but now she just looked her normal, desperate self.

"Aren't you going to hug me?" she asked him. He wanted to scoff. Sure, like they always hugged each other, but since the woman was in the hospital, Chuck thought he could humor her. He walked over and gave her an awkward hug.

"I'm glad you're here," his mother told him with zero indication of the happiness she spoke of. He nodded, turning his attention to his father, on the other side of the room. He was asleep. Gabriella had told him that he had finally come out of his coma about three days before. His father was sleeping now. Chuck walked to his bed and studied his father's sleeping face. Except for the color of his hair and eyes, Chuck looked like his father. He had the same full lips and wide shoulders and was the same height as his father. Same hardened features.

Chuck's eye caught a glimpse of a half-empty vodka bottle hiding behind his father's bed. *Unbelievable.* His mother was drinking in the hospital, and his father was covering up for her. Some things never changed, Chuck thought. Disgusted, Chuck turned to his mother. She quickly read his expression. She had seen it for many years. "I couldn't—," she began.

"I don't want to hear it." He cut her off sharply.

Luckily, three different steps echoed in the room. Seconds later, Lola, Gabriella and David arrived. Lola assessed Chuck in a second and stood beside him, pressing her hand against his cheek. She reassured him with her gaze. He grabbed her hand and kissed her palm. Her smile calmed him.

"Who is she?" his mother demanded rudely. Lola stiffened, and Chuck instinctively stood in front of her, hiding her from his mother's judgmental gaze. Lola slid her hand around his forearm, restraining him. As much as his mother might drive him to extremes, he would never hurt her. Chuck took Lola's hand from his forearm

307

and intertwined his fingers with her.

"She's Lola," Gabriella said—as if everyone already knew it and their mother was being slow—before he could say anything.

"Hi," he heard Lola say, and from the corner of his eye, he saw her do a little awkward wave. She was nervous; he felt her hand squeeze his as she waited for his mother's reaction. Chuck gently began stroking her hand with his thumb; her grip eased a little, and she gazed up at him with her sparkling brown eyes.

"I don't want her here," his mother said, glaring at Lola. Chuck glared at his mother. *How dare she?!* "Why can't you marry Silvia?"

"Because she doesn't want a family like you."

"Chuck, when will you grow up and realize Silvia doesn't want you because of you? Not me. I only met her once."

"Yeah and you were pissed drunk. Didn't make the best impression."

His mother glared at him and declared, "You will marry Silvia."

"No." Came his final reply on the matter.

"You will, and this skinny kid," his mother said, pointing at Gabriella, "will marry Sam."

"I told you Sam and I broke up!" Gabriella said, irritated. "

Well, call him and patch things up, and get rid of this David. And put on some pounds, will you? You're just bones!" his mother said, exasperated. She said David's name like it was some horrible infection. "And you," she said, pointing her finger at Chuck, "get rid of this Lola," she commanded, saying Lola's name just like she had said David's. "And marry Silvia. She's beautiful, not like *her*."

"Chuck, let's talk in the hallway," Gabriella announced, grabbing him by the arm before he snapped at his mother again. David walked over to stand with Lola. Although Chuck wasn't sure why David was there, he was happy he stood protectively by her.

Before Gabriella could say anything, Chuck asked her why David was there, feeling a jab of jealousy of the man Lola had called her boyfriend.

"It's complicated," Gabriella replied with an already-thought-out answer.

"Complicated?" Chuck raised an eyebrow, unconvinced. He knew better. He wouldn't think twice about hurting David if he hurt his sister.

Gabriella rolled her eyes.

"When did you and Sam break up?" he asked instead, knowing his sister had made up her mind about the answer she gave him. He would have thought she would have told him.

"It doesn't matter. Are you going to keep interrogating me?"

Chuck shook his head. Gabriella wouldn't say anything, and he didn't want to leave Lola in there for long. God knew what his mother might bark at her.

"Good. Are you calm?" He nodded. "Great. Then we should go back in before David and Lola get destroyed," Gabriella proposed, already walking into the hospital room. Chuck followed closely behind.

Lola saw him and went to stand by him. Actually, slightly hiding behind him, he noted.

"If you insist on loving my son, then give me a grandchild soon," his mother spat at Lola. "And that goes for you, too." She sneered at Gabriella.

Chuck felt both women stiffen and look down in shame. David gazed understandingly at Lola but flickered a confused look as he gazed at Gabriella. Why was he gazing at Chuck's sister, trying to understand her? Not a good sign. And what did David know about Lola and pregnancy? Did Lola have a child? Questions raced through Chuck's mind.

"And for god's sake, put some meat on you. You look horrible all skinny." His mother glared, disgusted, at Gabriella. Everyone winced.

Chuck had had enough. He was done with his mother; he was done with his past. Pressing a kiss on Gabriella's head, he whispered, "You look beautiful, kid. Call me if you need me, okay?"

Gabriella nodded and whispered, "Get out of here. I got this under control." Chuck nodded and grabbed Lola by the hand. He walked out with the intention of starting to truly live his life, instead of hiding and blaming old scars.

Chuck followed Lola up the stairs to their apartments quietly, like they had been for the whole car ride. Reaching their floor, they both made their way to their doors and turned to each other. Chuck had to ask, he just had to.

"Do you have a child?" he asked her. Lola looked completely surprised by his question. She hadn't expected that question. Did that mean she didn't?

"What? No. If I had a child, I wouldn't hide him or her. I would have told you, if I had a skeleton in my closet." She quoted him from earlier. "Why would you ask me that?" Lola asked, shaking her head, unable to understand.

"Your reaction confused me when my mother said, 'You better get pregnant soon.'"

Understanding dawned on Lola's face. She looked down and twisted her fingers and said, "I reacted like that," she paused, unsure, looking down at her twisting hands, "because I'm scared of getting pregnant," she admitted, letting go of her breath.

"Scared?" Chuck asked, surprised.

"My mother…," Lola began saying, but he understood before she finished. Her mother had died in childbirth; Lola must have been scared it would happen to her, too. Chuck took a step closer, wanting to hug her, reassure her it wouldn't happen. He was sure of it, but he couldn't explain why. Lola also took a step closer.

"It won't happen," he told her.

She smiled and said, "It doesn't mean I'm not still scared." *True.* Chuck nodded and took another step closer to her. Lola mimicked him. They were standing two feet away from each other.

Chuck gazed at Lola, wondering if she could love him. "Lola, did you hear what I said the other night through the door?"

Lola shook her head, her pink cheeks turning redder as she guiltily confessed, "I covered my ears and ran into the bathroom." Lola hadn't heard him. She didn't know how he felt. His heart whispered now. "Lola, I have wanted to tell you this for some time now. I want us to be a couple. I mean, I want you. I want us to be more than friends, want us to be a real couple instead of pretending to be one," he said. When he had told her the other night, it hadn't sounded so awkward, and his voice hadn't trembled with nervousness. He held his breath. "In short, would you like to go on a date with me? A real, non-pretending date?"

Lola grinned at him, her eyes sparkling like millions of stars in the night. "Sounds tempting."

"But I have to warn you this date will last longer than a weekend."

"How much longer?"

"A lifetime."

Lola took the final step, closing the space between them. "If you had said less time, I would have had to decline." She grinned, the most beautiful smile ever. "I would love to. I mean, love to go on this date with you." She blushed.

Chuck pressed a smiling kiss on Lola's grinning lips. The kiss was soft and tender, sealing their souls together.

The magnetic force hummed through them as it finally connected for eternity.

The end.

Epilogue

Lola struggled to place a light orange vase with a yellow fake flowers on the top shelve of her new bookcase, her giant belly kept getting in the way time after time. She was getting frustrated. She tried again but her belly bumped into the bookcase. She sighed.

"Chuck!" She called out loudly.

"Yes."

"I need your help," she whined, pouting her lips.

"Where are you?"

"In the sunset room," Lola answered.

Lola was finishing decorating the chalet. At first Lola had thought, she had to start from scratch but a month after she sarted dating Chuck, Lola moved into Chuck's apartment. It had been one of the easiest moves ever. While moving Chuck had found her designs for the last project she had done for Vance decorates, the one she worked hard on, the only she cared deeply about for no reason.

Well she found her reason, Lola had been designing for Chuck's chalet. "This looks just like my chalet" he had said and then checked his client number and matched it with the one on the designs. It was his chalet.

"How's my baby," Chuck said walking into the sunset room. The room was decorated inspired by the sunset she had seen the day Chuck and her shared their very first kiss.

"He keeps getting in the way," Lola said lovingly and caressed her giant belly.

"It wouldn't be the first time," Chuck teased making Lola grimace and laugh.

Chuck came and kissed her belly and then her.

"What do you need my help for?" he asked her stocking her face like he always did.

"I need to put the vase on the top shelve," she said. In less than five seconds Chuck put the vase on the top shelve and pulled Lola to the sofa by the large window. "You're going miss the sunset Mrs. Moran" he whispered in her ear.

Lola smiled loving when he called her Mrs. Moran. They had been married for a year now, and he never failed to make Lola's heart expand with love or make her crazy with desire with one look from his profound black eyes. They got married after a year of dating. Technically, it was a year and six month planning the wedding but bot considered themselves married when Chuck proposed. Lola had been right the sight of Chuck on knee was priceless.

They sat down, Lola rested her head on Chuck's shoulder and Chuck rested one head on the back of the sofa while the other rested on their unborn child, stroking rhythmically and gently.

They watched the sun slowly disappear in the horizon with orange, yellow and hints of purples clouds mixing in the sky and lingering in the sky and the soft darkness replaced it gradually.

"I love you," Chuck said and kissed her head as the sun disappeared.

"I love you," Lola said and titled her head looking at him. Smiling he kissed her waiting lips.

"I love you more."

"I love you more."

Ha! You wish! They thought together.

Acknowledgments

I would like to thank my mother first of all, for always being there for me. Thank you so much for believing in me, even when I didn't. Thank you for understanding me. I couldn't have done this without your support. I am forever grateful. I love you.

Secondly, I would like to give a special thanks my editor, Jane McAdams at Beaumont Hardy Editing, who not only has a keen eye but is filled with motivating compliments. Thank you so much.

Lastly, I would like to thank whoever you are. Thank you for reading The Truth In Pretending. I appreciate it with all my heart. I hope you enjoyed it as much as I did writing it. And make sure to stay tuned for more of the Valentine Weekend.

Thank You.

About Author

Juliana Jules is a romance novelist who enjoys dreaming about love any chance she gets. A secret hopeless romantic at heart, she is inspired by everything and anything, by everyone and no one.